He'd saved her life...for the price of a kiss

Though streaked with sweat and ashes, the Navajo man who held her was devastatingly handsome.

"Good. You're really with me now," he murmured. "Stick around this time." His smile was dazzling, filled with tender concern.

The warmth of his breath touched her face like a lover's caress.

"You're an irresistible temptation, woman. Forgive me for taking advantage of you," he murmured. Then he leaned over, taking her mouth with his own. Lanie was caught in a swirl of sensations; a tremor rippled through her. This man had sheltered her while they'd escaped the blaze, but in his arms she was finding another kind of fire—one with the power to blaze a path to her soul.

Lanie sat up, moving away from him as she looked around at the unfamiliar surroundings. "Who are you, and where am I?"

"You're safe, and you're in my town. I'm Sheriff Gabriel Blackhorse. Welcome to Four Winds."

Dear Reader,

Welcome to Four Winds, New Mexico! It's one of those magical towns where no one is who they seem to be...and everyone has a secret. And the sexy Blackhorse brothers are just the perfect tour guides we need.

Harlequin Intrigue is proud to present the FOUR WINDS miniseries by bestselling author Aimée Thurlo. She's been called a "master of the desert country as well as adventure" by Tony Hillerman, and a favorite author by you, our readers.

Join Aimée for all the stories of the Blackhorse brothers and the town in which they live. Don't miss *Her Hope* in November and *Her Shadow* in March.

Happy reading!

Sincerely,

Debra Matteucci
Senior Editor & Editorial Coordinator
Harlequin Books
300 East 42nd Street
New York, New York 10017

Aimée Thurlo
HER DESTINY

Harlequin Books

TORONTO • NEW YORK • LONDON
AMSTERDAM • PARIS • SYDNEY • HAMBURG
STOCKHOLM • ATHENS • TOKYO • MILAN
MADRID • WARSAW • BUDAPEST • AUCKLAND

To Bonnie Crisalli, who saw the promise of Four Winds and
gave me the chance to bring it to life.
And to Huntley Fitzpatrick, whose perceptive feedback has
guided and supported the series and kept it on track.
Thank you for being there!

With special thanks to Bill Hilburn for sharing his expertise.

ISBN 0-373-22427-3

HER DESTINY

Copyright © 1997 by Aimée Thurlo

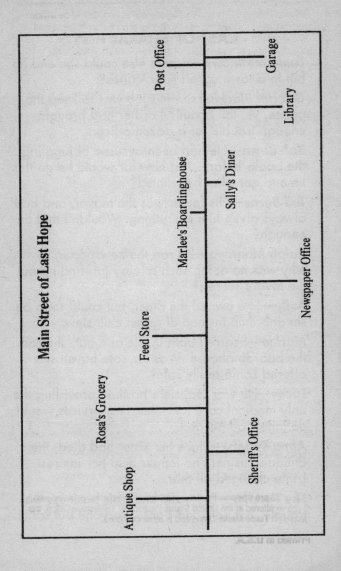

Main Street of Last Hope

Antique Shop

Sheriff's Office

Rosa's Grocery

Feed Store

Newspaper Office

Marlee's Boardinghouse

Sally's Diner

Post Office

Library

Garage

CAST OF CHARACTERS

Lanie Matthews—Where else could she end up but in a town called Four Winds?

Gabriel Blackhorse—His job was to keep the peace, yet the beautiful drifter had brought enough trouble for a dozen officers.

Bob Burns—He had been accused of juggling the books before. Just how far would he go this time to get what he wanted?

Ted Burns—His father was the mayor, and had always given him everything. Wouldn't that be enough?

Ralph Montoya—He ran the newspaper, so why was he doing such a lousy job finding out the town's secrets?

Sally—She owned the diner, but could soon be serving time instead of green chili stew.

Marlee—Scarred both inside and out, she ran the boardinghouse. Was the safe haven she offered Lanie really safe?

Lucas—He was Gabriel's brother, providing the only medical care for miles. His services would definitely be needed.

Alma Wright—Since her sister had died, their antique business no longer held her interest. Lanie changed all that.

The Peddler—Everyone knew his business was trouble, not pots and pans. Everyone but Lanie.

Prologue

Summer 1876

It had been another hot, dusty day. Sunset had left the New Mexico Territory skies the color of burning coals. Standing by the open window, hoping in vain for a breeze, Sheriff John Cooper stared outside, watching the orange-red horizon turn to violet over the Jemez Mountains.

Slow ripples of darkness battled the remnants of the day. Night would claim the land soon, and then the fights would start. It was a routine he was more than familiar with by now. Too much whiskey, pockets emptied too soon after several hands of poker at the saloon, and the boys from the Lazy L Ranch would get scrappy, hunting for trouble.

He returned to his desk, checked his Colt .44 six-shooter, then grabbed a handful of cartridges from the box and stuck them into his vest pocket. It never hurt to carry a couple of extra loads. Hearing footsteps and a loud thump outside his door, he cursed under his breath. He'd hoped to get dinner before things got too lively.

"Door's open," he roared, resting his hand over his revolver.

No one entered. Annoyed, he scooped up his Colt and crossed the room with quick, bold strides, throwing open

the door as he stepped back by the jamb to avoid pre-
senting a clear target. Hearing a moan, he glanced down.
An Indian man lay bleeding on the wooden steps, clearly
a victim of an unrelenting beating.

Cooper glanced around quickly, jamming the .44 into
the holster at his hip. The Navajo man's horse was lathered
with foam, indicating that rider and mount had just made
the run of their lives.

Cooper crouched beside the injured man and lifted him
enough to see his face. "Flinthawk!" The elderly medicine man's features were distorted by the cruel blows he'd
endured, and by trails of dust and caked blood. "Who did
this to you?"

His swollen lips moved, but no words came out.

Curly Jordan from the general store across the street
rushed up, his breath coming in short gasps. "I saw him
ride up all hunched over and slide right off his horse. I
yelled for the new doc. He's on his way."

"Good. Help me get him inside onto a bunk. From the
looks of that old horse of his, I have a feeling whoever
took a fist to him isn't long behind."

Cooper's young deputy forced his way through the gathering crowd. "What happened, Sheriff? This morning
Flinthawk said he was going over to the Lazy L to see
what was killing off their herd."

"Then you know as much as I do." As far as Cooper
knew, the Navajo healer had no enemies in town. His
herbs and remedies had cured almost everyone in Four
Winds at one time or another. During the winter of the
great fever, he'd been their only doc, and an effective one
at that.

Hearing the sound of galloping horses approaching,
Cooper squinted into the fading sun. "Looks like we're
about to get some answers." Cooper stepped out into the
street to meet the men riding in.

The group of five reined in beside Flinthawk's horse.

Dusty Calhoun, tall and lean, his face hardened by a network of lines that attested to long days in the territory's sun, tipped his hat back. "Sheriff, if you'll let us finish our business, we'd be much obliged. We want no trouble with you. Just turn the Indian over to us, and we'll be on our way."

"First, suppose you tell me what you want him for."

"Flinthawk killed our Indian blacksmith, one of his own people, if it's any of your concern. Then he beat my ten-year-old boy up real bad, and left him unconscious. Two of my hands saw him riding off in a real hurry. We took off after him. What I just told you happened on my ranch, on *my* land," he emphasized. "There, *I'm* the law, and we serve out our own justice."

"You're not on the Lazy L right now, Calhoun. You're in Four Winds. This is *my* town, and *I'm* the law here."

Calhoun dismounted slowly, never taking his eyes off the sheriff. He wore the expression of a man who knew a confrontation was at hand, and was ready to see it through. "I've heard you're good with a six-shooter, Cooper, and it's possible you'll shoot me dead before my Colt clears leather. But if I go down, one of my men will put a bullet in you, sure as can be. You can't outgun all of us. Just tell these good people to go home, then you and your deputy step back inside your office. You don't want any bloodshed."

The sheriff moved directly into Calhoun's path, blocking his way. "Mount up and ride off. Nobody needs to do any dying."

Calhoun stepped back, reaching for his Colt. Cooper was faster than Calhoun, but as he thumbed back the hammer on his .44, Calhoun's men drew their own weapons. Four Winchester rifles pointed at his chest.

"What'll it be, Sheriff?" Calhoun added softly, bringing his own revolver up. "Five against one are bad odds."

The ratcheting sound of a rifle shell being fed into its

chamber came from somewhere out in the street. Cooper glanced past Calhoun and stared at old Mrs. Riley, standing behind her buckboard. Until now, he'd never realized that the old schoolmarm knew how to use a rifle.

"I think it's best if you boys take the sheriff's advice and go home," she said in her firmest schoolteacher voice. "Do the figuring, Dusty, though you'll undoubtedly have to use your fingers and toes. You can't outrun the sheriff's bullet, and I'll subtract at least one of your hands, maybe two. Nobody's taking that medicine man anywhere, not without filling three or four graves first, maybe more. I owe Flinthawk, he saved my life. He's also done a lot of good things for the people of this town. My guess is you've got your story wrong. Flinthawk wouldn't harm anyone, especially a child."

Calhoun turned his head. "You don't want to do this, Mrs. Riley. You'll slow us down, but you'll die for your trouble."

"Oh, I don't think so," another voice piped in. "The odds against you seem to be growing by the minute."

Sheriff Cooper stared at Jensen, the owner of the saloon. He rested the butt of his double-barreled scattergun against his side as he stepped out from behind a porch post. Farther across the street, Cooper could see other rifle barrels poking through open windows, aimed at Calhoun's men.

Cooper smiled slowly. "You came to the wrong town looking for vigilante justice, Calhoun. Folks stick together here. Best you ride on. A jury will settle this matter in due time. If you press it now, there'll be more blood than you bargained for."

"I'll return with as many men as it takes, Cooper. Don't think this is over. The Indian is mine."

As Calhoun mounted his horse, a woman driving a red buckboard at a gallop thundered into town. By the time she had stopped the team of horses, the buckboard was right in front of the sheriff's office. When the dust settled,

Cooper saw a boy in the buckboard beside the dust-covered woman, his head bandaged.

"Mrs. Calhoun," the sheriff greeted with a nod.

She scarcely gave the sheriff a glance. Her attention was focused solely on Dusty Calhoun. "Husband, you didn't hurt that medicine man, did you?" she asked quickly.

Calhoun stepped back down from his mount. He glowered at his wife as he approached the buckboard from the boy's side. "What are you doing here, son? You should be at the doc's. Leave it to me to make sure the Indian gets what's coming to him."

"No, Pa, you don't understand. Flinthawk didn't hurt me. He saved my life."

Calhoun's eyes narrowed and he shifted his gaze, staring at his wife with open suspicion. "Have you been confusing the boy?"

"Pa, I'm telling the truth," the boy insisted. "I caught Beyale, the blacksmith, pouring something into our well. When I tried to stop him, he acted like a wild man, grabbing me by the throat. Flinthawk must have seen what was going on when he rode up. He ran over to help me. We almost had him, but then Beyale picked up a piece of firewood and hit me right over the head. I saw it coming, but I couldn't duck in time. Flinthawk pushed him back against the well. I heard Beyale's head hit the stone sides and saw blood. But then I guess I passed out. Next thing I knew, Beyale was dead, but I was still alive."

"I heard what you were planning to do, Luke Calhoun," his wife said, using his Christian name. "That's when I knew only your son could stay your hand. What you were after was nothing short of murder."

"If Flinthawk's as innocent as you claim, then why did he run away?" Calhoun said, shaking his head.

"I wasn't there, but I can tell you the answer to that one," Mrs. Riley, the old schoolteacher, offered. "Flinthawk's Navajo. His people are afraid of the dead and anything connected to them. You should know that, you've lived in the territory long enough.''

Before Calhoun could answer, Flinthawk staggered to the door. "I defended the boy and myself," he managed to say through swollen lips. "*Your* blacksmith was the one who attacked *me*. Then you and your men tried to finish the job.''

An ominous hush fell over the crowd.

"The blacksmith was evil," Flinthawk continued. "He was what my people call a skinwalker, a Navajo witch. He was poisoning your well because through your deaths his magic would have grown even more powerful. You don't understand our ways, but it happened as I say. If you don't believe me, perhaps you can believe your own child.''

Calhoun glanced at his son, who nodded, then back at Flinthawk. "Seems we wronged you, old man," Calhoun admitted slowly. "I'm in your debt now." He caught the eye of the storekeeper. "From now on, see that he gets whatever supplies he needs. You can put his bills on my account.''

Cooper glanced at Flinthawk. "Just say so, and I'll arrest these men. I don't know if the charges will stick, but I'll be happy to make their lives difficult for a day or two.''

Flinthawk leaned heavily against the wall for support, but somehow managed to stay on his feet without anyone's help. "That's not necessary. Let them go.''

As the group from the Lazy L rode off, Flinthawk looked around at the townspeople. "You risked your own lives to save mine," he acknowledged, his voice weak. "Once my injuries heal, I will repay this town. I will do a sing here. From this day on, Four Winds will be protected by the medicine of my people. The wicked who come here will never know peace, and if they remain, they will find that the cost is more than they ever dreamed they would pay.''

Cooper watched Flinthawk walk slowly but unaided toward his hogan near the stockyards. That was one proud man.

"Sheriff, what do you think he meant by that talk about the wicked paying for their ways?" the deputy asked.

"I'm not sure," Cooper answered, "but I know Flinthawk, and he's as good as his word."

Chapter One

Spring, 1997

Gabriel Blackhorse woke up in a gnarly mood. He coughed, sputtered and blinked back the sleep from his eyes. Damnation. He'd come out here to get away and relax. Why on earth was he waking up so early?

Tossing aside the top half of his sleeping bag, he sat up, half-naked, and sniffed the pungent air. He suddenly knew what had woken him up, and it wasn't good. Gabriel squinted through the haze of smoke that enveloped the forest clearing where he'd spent the night. The forest-service boys had been scheduled to make a prescribed burn in the area to clear away the underbrush, but from the looks of it, that fire had gotten out of hand. It shouldn't have come anywhere near this campsite.

Grabbing his jeans and pulling them on as he walked, he went to his Jeep and radioed the dispatcher back in town. It only took a moment to confirm that the fire had jumped the fire line. The rangers were scrambling to contain the blaze.

Well, from the looks of it, nobody was going to have a good day. He searched the ground next to the bedroll for his *jish*, the medicine bundle with the flint hawk, a fetish carved by an ancestor of his who'd also borne that name.

Following family tradition, Gabriel's father had handed it down to him a few months ago, and he'd kept it with him ever since. Finding the fetish, he quickly fastened the drawstring around his belt, then grabbed the sleeping bag and ground cloth, tossing both into the back of the Jeep. It was time to get out of here.

The Jeep bounced for a few minutes along the uneven dirt trail until Gabriel reached the graveled forestry road. As he began the final quarter-mile stretch before reaching the main highway, Gabriel caught a glimpse of something blue and metallic behind a cluster of pines. A car.

Someone else must have had the misfortune of choosing this area as a campsite. He had to go make sure they were awake and getting ready to leave.

Gabriel drove off the forest road, following the tire imprints left on the sandy soil. The camp was just a dozen or so yards off the road. He studied the site as he pulled up. The car was parked near a one-man tent, but no one was visible. "There's a brushfire!" he yelled, honking the horn. "You've got to get out of here now!"

Not receiving a response, he left his vehicle and walked to the tent. Whoever was in there was either stone deaf or just too hungover to care.

He peered inside the tent, but it was empty. A lace bra and lavender-colored panties stuck out of a bright pink laundry bag with a cartoon-chipmunk design on it.

He stepped back outside, curious now about the camper. Frilly things like the ones he'd found inside didn't fit his image of an outdoorswoman, particularly one who'd go camping alone.

The smoke was getting thicker, moving up from the valley below in a growing cloud.

"Anyone out here?" He shouted loud enough to be heard in the next county, but there was no response.

The woman couldn't have gone far, since her vehicle was still there. Problem was, he had no idea when the smoke had reached this spot. It was possible she'd gone off on a hike and then been unable to find her way back in the haze.

Gabriel muttered an oath. He'd have to go look for her. He crouched by the ground, studied the direction of the tracks, then returned to his Jeep. He'd cover ground faster that way.

Gabriel drove slowly into the forest, remembering a time long ago when he'd gone to rescue his two younger brothers from a similar situation. He'd broken Lucas's nose that time for taking good-natured Joshua along on a beer bust that had gone wrong. Not that Joshua needed his protection, even back then.

Gabriel kept his eyes on the trail ahead, focusing on the present. Duty defined him, as did the badge he carried, and he had a job to do. The last thing he needed now was a flat tire, and between the rocks and the smoke, the area was as safe as a minefield.

He'd been driving around for about an hour before he finally saw her. She'd climbed up onto a rock outcropping and was now trapped by a circle of burning brush and grass.

LANIE STARED in horror at the thick sheets of smoke that engulfed the desert floor. How could everything have gone so wrong? It had been beautiful this morning, a perfect time for a hike, the temperature cool and pleasant, the air stirred by a gentle breeze.

Then, within a half hour, everything had changed. The breeze had become a gust of wind, and smoke from several locations downhill had started filling up the canyons. An idyllic morning had suddenly turned into a nightmarish vision from Hell.

Lanie wasted no time, hurrying back toward her camp, always moving away from the smoke. Then the fire jumped the narrow canyon she'd been crossing, forcing her to climb the rocky slope as fire quickly surrounded her.

Smoke stung her eyes, her throat and lungs, making her cough despite the bandanna she'd tied over her nose and mouth. With each passing second, her thoughts were becoming more muddled, her mind encased in a fog as thick as the smoke encircling her.

It was all too clear, however, that nothing but a miracle would save her now. Her heart felt leaden. She'd made so many mistakes in her life, but she'd still dared to dream. In the past few months, those dreams had been pushed deep inside her, but not discarded. With sorrow, she faced the possibility that they'd never have a chance to become real.

She searched in desperation for a sign of hope. As a flicker of movement caught her attention, Lanie squinted, trying to focus. Swirling images swam before her.

Suddenly she saw a figure cloaked in gray, running through the ring of fire. He was coming directly toward her.

Wondering if she was hallucinating, she closed her eyes. When she opened them again, the specter she'd seen braving the flames had reached her and was lifting her into his arms. He pressed her against his hard, muscled chest until she could hear his heart drumming fast and strong. His breath touched her cheek above the bandanna as he whispered something she couldn't quite make out.

Maybe it was all a wild, wonderful fantasy before death. Yet as the thought formed, his arms wrapped even tighter around her, and she knew he was real.

Encircled by the flame-retardant blanket and her rescuer's strong embrace, she surrendered to the dark oblivion that called gently to her.

AWARENESS RETURNED slowly to Lanie. "Easy," she heard a man's deep voice say as he pulled down the ban-

danna she'd used to filter the air. "You passed out from
the heat and smoke, but you're okay now. Just don't rush
it."

Lanie's vision was still hazy, and she blinked madly,
trying to make out his face. She was resting against him,
but she had neither the desire nor the will to move away
from the strength and comfort of his arms. Slowly, like a
photograph developing before her eyes, her vision cleared.

Though streaked with sweat and ashes, the Navajo man
who held her was devastatingly handsome. His hair was
black, long enough to touch his shoulders. His eyes were
like a moonless night that seemed to explode from within
with a brilliance that made her breath catch in her throat.

"Good. You're really with me now," he murmured.
"Stick around this time." His smile was dazzling, filled
with tender concern.

The warmth of his breath touched her face like a lover's
caress. She moistened her dry lips with the tip of her
tongue, and heard him draw in a breath.

"You're an irresistible temptation, woman. Forgive me
for taking advantage of you," he murmured.

He leaned over, taking her mouth with his own. His lips
moved over hers, barely touching, yet so persuasive she
couldn't help but respond.

Caught in a swirl of sensations, she felt a tremor ripple
through her. He had sheltered her while they'd escaped
the blaze, but in his arms, she was finding another kind of
fire—one with the power to blaze a path to her soul.

He drew away slowly. "I hope you won't begrudge me
that reward."

"Not at all." Lanie took a deep breath and smiled. "But
now the debt's been paid. We're even."

He laughed. "If you say so."

Lanie sat up, moving away from him as she looked

around the unfamiliar room. "Who are you, and where am I?"

"You're safe and you're in my town. I'm Sheriff Gabriel Blackhorse. Welcome to Four Winds."

Chapter Two

Gabriel watched her appreciatively as she stood up, glad she hadn't been injured. She was a strikingly beautiful woman. Her eyes were light brown, almost the color of brown sugar. A man could drown in the sultry warmth of that gaze. Her hair fell softly down her shoulders in a cascade of brown and gold that tempted him with its promise of softness and femininity.

She looked around, taking in the empty infirmary. "What's this place?"

"My brother Lucas runs this first-aid station. He's out on a call right now, though he did check you over before he left. He said you should take it easy for a while."

"I'm okay, really." She walked slowly to the window and looked outside. "My car... my things?" she asked. "Did the fire destroy everything?"

Her voice became so taut, he was suddenly very sure that she'd carried everything she owned in that car. What this beauty was doing on the road definitely intrigued him. "Your car and possessions are probably just fine. The fire got out of hand for a while, but the worst of it, at least where your car was parked, was the smoke."

"Is it safe to return now? Even my purse is back there."

He nodded. "If you'd like, I can drive you back. The

forest service and the volunteer fire department have things under control now.''

''I'd appreciate a ride, if you don't mind.'' Lanie looked down at her watch, and was surprised to see it was after noon already.

''You know my name,'' he said casually, ''but I still don't know yours.''

She gave him an apologetic smile. ''I'm Lanie Mathews.''

''Were you on your way to Four Winds? You were camped just off the one road leading in and out of town. This place originally was the end of an old railway spur.''

''No, I was just passing through this part of the state. I took the wrong road out of Santa Fe, but didn't figure it out until late last night,'' she answered. ''If my car's okay, I intend to be on my way shortly.''

''Where to?''

She paused. ''East.''

''Vacation?'' he prodded.

''Just traveling,'' she answered with a shrug.

A woman of mystery. Well, he couldn't blame her. In fact, if anything, she fit right in around here. He should have been used to it. People in Four Winds always held back more than they shared about themselves.

Gabriel walked outside with Lanie and saw her glance around in confusion. He knew what she was thinking. There were no buildings around, except for the one they stood before. Her gaze darted around the low, pine-covered hills on either side of the narrow valley.

''Where's the rest of the town?'' she asked finally.

''Main street is on a stretch of highway farther west. My brother chose this spot for the clinic because it's so quiet.'' Although Lanie was clearly making a valiant effort at conversation, Gabriel could feel her tension. As they got under way, she sat rigid, worry clouding her features.

''What's troubling you?'' he asked.

"My car is very important to me. If anything has happened to my transportation, I don't know what I'm going to do."

"Don't worry. Four Winds is a hospitable town."

"I'm sure, but I have my own plans, and staying here for more than a day or two isn't part of them."

"Why the rush?" Gabriel's cop instinct was too sharply tuned to allow that comment to pass.

Lanie glanced at him, then back out the window, allowing the silence to stretch. "I'm very grateful that you helped me out during the fire and took care of me until I woke up," she said at last. "But what I choose to do with my life is my own business."

"Fine by me," he answered with a shrug. Lanie Mathews sure wasn't big on trusting people. Then again, he had to admit that wasn't exactly a bad thing, not for a beautiful woman traveling alone. She'd be safer that way.

The drive to the highway took them through Four Winds, and he couldn't resist showing off his town. "Most of the buildings have been modernized, but we still take pride in our sense of history here. The post office dates back to the early 1800s. If you look, you can see we kept the hitching post, though kids are the only ones who ever ride up on horseback these days."

"The narrow cobblestone streets are unusual. And everything is so clean," she said. "No litter. Anywhere."

"We're proud of our town, and that's one of the ways we show it."

"I like old adobe buildings. You don't see real adobe much anymore, with those thick, low walls bordering the front of the properties."

"I've always liked those, too."

As they reached the main highway and headed toward her camp, he gave her a long sideways glance. "Have you done much camping before?"

He saw her hesitate. The woman just wasn't much on talking about herself.

"I know what I'm doing," she answered at last. "If you're thinking that somehow I started the fire—"

He shook his head. "Relax. I'm not accusing you of anything," he interrupted. "I know you weren't responsible. The forest service was burning away some underbrush near here to avoid a bigger fire later on, and things got out of hand."

His answer seemed to reassure her, but her wariness continued to pique his interest and curiosity. Though she didn't seem afraid of him or of his badge, she was on the run from something, sure as anything.

He mulled it over as he turned off the highway and traveled across a smoking, charred meadow that had been overrun by fire. It was strange how Four Winds seemed to draw people with more than a fair share of secrets. Of course, he could include himself in that assessment.

Lanie leaned forward and gripped the dashboard of the Jeep as they approached her camp. "I got lucky! My car looks fine, and my tent wasn't touched!"

"Let's go take a closer look." He pulled to a stop and walked toward the camp with her.

Her car and tent were covered with ashes and soot, but both were undamaged. As he stopped beside the sedan, he noted the tires were almost bald, and the paint was so dull and faded, even the soot and dust didn't seem to matter much. It was a ten-year-old model that had seen a lot of miles.

"I'll be okay now," she assured him. "Thanks for the lift."

For some crazy reason, he hated the idea of leaving Lanie now. He glanced at her car and found himself hoping it really was on its last legs, as its appearance certainly seemed to suggest. "Before I leave, why don't you start up your car, just to make sure it's working?"

"If that car made it through the fire, it can handle anything. Don't worry." But she slipped behind the wheel and switched on the ignition. The car sputtered and almost caught a few times before the battery finally ran down.

Gabriel hooked up jumper cables, and Lanie tried several more times. Finally she leaned back on the seat dejectedly. "I don't understand. It was working before. The fire didn't come close enough to it to do any damage, and it's not like I parked it in the city where kids could have tampered with something."

"Let me see if I can figure out what's wrong." He checked the battery connections and a few other things, but there was nothing he could see to account for the car's refusal to start. Finally he gave up, admitting to himself that even if it made him a dirt bag, he was glad she'd be sticking around. "I'll get Charley out here for you. He runs the gas station in Four Winds. If he can't start it, he can tow it into town and take care of it there."

"Towing's expensive..." she said under her breath. "And I have a feeling that car repairs will be, too. But I don't have a choice."

"Charley's honest. He won't take advantage of a stranger."

"All right. While you contact him, I'll gather up my camping gear and put it in the car. I can't just leave my stuff out here."

"Give me a minute, and I'll help you break camp."

"No need." She glanced at her tent. "I only unloaded a few personal things."

He followed her gaze and glanced at her tent. The memory of her soft lace bra and the lavender panties taunted him, making his body tense. He looked at the ground and focused his thoughts on business. "Suit yourself."

She took down the tent like an expert while he radioed into town for a tow truck. By the time he finished, she was already loading her car. Boxes filled with textbooks and what appeared to be lesson plans were crammed into the back, along with boxes marked Shoes and Clothes.

"You're a teacher?" he asked.

"I used to be. I'm not anymore."

He noted there was a sad twist to her words, though her expression had remained neutral. "What do you do nowadays?"

"Any honest job that allows me to pick up enough cash to stay on the road."

Maybe it was that curious blend of vulnerability and toughness that drew him, or maybe he just knew what it was like to go it alone. This woman stirred him, touching him on more levels than he would have thought possible. The way she looked into his eyes when she spoke, and the haunted look there, really tugged at him. And that meant big trouble unless he watched himself.

"How long will it take Charley to drive out here?" Lanie asked, interrupting his thoughts.

"About an hour, maybe a little longer. But if you have no place in particular to go, why are you in such a rush?" he asked, even though he thought he knew the answer. Her hurry was so much like a *bilagáana*. Anglos were always fighting the clock, even when there was no need.

He saw her open her mouth as if to speak, then shut it. For that brief instant, the promise in her parted lips brought on the urge to kiss her again, to burst through that reserve of hers in the most primitive way of all. Cursing himself, he disciplined his thoughts. The time for them was already past. They'd shared an adventure and a moment. Now it was time to move on.

"I'm going to turn official now and check out the area making sure everything's okay and that there are no more stranded campers anywhere. Why don't you come with me? I can take you into town as soon as I'm done, and you can meet Charley there."

She shook her head. "I'll stay here. Thanks for everything, Sheriff, and good luck.'' She extended her hand to him.

It was a cool goodbye after their intimate kiss, but he took her hand, glad for the chance to touch her one last time. Her hand felt soft and small against his.

"Take care of yourself." He walked away, determined not to glance back. She didn't want him here, and he would never push himself on anyone. The fact that he wanted to stay was enough of a danger sign. She appealed to him in such a strong way that it made him jittery. As he stepped inside his vehicle, he heard her soft voice one more time.

"Goodbye, Gabriel." Her whisper barely rose over the rustle of the wind as it sighed through the pines.

Her voice echoed in his mind as he drove away, his gut in a knot. He couldn't remember the last time anyone had called his name in a voice as soft as that. He ran an exasperated hand through his hair. Brushing back the crazy emotions bouncing around inside of him, he kept his eyes on the road ahead.

LANIE SAT DOWN on an old stump several feet away from her car. Back on that rocky outcropping, she'd prayed for a miracle. What she'd received was a flesh-and-blood man who was equal parts lightning, fire and magic all at once. What a devastating package! She closed her eyes, remembering his kiss, and pictured him here with her now. He was big and strong, yet so tender as his roughened palms touched her skin. His mouth was gentle over hers, leading her down a path of fire and velvety soft caresses. A long, delicious shiver traveled up her spine.

She forced open her eyes. That was enough of that. A clear head. That's what she needed now. She glanced at her car, wondering anew why it wouldn't start. It seemed fate was against her. The darned thing had been just fine the evening before, and the fire hadn't even come close to it!

Here in the middle of nowhere, she wasn't sure what she'd do if the repairs and the tow cost more than the one hundred dollars she had left. Not many jobs would be available in a small town like Four Winds.

Time dragged, each minute increasing her irritation. She wanted—no, she needed—to keep moving. Where was that Charley?

Two hours had passed when Lanie finally heard the sound of a vehicle approaching from the direction of the highway. A moment later, a black-and-white tow truck appeared. A man in his early forties, wearing dark blue, grease-stained overalls climbed out of the truck and smiled at her.

"I'm Charley. You must be the lady Sheriff Blackhorse called about."

She nodded. "My name's Lanie. I had to leave my car here because of the fire, and though it looks okay, for some strange reason it just won't start."

"I'm the best mechanic around, don't you worry. If anyone can get it going, I can."

"I don't have a lot of money," she warned.

"That's okay. I take credit cards."

"I took a pair of scissors to mine months ago."

"No problem. We'll come to terms we can both agree on. Don't give it another thought."

His answer surprised her. It was certainly not what she'd expected him to say. Maybe in this sparsely populated area, working out terms of payment was a routine he'd grown accustomed to, something he took in stride.

He lifted the hood and checked inside for a full forty-five minutes, poking and prodding. He removed the battery and replaced it with a spare he had in his truck. "Would you try the ignition and see if it'll turn over while I try some things under the hood? Leave your foot off the gas."

Lanie did as he asked, but the battery wore down quickly without any results. Finally, Charley mumbled under his breath and slammed the hood shut. "You've been pushing this car pretty hard from the looks of it. Where you headed?"

Lanie shrugged. "Down the road." As the words left her mouth, she regretted them. Now there would be barrage of well-meaning questions and maybe even advice about women traveling alone. To her surprise, neither happened. A hooded look came over Charley's eyes, and he glanced away.

"You'll have to ride with me," he said, hooking up the sedan to the tow truck. "Your car is going nowhere on its own power. Not until you get a new battery, fuel pump, plugs and distributor cap, and maybe even a rebuilt carburetor."

Dismayed, she got into the truck and, as the miles stretched out before them, Lanie glanced back at the way they'd come. The highway was empty except for one dust-colored van just coming over a hill. Ahead of them, a stretch of vacant road wound into the hills.

"How long will it take for my car to be fixed?"

"Depends. Everything except the battery and plugs will have to be shipped in. I don't carry that many spare parts in stock. Costs too much, and people in Four Winds can usually catch a ride for a few days while they're waiting. Everything has to come in either by bus or U.S. mail. Shipping is expensive, and some distributors don't like messing with the schedules. I figure you should plan on staying at least a week, maybe more."

"Are there any campsites near town?"

He shook his head. "Just houses and private property. You'd be better off getting a room at Marlee's. She runs the boardinghouse and charges reasonable rates. I stayed there myself a few years back."

"Is that how long you've lived here?"

Charley's expression grew distant, and instead of answering her, he glanced out the window. "Her rooms are small, but really affordable. And the rates include kitchen privileges."

Though he'd evaded her question, she didn't press. She also didn't ask what "affordable" meant. First things first. "What's the repair on the car going to cost me?"

"My guess is about three hundred, including labor."

That cinched it. It looked as if she'd be in Four Winds for a while. She would have to get a job somewhere in order to earn enough cash to pay for the repairs and replenish her funds.

As they entered town, Lanie realized again just how small it was. Main Street was only a few blocks long. Unlike city stores that were bunched together, each business was housed in a separate building edged by a thin strip of land. Storefronts were brightly painted. The sun shone on doorways and windows trimmed with that vivid shade of blue seen all over the Southwest. That color was said to keep the evil spirits away.

Once they arrived at the garage, Lanie went into the rest room to clean up, although she suspected the charred smell would never come out of her clothes. Everything, including the upholstery of her car, was probably permeated with it. For now, it looked like that would be something else she'd have to learn to live with.

As she had so many other times in the past few weeks, she questioned the wisdom of having quit her teaching job. She missed her students and the challenges of the classroom. If only she could have had a second chance, she would have done things differently. As it was, Lanie knew she'd never teach again.

She splashed cold water on her face, hoping to replenish her energy and drive the memories away. She needed to come up with a plan. The last thing she'd expected was for her car to break down. It had never failed her before, and in fact, last time she'd had it checked, they'd told her everything was okay. Having it break down now, with no previous warning, seemed strange. Of course, she'd put a lot of miles on it since then.

Lanie placed the lavatory keys back on their hook, then left the garage. Charley already had his head back under the hood, working on her car. "I'm going to find a room. I'll be back for my things later on. Is that okay?"

"Sure. Take your time. Marlee's place is on up the road a ways. Just keep going straight until you see an adobe home surrounded by piñon pines.

Lanie walked down the street, looking around and trying to orient herself. It was only five-thirty, but everything appeared closed except for a diner. No cars were moving, though there were a few parked along the curb. The only sound she could hear was that of the wind rustling the leaves of an old aspen outside the library a few doors down. As she looked at the adobe building, clearly marked Four Winds Public Library, she smiled. It looked prim and proper in comparison to the Old West, false-fronted construction of most of the other buildings.

As Lanie approached the diner along the weather beaten, uneven sidewalk, she caught a glimpse of movement out of the corner of her eye. Farther down the street, on the same side as the diner, she saw someone getting out of a beat-up, dust-colored van. She couldn't see the driver, just his outline. She wondered if it was the same person who'd been behind them on the highway.

The alluring scent of fried sopaipillas wafting through the diner's open window distracted her. She was famished. Lanie hesitated for a moment, tempted to eat before going to Marlee's boardinghouse. Before she could make up her mind, a slim blonde wearing jeans and an apron glanced through the window and waved. "Come in, hon." The blonde went to the screen door and held it open for Lanie. "Just have a seat anywhere."

Lanie went inside. Several small wooden tables covered with gingham tablecloths were in the process of being cleared, though there were still a few tables with customers quietly enjoying their meals. It appeared that people in Four Winds ate early.

"You're the lady who was caught in the fire, aren't you?" When Lanie nodded, she continued. "I'm Sally, I own this place. You just relax now. You've been through enough for one day."

Lanie nodded, introduced herself and chose a stool at the counter. It wasn't surprising that Sally knew all about her though they'd only just met. In a town this size, news would travel fast. She glanced at the menu and ordered a sandwich to go. "I still have to go find a room," she explained, "but I was just too hungry to wait."

Sally came back with a huge platter of enchiladas. Massive tortillas smothered with chicken, cheese and green chili filled the plate. "Here you go. Forget takeout for tonight. Relax and eat, it's on the house. Think of this as one of many ways Four Winds is going to change the way your luck's been running. Happens that way for a lot of us." She paused and smiled. "Well, come to think of it, you did have one bit of *great* luck already."

Lanie glanced at her quizzically, savoring the delicious enchilada. "What?"

"You got close to Gabriel, honey." Sally laughed. "The three Blackhorse brothers sure can make a woman's pulse race, I'll tell you."

"I've only met the sheriff."

"You'll meet the others sooner or later. Gabriel and Lucas, the two oldest, are scrappers. Those two don't know how to back down from a fight. Men step aside when they come into the room. But one smile from either one of them, and you can hear women's hearts beating faster all around the room."

Lanie said nothing, though she doubted any smile could have the impact Gabriel's did.

"Some say Joshua, the youngest, is the handsomest," Sally continued, "but I don't know about that. He's certainly the gentlest, though bigger and stronger than his two brothers. As far as I know, he's never so much as raised his voice to anyone. Of course, no one's ever been fool enough to get him riled." Sally smiled. "If I was ten years younger, I'd risk a few flames for the chance to be carried off in the arms of one of the Blackhorse brothers."

The outrageous statement made Lanie laugh. "As I said, Gabriel is the only one I've met, but I can certainly understand women's reactions to him."

"He's also a good sheriff, you know. According to the ones who lived here awhile, he's even better than his father, who was sheriff before him."

"So you're not a native?" Lanie asked, making small talk.

A guarded look came over Sally's eyes, and to Lanie's surprise, her friendliness seemed to cool considerably. "Nope." Sally moved over to a nearby table, freshening the iced tea of a customer.

As it had been with Charley, talk about the past seemed to be definitely off-limits with Sally. Lanie began to wonder if that was going to be a trend in Four Winds.

As Sally stepped through the half doors leading to the kitchen, Lanie saw a teenager inside, washing pots and pans. Sally's voice was stern as she admonished the boy for making too much of a mess.

Lanie had meant to ask about a job, anything from waitressing to cleaning, but the opportunity had suddenly come and gone. She'd be better off waiting and asking Sally another time. As Lanie finished the last of her food, she fought back the intense weariness stealing over her. Her body ached, and she was having a hard time staying alert. She needed to get some sleep, and soon.

Chapter Three

Lanie turned and saw a familiar Jeep with official markings and flashers on the top. A moment later, Gabriel pulled up and opened the passenger's door.

"You look beat. Want a ride to Marlee's?"

She hesitated. He'd done enough; it didn't feel right to keep accepting his help, though it would sure come in handy right now.

"Come on. Don't be so squirrelly. We're past that, you and I."

His smile was as devastating as she remembered, and she felt a thrill course through her. "Okay, but since all my clothes are still inside my car, and I'm not sure when Charley closes, how about taking me there first. Then I can take my things to Marlee's at the same time."

"No problem."

Ten minutes later, with her clothes boxes in the back of his Jeep, they were on their way to Marlee's.

"I'm going to have to find some work here to pay for lodging and the car repairs. Do you happen to know if anyone in town is hiring?"

"For starters, Marlee might be willing to strike up a deal with you," he said. "She broke her leg about two weeks ago, and she can't get around too easily. She may be willing to give you free board in exchange for some help around the house.''

"Thanks. I appreciate the tip.'' She smiled ruefully. ''Of course, it's to your advantage, too. I'm sure you don't want a deadbeat hanging around your town.''

He never cracked a smile. "One thing you'll learn soon enough is that people here work together and help each other out. Who knows, you may even end up deciding to stay. It wouldn't be the first time. This is a special place, believe me. Not many leave for good after they've lived here awhile.''

There was something about the way he said it that made her extremely nervous. She didn't want to like it here; she wanted to leave as soon as possible. She needed to keep moving, and not look back. She had no ties to anyone and belonged nowhere, at least not anymore. And that's the way she wanted to keep it.

"You said you were a teacher,'' Gabriel said. "The town's been looking for a substitute teacher for quite some time. Your skills would come in handy here. Are you qualified to teach history?''

"Among other subjects,'' she answered slowly.

"And you have references?''

"Excellent ones, but I'm not interested in a teaching post. Not now, not ever.'' She refused to meet his eyes.

"It's only a substitute job, not a permanent thing. And it would pay pretty well,'' he urged.

"No, thanks.'' Her tone was cold and final.

"Okay.'' Gabriel shrugged. It might not make sense to him, but it was really none of his business.

As he parked in front of the boardinghouse, his radio crackled to life. She couldn't make out a word, though Gabriel seemed to understand everything despite the static.

"I need to get over to the mayor's house,'' he said, quickly unloading her belongings from the back. "I'll give you a hand taking these inside, then be on my way.''

"I can take care of that. It's no problem."

"Okay. See you later, then."

As he sped away, she glanced up and down the narrow, empty street. What a strange town this was. It was only a little after seven, yet nobody was around. She wondered where everyone went after sundown. After teaching in a city plagued with youth gangs, she found the stillness here uncanny, but welcoming. Yet she couldn't help feeling there was something odd about the town and the people of Four Winds.

Lanie shook her head, brushing the thought aside. She was exhausted, allowing her imagination to run away with her—that was all. She looked ahead at the brightly lit portal of the adobe boardinghouse. A wooden sign, announcing rooms to rent, hung from two massive wood vigas. Silk orange mums in containers were placed on both sides of the front door, welcoming visitors. Nothing sinister there.

She knocked on the glass storm door, glancing inside as she did. A young woman sitting on the sofa across from a television set waved and said, "Come on in."

"I'm looking for Marlee," Lanie said, stepping into the brick-floored living room.

"I'm Marlee. Are you looking for a place to stay?" she asked, not getting up.

Lanie studied the hazel eyes that regarded her. There was a defensive tightening there, a quick, almost reflex action.

"I'm told you're looking for help with the upkeep here, and that you might be willing to exchange that for room and board."

"Not board, no, I can't afford it, but for a room, yes. I've got one vacant right now."

Marlee stood up with effort, the cast on her right leg affecting her movements. As she faced Lanie straight on, the light from the lamp illuminated her face. Lanie saw the scar that ran from her left temple all the way down to her chin.

"Don't let it bother you," Marlee said casually, as if used to people's reactions. "It happened a long time ago, before I came here." Her voice grew distant. "A lifetime ago." She shrugged, then focused back on Lanie. "Now tell me, what brings you here to Four Winds?"

"An accident." She recounted the events.

"A lot of our residents are people who were just passing through at one time or another," Marlee observed simply. "This town has a lot to offer."

"Not to me. I'll be back on the road just as soon as I can."

"Funny, that's what I said, too."

Something about her tone gave Lanie goose bumps. Before she had much of a chance to think about it, Marlee returned to her chair and waved for her to sit down. "What I *need* is someone to carry laundry, do the shopping and help me with the housework. It's time-consuming, believe me, and I don't have much patience with slackers."

There was a hard edge in her tone, but somehow that harshness didn't reach her eyes. All Lanie saw reflected there was an ingrained caution about strangers, not cruelty.

A careful look around the room told her even more about Marlee. If the woman was demanding of others, it was simply because she was so demanding with herself. Even now, when getting around was difficult for her, there wasn't a speck of dust anywhere, nor was anything out of place. The room was immaculate.

"I can handle hard work," Lanie said, "but I'm going to have to look for another job in addition to working for you here. I'll need some money to pay for the repairs to my car, and to cover my other expenses. I'd like to get back on the road as soon as possible."

"Fair enough," Marlee answered. "Looks like it'll be a good arrangement for both of us." Marlee waved toward the rolltop desk in the corner. "Open that and take the key that's still on a hook. Your room is just down the hall, second door to the last on your right. I'm sure you'll like it. It's got a great big poster bed with a very comfortable mattress."

At the moment, the description sounded like heaven to her. Lanie found the key. "Is there anything you'd like me to do right away?"

Marlee crinkled her nose. "How about washing those clothes you're wearing? I hate the smell of smoke. It gets into everything."

"I haven't got anything else right now that smells better. All my things were in my car at the time of the fire. Everything got smoked, just like a big camp fire."

"There's just you and me here tonight, so you can borrow my bathrobe and walk around in that while your clothes are washing. I only have one full-time boarder right now, besides you."

"How many rooms do you have here?"

"This is a four-bedroom house, but one of them is my sewing room. I opened up my home as a boardinghouse because I found out I really didn't like living alone." Marlee stood up slowly, favoring her leg. "Come on. I'll get you my robe and some towels."

"Please, don't get up," Lanie said quickly. "Just tell me where they are."

"No, it's okay, really. I have to move around every once in a while, or I get really stiff."

FIFTEEN MINUTES LATER, Lanie was in the shower. Marlee's bathrobe was draped over the towel rack. The hot water and the clean bathroom equipped with all the amenities reminded her of how wonderful simple conveniences could be. Nothing like a long trip to make her appreciate things she'd once taken for granted. She thought of the past few weeks, all that driving and going nowhere. No matter how far or how fast she'd gone, she had yet to outrun the pain that haunted her. And she knew that until she could find some peace within herself, her journey would not end.

Lanie stepped out of the shower, and towel-dried her hair. Wearing Marlee's bathrobe, she picked up her clothes and the items she'd selected from her boxes to fill out the load and started down the hall. She was about halfway down when she saw Gabriel.

He strode toward her, his eyes bright with a fire that made her body tingle. She hugged the bundle of soiled clothing closer to her, aware that the belt of the bathrobe was too loose for comfort.

"I see you've settled in."

He stopped so close to her she could feel the warmth from his body wrap itself around her. Despite the robe, she felt naked under the constant gaze that held her captive.

"What brings you here?" she asked, amazed at how steady her voice sounded.

"I live here."

The news was as alarming as it was thrilling. Trapped between conflicting emotions, she struggled to hold on to her focus. "The town doesn't pay the sheriff enough for a place of his own?" she added quickly, realizing she'd remained silent too long.

"It's not necessary, at least not in my case. A house is something that goes better with a wife and family. A place like this suits all my needs." He grinned slowly. "Well, almost."

She felt her cheeks grow hot. "Well, your needs are *your* problem. Now, if you'll let me pass, I've got clothes to wash."

He laughed. "Testy, aren't we?"

"I've had a long, difficult day. Then there's this sheriff,

you see, who keeps getting in my way." She glared at him.

"You didn't mind so much when I carried you out of the fire." He stepped closer, his voice a husky murmur.

She moved back and bumped into the hall table behind her with a thump. Her heart began pounding; her hands were trembling. It was hard to think with him only inches away.

He placed one finger beneath her chin, and tilted her face up toward his own. "What? No snappy comeback?"

Giving him the haughtiest look she could manage, she edged past him and continued down the hall. Her attention was suddenly diverted as she walked past the window. Headlights illuminated the front room. Lanie glanced outside and saw a familiar vehicle driving by slowly. "There's that van again."

Gabriel went to the window and glanced out. "You've seen that van before?" he asked.

"Twice now. Why?"

"I don't recognize it, and we don't get many strangers around here. If Four Winds had burglaries, I'd swear he was casing the place. I'll be back." He slipped out the door.

Marlee came out of the kitchen and hurried unsteadily toward Lanie. "What happened?"

Lanie gestured outside. "There's this van I keep seeing," she said. "I think it came into town when I did, but for some reason it keeps popping up every time I turn around."

"A van?" Marlee's voice shook slightly. "Did you see the driver?"

She shook her head. "Just his outline."

"What kind of van was it?"

"Nothing special. Just an old VW model without any back windows."

Marlee's face paled. She went to the window and stared out. "So it's time again," she whispered under her breath.

"Time?" Marlee's tone was enough to send a chill up Lanie's spine.

"Time for the trouble to start," Marlee answered. Suddenly she turned around and gave Lanie a disarming smile. "Don't listen to me. I'm just crabby because of my leg. Why don't you put your clothes in the washer, and then come into the kitchen and have something warm to drink?"

"I think I better go back to my room while my clothes are washing. I feel almost naked just wearing this."

"Okay. Tell you what, I'll bring you a mug of hot chocolate. How's that?"

"I hate for you to go to any trouble...."

"No trouble at all," Marlee insisted.

"Okay."

Lanie went to the laundry room, started her first load, then returned to her room to sort the rest. Her thoughts were racing. Marlee's reaction to the van had piqued her curiosity, and she was eager for a chance to find out more.

Speculations filled her mind. Something wasn't right here in Four Winds. Just beneath the people's friendliness was an edge of tension that never went away. Their insistence on treating her as if she intended to stay in Four Winds was as disturbing as it was disarming. Even Gabriel seemed to be intent on making her an instant member of the community. She would have liked to think it was because he found her attractive, but she was beginning to realize that nothing in this town was as simple as it appeared at first glance. There were secrets here, and no one was sharing any with her.

Dejected, she sat down on the edge of her bed heavily. One thing was clear. She was trapped here, at least for now, and she'd have to make do.

Marlee knocked, then came in slowly, favoring her injured leg. In one hand was a steaming cup of cocoa. "It's an old family recipe. I hope you'll enjoy it."

Lanie sipped it slowly. "It's very good. Very rich. What's in it? It has an undertaste I can't quite place."

"I make it with half-and-half and some spices. I use a special cocoa, too." She watched Lanie savor it. "The exact recipe is a family secret," Marlee answered with a mysterious smile. "Just enjoy it."

Lanie had finished almost all of it when she saw the look of smug satisfaction etched on Marlee's face. Uneasy, Lanie set the mug down.

"I better be going and let you rest," Marlee said, moving toward the door. "Just remember, Lanie, that you're here now and part of this town. No matter how crazy it seems, you'll find things always work out in Four Winds." With those cryptic words, Marlee went down the hall.

Lanie stared at the cocoa suspiciously, her eyelids growing heavy, her thoughts fuzzy. She was tired; that was all. Marlee had no reason to harm her. The cocoa had been a gesture of friendliness, warm and caring.

Lanie leaned back on the bed, an intense weariness stealing over her. She couldn't stay awake anymore. She closed her eyes, intending to rest them for just a moment or two.

The next thing she knew, sunlight was peering through the curtains. Lanie sat up with a gasp. All her clothes were clean, not just the load she'd started last night, and were folded by the chair. She stumbled out of bed quickly and tried to clear the cobwebs from her mind. She'd never slept *that* soundly. She splashed cold water on her face. The first thing she intended to do was find Marlee and ask a few pointed questions about that secret cocoa recipe.

Chapter Four

Lanie helped herself to some coffee from the pot. "I'd intended to be a bit more useful last night, but it seems I just conked out. Though I'm normally not a heavy sleeper, I had the kind of rest that goes well with a headstone," she added, watching Marlee's reaction.

Marlee smiled sheepishly. "I'm really sorry about that. It's my cocoa. The special recipe includes some herbs that help soothe and relax, but I guess I made it too strong. When I saw you fast asleep, I realized what had happened. I was hoping you wouldn't hold it against me. That's why I decided to make up for it by finishing the wash for you."

Lanie forced a grudging smile. There wasn't much point in staying angry. "Well, I needed the sleep anyway."

"Good. I'm glad that's settled." Marlee walked inside the pantry. "I've got a list of things I'd like you to pick up for me at the grocer's," she called back. "Can you go first thing this morning?"

"Sure." Lanie turned to add milk to her coffee cup and caught sight of Gabriel in the kitchen doorway. "Good morning. Did you find out anything about the van?"

Gabriel shook his head. "I didn't think I was too far behind, but I couldn't find any trace of it last night. There aren't that many vans here in town, either, so you'd think it would stand out."

Marlee came out of the pantry and smiled at Gabriel. "Help yourself to some rolls while I go find my grocery list." Marlee walked out of the kitchen and down the hall.

"What's with Marlee's cocoa? Have you ever had some?" she asked softly.

"You've got to watch that. She laces it with some herbs said to be natural tranquilizers. I had a cup analyzed once. Everything in it is harmless, but it'll put you out like a light, particularly if you're the least bit tired."

"You should have warned me earlier," Lanie said.

Marlee came back into the room before Lanie could say anything more, and handed Lanie the list. "Here you go. The grocery store is a little ways down the street, on your right. It's easy to find. Just have Rosa put everything on my account."

Gabriel set his cup down, then went to the door with Lanie. "Time for me to get to work. Do you want a ride?"

"No, thanks. I'll walk. A little fresh air is just what I need this morning." As she stepped outside into the crisp morning air, a school bus drove by slowly. She watched it for a moment, her heart pounding like a hammer in her chest.

"Why are you so intent on *not* teaching? It's obviously something you miss."

The question was spoken in a soft, oddly persuasive tone, and Lanie almost answered before she realized what she was doing. "It's a private matter," she finally said in a clipped tone.

"And painful, too," he observed. "What are you running from, woman?"

"I'm not running."

"But you don't stay any place for long?"

"That's my choice." Although she didn't look at him directly, she knew he was studying her, trying to read her thoughts.

"Marlee told me she can give you room, but not board.

Does that mean you'll be job hunting in town today?'' he asked.

She nodded. "I'm hoping I can find some odd jobs I can do for cash, or even better, a temporary job."

"You'll be able to get work. People will help you. It's just the way they are here."

The way he said it made Four Winds sound like just another particularly friendly small town, but Lanie suspected it was much more than that. "How long have *you* lived here?" The question slipped out, but unlike the others she'd spoken to here, Gabriel didn't seem to mind.

"I grew up here, left for some time, then came back to stay about four months ago. My family's always lived in this area. Lucas, my brother, is the medic. He got his training in the Marines, then he came back here and set up that clinic you saw. The town needed one, since we have no doctor here.

"Joshua, my youngest brother, wants to be a medicine man." Gabriel placed his hand on the leather pouch at his waist. Lanie noticed the gesture, but didn't interrupt him. "He's still training, but he shows great promise, I'm told. He and my dad are off on the reservation now, but they'll be back eventually. There's something about this place that always draws us back."

"Small-town living isn't for me," she answered. "If I ever do settle down, it'll be in a more urban area."

"Where you can get easily lost in the crowd?"

She shrugged, but remained silent.

"By the way, you might ask Alma at the antique shop about a job. This is her busy time of year. Her business is mostly mail order. She makes up catalogs and sends them all over the U.S." His gaze stayed on her, his eyes filled with a dark intent she couldn't define. "If you need help with anything, let me know."

"You're so helpful, it almost sounds as if you want me to stay," she said slowly. She was aware that what she was doing was as dangerous as baiting a bear, but she felt compelled to learn what was on his mind.

"You're here, woman," he said after a moment. "That's a fact. All I'm doing is trying to give you a hand." Gabriel regarded her for several seconds. "Is that what worries you? You're not used to having someone help you without trying to take advantage of you?"

"What makes you say that?" she demanded.

"You're traveling alone, running from something, and defensive more often than not." He held up one hand, stemming her protests. "Caution is a learned response that usually comes from experience."

There was no criticism implied in his words. It was an observation and one, she had to admit, that was remarkably accurate. "I'm a survivor. You don't have to concern yourself about me."

"A survivor is just someone who has lived through great pain. The ability to get through it and go on is often nothing more than a mark of patience."

Gabriel's eyes met hers, and the warmth and understanding in his gaze penetrated the walls she'd so carefully constructed. Though she didn't know his story, intuition told her they were kindred spirits.

She broke eye contact suddenly, thinking she was going crazy. The last thing she needed was to entertain fanciful notions that only led to trouble.

"Don't be so wary around me. There's no need," he said in a quiet voice. "I'm not looking to seduce you. If I were, I'd do a better job."

She nearly choked. "Your ego is certainly healthy, but let me bring you back to earth. To get anywhere with me, I'd have to be interested in you, and I'm not."

"If you say so." Gabriel gave her a cocky grin that told her he hadn't been fooled.

"You're free to dream, I suppose." Lanie shrugged.

"I'm not a dreamer. I live in the present, pretty woman, and deal with things as they happen."

She buttoned up her jacket. He was making her feel as nervous and awkward as a teenager. "I better get started," she said. "Thanks for tipping me off about the job." She crossed the street then, and as she reached the sidewalk, she glanced back.

She regretted it immediately. Gabriel caught her glance, smiled and winked. Feeling her cheeks grow hot, she doubled her pace. There was chemistry between them, pure and simple, and that was what made him dangerous to her. The last thing she needed in her life now was romance. That only led to pain, and she'd had her share of that already.

Main Street was a ten-minute walk, five if you hurried, but the charm lasted longer. Struggling to keep herself from finding the town too appealing, Lanie forced herself to list its limited assets. In addition to the boardinghouse and library, there was a post office, a feed store that also carried clothing, the sheriff's office, the diner, the antique store Gabriel had mentioned, a small grocery store and the garage where her car was being held captive. As she passed one small intersection, she noted a one-story bank and some other businesses on the next street over. Most of the other buildings she could see looked like homes.

Despite her determination to resist Four Winds's folksy appeal, Lanie couldn't shake a crazy sense of homecoming. She'd never been here, didn't want to be here now, yet it felt as if she'd finally found the place where she belonged. Discarding that unsettling thought, she concentrated on the tasks ahead of her today.

As she reached the feed store, an old van parked on the street caught her eye. It looked to be the same one she'd seen before. Giving in to curiosity, she took a closer look. An elderly man wearing a cotton tunic shirt and faded jeans pulled open the side door of the vehicle, reached inside and brought down a hinged piece of plywood, unfolding two attached legs. It looked a little like an old-style Murphy bed and obviously served as a display counter. He then began arranging some pottery and crafts on the wooden table.

As she watched, Lanie could hear two women talking inside the feed store.

"He's back," said one. "I don't think that peddler has been through here in what, two years?"

"I wonder what he's brought us this time?"

"Good things wrapped up in a parcel of trouble, no doubt."

More curious than ever, Lanie found herself walking closer to the van. She really wasn't positive it was the same one she'd seen the day before, but it intrigued her. She read the peddler's sign. Curious Goods—Prices To Fit Every Customer.

Her gaze traveled over the pottery collection he'd just laid out. One bowl in particular caught her eye. Maybe it was the strange markings that adorned it, or perhaps it was the color, which seemed to be just one shade darker than silver gray. She couldn't resist taking a closer look.

The peddler smiled, noting her interest, and waved for her to approach. "Come look."

Lanie strolled to where he was. The peddler appeared to be an Indian man, though she wasn't certain from which tribe, and he wasn't nearly as old as she'd thought initially. His face looked weathered, but had a timeless quality. His eyes were dark gray, almost the color of the bowl that had interested her.

Lanie picked up a few of the smaller bowls, but none captured her attention to the same degree.

The peddler reached for the bowl she'd wanted and held it out to her. "I can see this is the one you're really interested in. I think it's meant for you."

Lanie knew she should walk away. She really didn't

have the money to spend on whims. Yet, driven by an urge too strong to resist, she took it from his hands.

The clay felt smooth and cool to the touch, like soft silk or smooth velvet, and she found handling it oddly compelling. Reluctantly she held it out to him. "I'm sorry. I wish I could buy it, but I can't afford it. I haven't got any money to spare, or even a job. I'm new in town. In fact, I think you and I arrived about the same time."

He nodded. "We're both wanderers, then," he said with a smile. "Since prices are set to meet the individual, for you, miss, it's free. A gift."

"I couldn't possibly," she started to protest, when the bowl was pressed into her hands.

"Accept it, to make an old man happy." he insisted.

His eyes entreated her. Lanie realized that it was important to him that she accept. In many Indian cultures, turning down a gift was an insult. Unwilling to hurt the man's feelings by refusing his generosity, and really wanting the beautiful bowl, she accepted it. "Thank you very much."

His expression changed the instant she accepted it. He looked at her in triumph, as if he'd just met a life-long goal.

"It is yours for life now," he said quietly. "Its fate and yours are intertwined. I must caution you that this particular piece has a legend attached to it. The pot is said to have belonged to a Navajo skinwalker, a witch, and some believe it brings trouble. You will either control it, or it will control you."

Now she understood why the Indian man had been eager to get rid of it. It was obvious he believed the legend. "Thanks for the warning, but I don't believe in things like that."

"Whether you believe or not doesn't make much difference to the spirit world. But I should warn you that others may try to take it from you. Keep it safe and away from curious eyes."

"It's valuable, then?"

He nodded slowly. "To some more than others." Abruptly he smiled. "Or perhaps it's simply a pottery bowl an old man wanted to give a pretty lady so she'd remember him," he added, a mischievous twinkle in his eyes.

Lanie laughed. The old man was a crafty one, all right. He'd woven a tale to pique her interest and make the gift more valuable in her eyes. "I thank you for the gift."

"Go in beauty," he said in the way she'd heard the Navajos say goodbye.

Wrapping the bowl in her handkerchief, she placed it carefully into her tote bag and walked to the grocery store. As she strolled past the other stores, Lanie noticed some of the townspeople watching her, though no one approached her or said anything. When she made eye contact, they quickly glanced away.

As Lanie arrived at the small grocery store, a middle-aged Hispanic woman came out from behind the counter. "I'm Rosa Gomez. That peddler sure is an odd one. He comes and goes and always has something interesting to show for his travels. What was it he gave you?"

Lanie unwrapped her bowl and held it out. As she did so, surprisingly she realized that she didn't really want anyone else handling it. Without making it obvious, she drew the bowl closer to herself, while still making it easy for Rosa to look at.

Rosa looked at the pottery piece with open distrust. She seemed about to make a comment when Gabriel came into the store.

"Hello, Sheriff," Rosa greeted. "Maybe you better come look at this." She cocked her head toward the bowl in Lanie's hand. "I don't know very much about Native American crafts."

Gabriel glanced down at the pottery, but made no move to touch the bowl. "Where did you get it?" he asked Lanie.

"A gift from the peddler," she answered, telling them what the man had said about it. As she spoke, another woman came over and joined them.

Lanie fought the urge to wrap the bowl back inside the handkerchief and stow it inside her bag. Though she was at a loss to explain it, the idea of having so many people looking at her gift was making her nervous.

"Rosa, do you have any of those pears I like?" The woman was in her late fifties. Her long denim skirt and loose, short-sleeved top looked stylish and comfortable.

"I'll get them for you in a minute, Alma. Why don't you take a closer look at this bowl?"

Alma glanced down at it casually but, as if sensing Lanie's reluctance, made no move to touch it. "Where did you get it?"

Lanie began to wrap her handkerchief around it. "It's just a gift from the peddler."

"Some of those old Navajo pieces sometimes have curses on them. Maybe you shouldn't have accepted it," Rosa said.

Alma rolled her eyes. "That's ridiculous." She gave Lanie a warm smile. "I'm Alma Wright. You must be our new resident."

Lanie tried to bite back her annoyance. Being referred to as the new resident was starting to get on her nerves. "I'm just passing through," she said firmly.

"Are you perhaps interested in a temporary job?"

"Yes, as a matter of fact, I am."

"Oh, good! I could use some help in my shop right now. In this small town, it's nearly impossible for me to find someone who will come in every morning and work all day. People have their own businesses to tend to. I have one young man who helps out when he can, but he works as a courier for his dad, the mayor, and he's not available most of the time.''

"Where's your shop?"

"Right next door. Come in after you're finished here. I'll show you around, and we can talk."

"Thanks. I will."

As Alma went to pay for her groceries, Lanie glanced at Gabriel. He had moved off and was picking up a small carton of juice from the refrigerated section.

"You didn't say much."

He shrugged. "I really don't know much about pottery. But to be honest, I'm not convinced that bowl is Navajo in origin, let alone a skinwalker's. It does look old, but that's about the only thing I can say for sure." He placed the juice on the counter and reached for his wallet. "I'm going to go find the peddler and introduce myself. If he's going to do business in my town, it's time for us to meet."

Lanie said goodbye to him, then finished her shopping for Marlee. As she stepped out onto the sidewalk, she saw Alma cleaning the glass window of her store, Golden Days Antique Store. Antique crosses, some made of wood and others from red and green glass, filled the display area.

Alma smiled and waved an invitation.

Lanie stepped into the store. Shelves filled with curios, from matchboxes to wooden, hand-carved cookie molds lined the walls. On the counter, however, papers were scattered several inches deep. Photographic equipment had been placed on top of them.

Alma smiled. "As you can see, I can use some help." She waved a hand around the room. "I'm in the middle of making up new catalogs. That means taking photos of the different pieces I have in here and on consignment around town, then writing descriptions for the catalog copy while I'm taking phone orders and doing the bookkeeping. I can afford to pay five dollars an hour. If you're interested, you can start tomorrow."

"When would you need me? I've agreed to do housework and run errands for Marlee in exchange for my room, so I'll have to coordinate it with that."

"I'm flexible about time, as long as the work for the day gets done. You can shuffle your hours around to suit."

"That would be perfect. But I should warn you that I don't know very much about antiques."

"You'll learn—I've got a lot of reference books here. And who knows, you may end up falling in love with the business like my sister Emily did."

Lanie found the thought of dealing with objects rather than people or, more to the point, students, comforting. Damaging a piece of furniture or curio by accident could be a great loss, but it couldn't compare to the responsibility of making a mistake that destroyed a young life. "I'll be here tomorrow, then."

"I thought flexible hours would appeal to a free spirit like you," Alma said with a twinkle in her eye.

"Free spirit?" The assessment surprised her. If there was something she was not, that was it. Not free from memories, or guilt...

"You're on the road, no ties, traveling from place to place. How else would you describe yourself?" Alma asked.

"Someone who has nothing she can't afford to lose, and likes it that way," Lanie answered softly.

"But every once in a while, life forces you to stop and take stock of things, doesn't it? Maybe this is one of those times. Your stay in Four Winds could be the opportunity to learn new things."

"That's one way to look at it," Lanie replied with a ghost of a smile.

The bell above the shop door rang as a customer entered. "I better get back to work now. You can come in anytime after nine tomorrow, and I'll get you started,"

Alma told Lanie, then turned to see what she could do to make a sale.

Lanie balanced the two grocery sacks carefully as she walked back to the boardinghouse. She was halfway there when she heard her name being called from a passing vehicle.

Gabriel pulled up next to her in his police car. "The peddler seems to have vanished into thin air. I didn't get a good enough look at him to make a positive ID. Could you ride along with me while I try to track him down? I want to ask him a few questions. Like where, for instance, he got that bowl he gave you."

"Why is that important?"

"Some places around here are sacred, and that bowl looked old enough to have come from an archaeological site. I just want to make sure he's not stealing from any of the tribes."

"Okay, I'll come. There's nothing perishable in these groceries, so they'll be fine for a while."

Gabriel helped her load the bags into the Jeep, then held the door for her. "I've been asking about this peddler. Everyone knows about him, but nobody really knows him. What they remember most are the things that happened after he left last time he was here."

"Like what?"

"Two years ago, when the peddler came through, old man Simmons bought a shovel from him. First time he used it digging for fishing worms, Simmons found a man's body someone had buried decades ago. The body was eventually identified, and the man's family came to claim him. Turns out they were so grateful to finally find out what happened to their dad that they set up a trust fund for old Simmons." Gabriel shook his head in disbelief. "The end result is that Simmons doesn't have to go fishing anymore to get meat on the table. He has steaks shipped in."

"Well, surely no one thinks the peddler's shovel had anything to do with what happened."

He smiled. "If you talk to the old-timers, they'll tell you the peddler is part of this town's history. Depending on who you talk to, they'll even try to convince you he's this town's soul. For some reason no one can explain, he stopped coming thirty or so years ago, after years of visits. Then, out of the blue, he showed up again two years ago and sold Simmons that shovel. Now he's back again. They insist that time hasn't changed anything, that strange things will always happen after the peddler visits."

"Oh, please!" she scoffed. "That man was not a creature out of a legend or some kind of spirit. He was just an old man making a living the best way he can."

"Well, tales do change the more they're carried, and this might not even be the same fellow. I don't know how much of it, if any, to believe, but I do want to find this guy. If he's selling artifacts he dug up someplace he had no business being, then I've got to put a stop to it."

"Something about that bowl really bothers you, doesn't it? What is it?"

"I don't know. I just can't put my finger on it. Maybe it's because I'm Navajo, and according to the story he told you, that thing is connected to skinwalkers. That's not a plus where I come from."

They headed down the main highway awhile, but found no trace of the peddler or his van. Frustrated, Gabriel drove to a high point and studied the surrounding area. "This doesn't make any sense. He's got to be out here somewhere."

"We can't really see into the forested area west of here. Maybe he went in there," Lanie suggested.

"But he would have had to be going eighty, at least, to have made it that far in this short time," Gabriel countered. "That old van wasn't built for speed."

Lanie stared at the way Gabriel's hand rubbed the steering wheel, his palm running back and forth over the surface. For a moment, she pictured him touching her that way, caressing. She pushed the thought back vehemently. "You have another suggestion?" she answered, annoyed with herself.

"Not at the moment."

"Do you know if it was the same van we saw driving by Marlee's?"

"I only caught a glimpse, but how many old VWs like that are still around?"

"So, what now? It's not like the guy has done anything wrong. Couldn't you just leave him in peace?"

"I suppose so. Let's go back to town. There's nothing else we can do now."

"I know you've got questions about the peddler, but there's something you have to remember. The peddler didn't *sell* me the bowl, he *gave* it to me. If he were stealing from a sacred site, don't you think he would have tried to make a profit from it to compensate for the risks he'd taken?"

"Yeah, maybe. But my gut instinct tells me that this peddler is trouble. I was a cop in L.A. for five years before coming back to Four Winds. In that time, I learned a lot about people, and there's something about this guy that's not right. I can feel it. For one thing, honest folks aren't this good at disappearing. They don't get the practice."

"I'll tell you one thing about him," Lanie said, a little annoyed at Gabriel's pessimistic view of the harmless old man, and focusing on that to stop her mind from wandering down more-dangerous avenues. "That peddler seemed as honest as anyone else I've met in Four Winds. Why don't you cut him a little slack?"

Surprised by her vehement defense of the old man, Gabriel glanced over at her. "Though you're pretty suspicious of people's motives, you're not in the least worried about the peddler's. How come?"

She considered it for a moment. "It's my impression of him. If he's been stealing from sacred sites, he certainly hasn't been making oodles of money at it. My guess is that he barely gets by. That van of his is at least thirty years old, and his clothes were faded and threadbare."

Before he could counter that argument, a call came over his radio. This time the dispatcher's voice came through clearly. "Unit One, this is Home Base. Do you copy?"

"Go ahead, Base."

"Marlee called from the boardinghouse. Someone's broken in over there. The intruders might still be inside, so she called in from next door and she'll wait for you out by the apple tree until you check out the place."

"I'll be there. Ten-four."

"Ten-four. Base out."

"I thought you said you didn't have crime here," Lanie muttered.

"We don't," Gabriel answered. "Or at least we didn't, until now." He turned off on a side road and slowed the unit to a stop at a bend in the road about three blocks from the boardinghouse. "I'll drop you off here. You'll be okay."

"I'm not getting out. I don't know Marlee all that well, but she's been decent to me, and if she's in trouble, I'd like to be there for her. She might need help."

From the determined look on her face, Gabriel knew that the only way he'd get her to leave was if he physically forced her out. He didn't have time for that.

"Suit yourself," he snapped.

He whipped around the bend in the road and drove up a rutted trail to the rear of the house. Stopping about thirty yards away, behind the cover of some piñons, he left the Jeep, staying low to the ground.

"Stay here," he whispered.

Lanie strained to see ahead, figuring four eyes were better than two. As she shifted to one side, she spotted a dark shape near a window. Concentrating to recall the floor plan, she suddenly realized it was her bedroom window. Moving quickly, she left the car and caught up with Gabriel. "Look over there. A man's standing by my window."

"I saw him," Gabriel whispered, then glowered at her. "I thought I told you to stay put."

"I was trying to help—don't be so ungrateful," she said defensively. "I wonder what he's doing there. There's nothing in my room worth stealing." The peddler's warning suddenly rang in Lanie's mind. She glanced back through the open door of the Jeep at the tote bag she'd left on the seat. "Not yet, anyway."

Gabriel followed her line of vision. Was the pot already attracting interest in town? His gut feeling that it meant trouble might be turning out to be right. "We'll look into that angle later. Right now, I've got a job to do."

Lanie walked quietly back to the Jeep, watching Gabriel as he moved toward the boardinghouse. He soon became one with the shadows and disappeared from her view.

Chapter Five

Gabriel crept forward, senses attuned to danger. Years of hunting in the desert had made him a good stalker. But now, memories from another time and place crowded his mind, taunting his confidence and courage. A woman back in L.A., a shotgun blast, the blood that had poured from her in a never ending stream.

He shook his head, pushing back the thoughts. This wasn't the time. He had to stay sharp. Things were sure getting weird in Four Winds all of a sudden. First the fire and Lanie, next the peddler with the crazy legacy and now a prowler.

He was about eight yards away from Lanie's window when he realized the dark shape there wasn't a person. It was a bulging blue pillowcase that had been snagged by the pyracantha bush beside it.

He kept his back pressed to the house wall as he moved forward, gun drawn. No sounds came from inside the room. He raised his head slowly and peered through the broken window. Lanie's room was in shambles, but there was no one inside. Even the closet door stood ajar. Whoever had broken in had left in one heck of a hurry, judging by the booty left behind.

Holstering his weapon, he crouched down and studied the ground for tracks. He found some immediately. Two men wearing sneakers, approximately size nine, had gained entry here. Of course, sneakers were a dime a dozen in town, since those were the cheapest shoes Darren Wilson carried in his store.

Gabriel hoisted himself through the window, careful of the glass. Once inside, he searched the house methodically. Satisfied no one was there, he stepped out the front door and looked around. Lanie was standing with Marlee by the apple tree near the fence. Fear was etched on Marlee's face. Lanie seemed flushed with anger and determination. Full of fire, she seemed even more beautiful than usual.

He signaled them it was safe to approach and watched Lanie help Marlee cross the uneven ground. Lanie continued to be a fascinating puzzle to him. He had initiated a background check on her, but so far hadn't found out much. As far as he could tell, Lanie had never even been cited for a traffic violation. Yet there was no doubt she was on the run, though evidently not from the law.

"Whoever was here is long gone," he assured them as they came into the house. "And it looks like only Lanie's room was disturbed."

Marlee's anxiety was evident as she hurried to Lanie's room. "Why would they break into the boardinghouse?" She stepped inside Lanie's room and glanced back at her. "Can you answer that?"

Lanie shook her head, then gestured toward the pillowcase filled with loot that Gabriel had set on top of the bed. "Let's see what they tried to take. Maybe we can figure out from that what it is they wanted."

Gabriel held the sack open for them. "Be careful not to touch anything in here. This isn't the work of someone passing through. Strangers stick out in Four Winds. Since we have no professional thieves in Four Winds, my guess is that they left fingerprints on everything. None of the kids in town have criminal records that I know of, so these fingerprints will probably not be on file. But they're still evidence that might come in handy at some point if we need to confirm the involvement of a particular suspect.''

Lanie studied the contents of the pillowcase. They'd taken the small notebook she used for recording expenses, her travel journal, which simply listed the places she'd passed through, some towels and two small sandpaintings Marlee had used as room decorations. "Not exactly a treasure trove, is it?" she mused.

"Why would anyone break in just for that stuff?" Marlee asked. "Those sandpaintings are in every booth at the county-fair craft show, and the towels are nothing special.''

"Maybe they came in expecting to find more but had to settle for that instead," Gabriel said, then looked at Lanie. "Who was around when the peddler gave you that pottery bowl?"

She shrugged. "I don't know. I haven't met very many of the townsfolk yet. I remember seeing several people around, but I wasn't looking at anyone closely."

Gabriel weighed everything in his mind. There was definitely something going on in his town. When he'd returned four months ago, he'd assumed his biggest worry as sheriff would be boredom, but things were changing. He could feel it. The sense of danger was unmistakable, like the electrically charged air that would make a person's hair stand on end right before a lightning strike.

"Wait a minute," Marlee said, interrupting his thoughts. "Did I understand this right?" She looked directly at Lanie. "You accepted a gift from the *peddler?*"

"Yes." Lanie pulled the bowl from her tote bag. "It's just a small piece." Seeing the wariness on Marlee's face, she added, "Does it bother you?"

"Worries me is more like it," Marlee answered. "Tell me this, the van you said you kept seeing, could it have been the peddler's?"

Lanie shrugged. "I think so, but I can't swear to it."

"It seems to me that he might have selected you long before he gave you the pot." Marlee's eyes narrowed in thought. "People around here say that nothing ever happens by chance in Four Winds. They believe our town calls people to it so they can fulfill their destinies. I think that bowl is part of yours."

Gabriel exhaled loudly. "I've never believed that people are forced to do anything by unseen powers. We all have choices."

"I agree with you up to a point. I do believe that Four Winds brings people here, but how they shape their destiny is up to them," Marlee said quietly.

"So what are you saying?" Lanie asked. "That the fire and my car breaking down were all part of my fate? That Four Winds called me?"

"Yes. That much, I'd say, is obvious. What remains to be seen is why it's important for you to have that pot, and what happens now that you have it."

Gabriel studied Lanie's expression. He could see that she wasn't sure how much to believe, and how much was Marlee's very convincing imagination. He couldn't blame her.

"Well, it's time to get to work repairing that window. Otherwise, we're all in for a cold night." Marlee glanced at Gabriel. "Could you help me out with this? I've got some tools in the kitchen closet."

"Sure," Gabriel agreed. "You two can go inside if you want."

"I'll bring in the groceries I left in Gabriel's vehicle," Lanie said, "and I'll meet you inside, Marlee. We can put the food away while Gabriel is busy here."

"I'll work as quickly as I can with my investigation, then fix the damage," Gabriel answered.

As Lanie headed back to the patrol vehicle, Gabriel joined her. "Let's both ride in," Gabriel suggested. "I

need the evidence box I keep in the Jeep, so I might as
well bring the vehicle around and park in my usual spot.''

A few moments later, they were driving back to the
house. "I just don't buy Marlee's story about that peddler," Lanie said. "He's a stranger who comes and goes
as he pleases, and that's why he's such an easy target for
the townspeople. He's a mystery to them, so they blame
him for everything that happens that they can't explain."

Gabriel said nothing. There were too many questions
running through his mind. He stole a look at Lanie as he
pulled up to the house and parked. He was starting to
realize that when he'd gone to her rescue in that fire, he'd
found far more than he'd expected. He'd carried this
woman of passion and courage out of that inferno and into
his life. Now he wasn't at all sure what to do with her. In
so many ways, she seemed vulnerable, and that aroused
his protective instincts. But he would have been a fool not
to notice that Lanie was at the center of all the trouble
he'd seen lately in Four Winds. She either attracted it like
a magnet, or caused it. He just wasn't sure which.

He grabbed his investigation box from the rear of the
vehicle and walked toward the boardinghouse. It was time
to concentrate on his job, not on her. "I'm going to search
your room for prints and other evidence. After I'm
through, I'll let you know and you can come in and clean
up. Then we'll have a go at that window."

Gabriel went into Lanie's room and closed the door behind him. First he searched the room methodically. There
weren't many clues, but he did manage to lift a few prints.
As he considered the significance of the items the thieves
had tried to take, he felt sure that they'd come to learn
about Lanie. The sandpaintings and the towels had probably been taken out of frustration since there wasn't much
here of a personal nature. But why the curiosity about her?
That remained to be answered.

Finished, he walked out into the hall and called out, "I'm through here. You two can come in."

Lanie and Marlee came down the hall. Lanie was carrying a plastic bucket containing a few basic tools. "First thing we have to do is measure that window so we can come up with something to cover it for tonight," Marlee said, reaching into the bucket for a tape measure.

"I think there's a piece of plywood out by the woodpile," Gabriel said. "I'll get it."

While Gabriel was looking for the plywood, Marlee swept the floor and Lanie picked up.

Gabriel returned with a thin piece of wood about the right size as Lanie took the small bowl from her tote bag and placed it on the dresser.

"Let me hold that tape measure, Marlee," she said, moving toward the window.

While the women were occupied, Gabriel walked over to where Lanie had placed the bowl and studied it without picking it up.

He saw Lanie watching him from the corner of her eye as she continued to help Marlee. He was aware of the way her gaze drifted over him appreciatively. He tried not to smile. He caught her glance and held it for a moment longer than was necessary, and saw her blush and look away.

"I've been thinking about that peddler," she said quickly. "If he followed me into town, he must have known about the fire. I wonder if the reason he gave me the bowl was because he figured anyone lucky enough to survive that could deal with any bad luck it would bring."

Marlee shrugged. "Maybe he just accepted that the fire hadn't gotten out of hand by accident, that it was Four Winds's way of drawing you here."

"I don't know if I buy that, Marlee," she said, glancing at Gabriel.

Overcoming his reluctance, Gabriel picked up the pot.

He turned it slowly around in his hands, but as his palm brushed against a rough spot on the top edge, a burning sensation began in his palm and grew swiftly until he could hardly bear to move his arm. He bit down on his lip to keep from groaning and somehow, instead of dropping the bowl, he managed to set it down.

"You okay?" Lanie asked.

"Yeah. Look, I'm going to nail up that plywood, then give my brother a call. I'd like him to take a look at your bowl, if you don't mind. He knows more about things like this than I do."

"Not at all. I'd like to find out more about it."

A few minutes later, Gabriel walked to his room, hugging his injured hand. It had reddened and blistered as though he'd touched a hot coal. He wasn't sure what had happened. Lanie had handled the bowl all day long, apparently without any ill effects. A legend he'd heard a long time ago played at the corners of his mind, but he was having difficulty remembering some of the details.

Certain Lucas would, he picked up the phone and dialed. He'd have some answers soon, but somehow he had a feeling knowing what was going on wouldn't make things any better.

WITHIN THIRTY MINUTES, he heard his brother's truck drive up. It was hard to miss the backfires that were as much part of it as the nearly bald tires or the ancient engine.

He went outside just as Lucas got out of the truck. "Hey, Shadow." Lucas had earned the nickname as a kid, always following Gabriel, his older brother, wherever he went.

"Fuzz?" Gabriel had always wanted to be a cop, hence the nickname. "What's going on? I've been hearing all sorts of things from the folks I've been treating, and now

I get this call from you on my mobile number asking me to head over here on the double.''

"I wouldn't have called if it wasn't important.''

"I wouldn't be here if I didn't believe that,'' Lucas countered with a grin.

As they walked inside, Marlee and Lanie came to the front door. Gabriel saw the look Marlee gave his brother. She'd always had a soft spot for him.

He introduced Lanie, then watched her reaction to the newcomer. Lucas's tall, lean build had always drawn a fair share of attention from women. The possibility that Lanie might find his little brother appealing disturbed Gabriel, though he wasn't at all sure why he should care. To his immense relief, Lanie scarcely gave Lucas more than a glance.

"Shall I bring the bowl?'' she asked Gabriel.

"Please,'' he said.

Marlee looked at Lucas. "I can see you two want a chance to talk alone,'' she said, disappointment obvious in her tone. "But don't rush off afterward, okay, Lucas? I've baked you some chocolate-chip cookies.''

Lucas gave her a smile. "That's my favorite kind of invitation.''

Marlee laughed. "One of them, at least,'' she teased, then left the room.

The moment they were alone, Gabriel hurried to fill Lucas in on everything that had happened since Lanie had accepted the bowl.

"Trouble follows that peddler. I've heard too much from too many people over the years to assume it's all just nonsense.'' Lucas glanced at his brother's hand. "That burn looks nasty. I'd better put something on it.''

Gabriel winced as he flexed his hand. "That's another thing,'' he added. "The woman's been handling that bowl all day, and nothing's happened to her. I didn't tell her about this, and to be honest, I'm not sure she'd believe this burn had anything to do with the bowl. Hell, I'm not sure *I* believe it, and I know there's no other explanation. There was nothing on that plywood I handled, that's for sure.''

Lucas looked up from bandaging the burn, then noted the medicine bundle Gabriel had at his waist. "Good thing you're keeping the *jish* with you," he said, meeting his brother's gaze. "Remember the story our uncle told us?"

He nodded slowly. "Yes, but I wanted to ask you about some of the details. To be honest, I never paid much attention to the story. It didn't even scare me much, since I thought it was nonsense. I know that a lot of our family's history, from our father's side, was lost after Grandfather and his brothers were killed during World War I. I always figured that our uncle's story was a way to generate family history, nothing more. Now I'm not so sure.''

Lanie came back in before Lucas could respond. She set the bowl down on the table before them. "It's got this little rough spot here," she said brushing the loose clay from it, "so if you handle it, be careful.''

Lucas and Gabriel exchanged a quick glance. "I saw that look, guys. What's going on? Is it stolen?"

Lucas glanced at Gabriel, deferring the question with raised eyebrows.

Gabriel considered it for a moment. He wouldn't tell her the whole story, since he wasn't sure how much he could trust her yet, but not telling her anything at all could be even worse. She'd search for answers on her own then, and there was no telling what trouble that would cause.

"A long time ago, our uncle told us a story," Gabriel said, motioning for her to have a seat. "It's a tale about one of our clan and the past that touches our present." His voice grew soft as he remembered and shared the tale in the tradition of his people. "Our great-great-grandfather, a great *hataalii*, a medicine man, was called upon to battle a powerful skinwalker. Our ancestor fought bravely, but his victory was limited. He escaped with his life, but he never truly defeated his enemy because he never found the root of his power, the bowl the skinwalker had made from the ashes of the woman the skinwalker had loved and killed.'' He watched Lanie's eyes light up in fascination. To her, it was simply a ghost story. Unfortunately, if he was right, there was a lot more to it than that.

''What makes you think it's the same bowl?'' she asked.

''There's the coyote figure on the side,'' Lucas said, pointing to save his brother the need to explain the burn on his hand. ''Also, there's the figure with a bandanna on his head.''

She looked carefully at the pottery designs. ''I guess they could be what you say, but neither is really well defined.''

''True,'' Lucas admitted. ''But the possibility is there.''

''So are you saying it belongs to your clan?'' Lanie glanced at Gabriel.

''No, not at all. It's yours.''

''Well, that's good, because I really do like it, and I took it to heart when the peddler said it was mine for life,'' she said with a tiny smile.

''He said that, and you didn't try to give it back to him?'' Lucas stared at her in surprise. ''You have a lot to learn about our ways, woman.''

Gabriel caught the precaution in Lucas's phrase. Names had power, and were not to be used freely. His brother Lucas normally didn't pay attention to things like that. The fact that he was doing so now made Gabriel jittery.

''I don't understand,'' Lanie said. ''Why should I have given the bowl back?''

''Our legends are filled with warnings like that. We don't take things of that nature lightly,'' Lucas said.

Gabriel stepped closer to Lanie and gave his brother a stern look. ''What my brother means is that an object like that bowl could be linked to our history as a people and could be of great value," Gabriel said, turning to give Lanie a reassuring smile.

Lucas glanced from the woman to his brother, then smiled slowly.

Gabriel looked down at the bowl, then back to Lanie. "You better take that with you and find somewhere safe to keep it. In the meantime, my brother and I have some family business to discuss." He led Lucas down the hall to his room.

Once they were both inside, Gabriel shut the door quickly and faced Lucas. "What do you know about the peddler? Do you have any idea where he goes after he makes an appearance in our town?"

"The last time he came to Four Winds, I was still in the Marines. Dad was the sheriff back then. I remember hearing that Dad had wanted to question him about something, but wasn't able to locate him. You know as well as I do that Dad can track anyone, but that time he failed. He didn't take it gracefully, either. He was really ticked off that the peddler gave him the slip."

"I have to find Dad and Joshua. Between them, they should be able to tell me everything I need to know about the peddler and that damned bowl."

"You do remember the last of the story, don't you? Or is that why you called me?"

"Refresh my memory," Gabriel said.

"It was foretold that the bowl would be found again someday, and that another member of our clan would be called to defeat its power or die." He took a deep breath. "The problem is that the bowl is linked to its owner, and their fates are intertwined. There's more, but I just can't remember the rest. Finding Dad could be a big help to you, but it's going to take a while. Josh talked Dad into trying to track down Rudolph Harvey, the *hataalii* who's said to live down by Mount Taylor. He's the only one

around who knows the songs that Josh wants to learn."
Lucas stared at an indeterminate spot across the room. "I
can probably find our uncle easier, but I'll search for all
three. At least one of them is bound to turn up."

"Thanks."

Lucas walked to the door and stopped before opening
it. "Remember one thing. You can't take the pot from the
woman. It has to remain with her, since she's accepted it.
To do otherwise is to risk her life."

"*If* the legend is true, and *if* it's the same pot."

Lucas glanced down at his brother's injured hand. "Do
you doubt it?"

"I don't know. But for starters, I intend to have that
clay analyzed."

"You're willing to risk the woman's life to do it?"

Gabriel took a deep breath and let it out slowly. "No.
The bowl will remain with her. I'll just take a sample from
that roughened spot."

Lucas smiled and nodded. "I figured you'd protect your
woman."

"*My* woman?" He shook his head. "You're mistaken."

Lucas raised one eyebrow. "I don't think so. You may
not have made your move on her yet, but she's the one
you want."

"You're full of it, Shadow."

"Maybe, but you know it's true."

"If this is the legendary bowl, why do you think *she*
was chosen?"

"I have no idea. Maybe it has something to do with the
bond between you."

Gabriel started to deny that any bond existed, then
changed his mind. He wasn't good at lying.

The two brothers walked back to the living room. "How
soon will you be leaving?" Gabriel asked.

"I've just about finished my rounds. Once I've checked
on Marlee's leg, I'll pack my gear, gather some supplies,

then go. I'm going to have to hike quite a ways, so I want to be prepared.''

"Intimidated by a little walk?" Gabriel grinned. "That's what you get when you have too many women all trying to feed you."

Lucas glowered at Gabriel. "You're a real…"

Marlee came into the room just then, carrying a tray of chocolate-chip cookies. Seeing Lucas near the door, she gave him a hopeful smile. "Ready for a snack?"

Lucas glared at his brother as if daring him to open his mouth, then turned and smiled back at Marlee. "I can't stay long today. I've got a long trip to make," he said gently. "But before I go, I should see how my patient is doing. How's the leg?"

"Much better, thanks."

Lucas helped Marlee to a chair, then helped her flex the knee. Working carefully, he checked for signs of swelling around the cast. "You seem to be doing much better than last time. In about a month, the cast will come off, and all this will be behind you."

"But you'll come by once in a while as a follow-up?" she asked with a hesitant smile.

"Oh, I'll be around from time to time."

Gabriel watched his brother try to sidestep Marlee's questions. If there ever was a confirmed bachelor, Lucas was it. But women always looked at him wistfully, as if the fairer sex simply couldn't resist trying to tame something wild.

Lanie came into the room as Lucas stood up. "I've got the bowl tucked away now," she said, looking at Gabriel, then at Lucas.

"That's good," Gabriel answered, his mood somber.

"Why do I get the feeling that you two are keeping something else from me? What *is* it about that bowl?"

Fear shadowed Lanie's eyes. Gabriel fought the sudden urge to kiss her and let desire replace the dark emotions mirrored there. "We don't really know much yet. Hang tight. We'll let you know more as soon as we can. Until then, just stay on your guard."

As he looked into her worried eyes, he felt a fierce protectiveness stealing over him. He had saved this woman and brought her here. He would not allow anyone or anything to harm her. Whoever or whatever threatened her would have to get past him first.

"Maybe I shouldn't keep the bowl here," she said hesitantly. "I don't want anyone hurt because of it. Let me give it to you so you can put it someplace safe."

Though her voice was even, he could see the uncertainty mirrored in her gaze. "I can't take it. It's yours now, and with it, the responsibility." Seeing her confusion, he added, "Let me say goodbye to my brother. When I come back, I'll try to explain."

Gabriel matched his brother's strides as they walked out to the truck. "I know it's a lot to ask of someone used to hot meals and a soft bed, but hike in and out of the desert as fast as possible, okay?"

"That's it," Lucas said, stopping in midstride and facing his brother. "You've hassled me enough today. Want to take me on, Fuzz?"

Gabriel grinned. They'd done this a million times, and he was hard-pressed to say which of them enjoyed it most. "Sorry, little Shadow. I'm going to have to pass this time. If I break your legs, then you won't be able to help me by finding the people I need to talk to," he said, knowing the reply would irritate Lucas.

"You're just getting old," Lucas replied. "Can't back up your words anymore, can you?"

Gabriel was just about to answer when he heard a soft rustle to their right. "Trouble," he warned just as two men wearing ski masks jumped out of the shadows.

As one swung a two-by-four at Lucas's back, the other aimed a kick at Gabriel's jaw. Gabriel ducked, evading the blow, and slammed his fist hard into the man's midsection. His opponent recovered quickly and, recapturing his balance, took a quick jab at Gabriel.

Gabriel saw the punch coming and stepped back, blocking with his forearm, blunting the attack. As he glanced to the side, he saw his brother hadn't escaped the initial attack unscathed. The strike from the piece of lumber had knocked the breath out of him.

Lucas was still gasping as he evaded another wild swing, then kicked up, knocking the piece of wood from his opponent's hands. "Don't worry, Fuzz." He panted. "Now that I've disarmed this idiot, I'll finish up quick and come save your butt."

His brother's goading inspired Gabriel to make quick work of the thug attacking him. Moving fast, Gabriel grabbed his opponent's arm and, with a quick sidestep, threw the man to the ground. As the thug scrambled back to his feet, Gabriel caught a glimpse of Lucas tackling his own opponent and reaching for the concealing mask.

Gabriel moved toward his own attacker, intending to finish the fight once and for all, when the blast of a shotgun exploded behind him.

Lucas jumped behind cover as Gabriel spun around, drawing his pistol. Gabriel stared at Lanie in surprise. The pair who'd jumped them had taken off in a run. He lowered his weapon and scowled at her.

"Take this shotgun, will you?" she managed to say in a shaky voice. "Marlee insisted I help you two by firing off a round into the air. I've done it, but I'm never touching this thing again."

Chapter Six

Gabriel holstered his handgun and took the shotgun from her shaking hands. "Why did you fire? It wasn't necessary. In another minute, we would have had them." Gabriel's eyes narrowed as he watched Lanie's expression, searching for nuances that would reveal her thoughts far more than words.

"I was just trying to help. From inside the house, it didn't look like either of you was doing so great."

Gabriel could hear Lucas sprinting through the woods, chasing after the pair. He wouldn't have a chance. Lanie's move had given the men the opportunity they needed to escape. "If you hadn't interfered, we would have had both suspects in custody right now. Instead, we have nothing except a vague description that could fit half the known world."

"Next time I'll be sure to stand back and watch you get your heads pounded in."

"None of the Blackhorse brothers have ever lost a fight," he answered, his voice matter-of-fact.

She rolled her eyes. "Oh, please. Testosterone doesn't impress me."

"It should. That one hormone can compel much more than a fight. I'd love to demonstrate sometime." He watched her face turn a lovely shade of pink, and he had to smile.

Hearing running footsteps, Gabriel turned his head. Lucas returned, short of breath. "I couldn't catch up. They drove off long before I even got close. They'd parked about fifty yards from here."

"I'll go back there in a minute. Maybe I can tell what kind of vehicle they had."

"I already checked that for you. I never saw it, but to me it sounded like a pickup," Lucas answered.

"Which won't give us much. Around here, everyone has at least one truck."

Marlee came out slowly, favoring her leg. "Are you two all right?" Her gaze strayed over Lucas gently.

Lucas smiled at her. "Sure, we are. We can take a few punches."

"But they still hurt," she added, her voice whisper soft.

Gabriel saw the concern in Marlee's eyes and wished he could have seen the same in Lanie's when she looked at him. What he had seen in hers was annoyance. Of course, that was his fault. Maybe he should have thanked her first before pointing out the dismal results of her actions.

"Do you think this all happened because of my bowl?" Lanie asked.

Gabriel took a deep breath and let it out slowly. "I don't know. They had no intention of killing us—otherwise they would have tried to grab my pistol, or they'd have been armed. I think they were hoping to rough us up enough to get us out of the way for a while."

"Optimistic of them," Lucas scoffed.

Gabriel flexed his hand. His knuckles were raw and skinned, and his burn throbbed. Meanwhile, Marlee was holding his brother's hand, fussing over him, and Lucas was eating it up.

He looked at Lanie, and she gave him a haughty stare.

"Don't expect any sympathy from me," she snapped. "Didn't you say you had the fight under control?" She continued, not expecting an answer. "Well, then, I'm sure bruises were all part of your plan, too." She turned and strode back into the house.

Gabriel followed her back into the boardinghouse, then went to his room to wash up. Lucas came in a moment later. He closed the door, then burst out laughing.

Gabriel glowered at him. "What's with you?"

"You looked like a pup who has lost his supper dish."

Gabriel washed the blood from his knuckles, careful to avoid wetting the bandage Lucas had placed over his burn. "Women don't fuss over me, because they know I'm not a wuss."

"Right. That's why you're so jealous you can't see straight."

"Of you? Give me a break." Gabriel dried off his hands, trying to think of something constructive. "Did you get in at least one solid punch, something hard enough to leave a mark?"

"You mean like a black eye, or something that'll make whoever it was easier to identify?" Lucas shook his head. "Not really. How about you?"

"I don't think so, but if I see anyone around town sporting bruises, he and I are going to have a chat." Gabriel walked with his brother back down the hall. "You better get going and see if you can find our uncle, or Dad and Josh. I'm going to need all the information I can get, and as fast as possible."

As Lucas drove away, another truck pulled in. A moment later, Ralph Montoya got out and strode toward the boardinghouse, notepad and tape recorder in hand.

Gabriel saw him approach and had to force himself not to duck away from the entrance. He didn't personally dislike the man but, as a general rule, he hated reporters.

"Hey, I'm in luck! It's the real-life hero of the day!"

Ralph greeted. "I was hoping to catch up to you!" Ralph glanced down at Gabriel's tan shirt and noted the torn pocket. His gaze swept over him with the meticulousness of a trained observer, marking his bruised knuckles. "Trouble again?" Not getting a fast enough response, he glanced past Gabriel at the women. "Is everyone here all right? I saw Lucas take off just a moment ago, so I assumed he'd been here taking a look at Marlee's leg. But it looks like there was a fight."

"We had some excitement," Marlee said. "Two burglars—" She stopped speaking abruptly, seeing the warning look on Gabriel's face. "Maybe you better ask the sheriff," she said, leaving the room.

"I came here to get the details of how you rescued our newest resident, but it looks like I'm on a lucky streak today." Ralph smiled at Lanie as she came into the room.

Gabriel saw the hungry spark in Ralph's eyes. He'd seen that look on members of the press before. Ralph would be genetically incapable of letting it go without an explanation now. "It was just a couple of kids looking for trouble," Gabriel said, deliberately downplaying the attack. "Not exactly front-page news."

"What were they after? The pottery bowl?" He glanced at Lanie, then at Gabriel.

Lanie gasped. "How on earth could you know about the bowl?"

Gabriel just shook his head slowly. Too late to do anything now. Ralph knew how to get people talking, and he'd certainly pushed the right buttons today.

"The peddler is a favorite subject of conversation in Four Winds," Ralph told Lanie.

"What do you know about him?" Lanie asked.

"No more than the sheriff does, I'm sure," Ralph answered with a glance at Gabriel. "Newsworthy events seem to follow this man's visits as sunshine follows the rain, kind of like the Pied Piper. But sometimes he brings the rats, too. Would you mind if I took a look at the bowl he gave you?''

Lanie hesitated. "I'll make a deal with you. I'll show it to you if you promise to find out all you can about it.'' She glanced at Gabriel, who nodded.

As Lanie left the room, Gabriel glanced at Ralph. "I'd appreciate it if you'd show me what you find out before you print it.''

Ralph considered the request. "In turn, will you cut me some slack about parking in front of my office?''

"It's a fire zone, not a parking area. But okay. Just *your* vehicle, though.''

Lanie came out, holding the bowl in the palm of her hand, then set it on a shelf that was eye level. Ralph studied the pottery, but when he reached for it, Gabriel quickly intervened. "No, don't handle it. Oils from your hand might discolor it. Until I'm sure of where it came from, and what its value is, I think it's best if Lanie is the only one to touch it. It'll minimize any risk to the piece.''

Ralph made a sketch of the bowl and its markings, then flipped his small notebook shut. "I'll let you know as soon as I find something out.''

Gabriel waited until Ralph got into his pickup before walking back into the room. When he saw Lanie, a prickle of unease went up his spine. She was holding the bowl, staring at it as if entranced.

"Will you let me take a sample of the clay from that rough spot to send in for analysis?''

"What are you hoping to find?'' she asked, her voice wary.

"'Hoping' is the wrong word,'' he answered. "It's more a case of trying to narrow down a few things. For instance, the materials used could tell us where it came from and maybe even its intended purpose. If it *is* made from ashes, that would definitely indicate that is a skinwalker bowl. Admittedly I'm just fishing, but I figure it's worth a shot."

"How do you want to do this? Shall I break off a small sliver from the rough spot?"

"I'll go get a vial from my evidence kit. Then I'd like you to scrape a little loose clay into it with your fingernail."

Gabriel retrieved his evidence kit from his patrol vehicle and came in a moment later. He held the vial steady while she scraped a tiny sample of clay dust into it.

"Thanks," he said, sealing the lid.

"Let me know what you learn?" she asked.

"You've got it." The worry in her eyes stabbed through him. He wanted to take her into his arms, to reassure her, to fill her with other emotions that would leave no room for fear.

But there were matters he had to take care of now. The best way he could protect her was by sticking to his job as sheriff.

"You're not alone in this," Gabriel said finally, wishing he were better with the sweet talk women loved. "Remember that."

As he walked away, he could feel her gaze on him. He couldn't remember ever feeling this way about a woman. There was a special bond between them. Lanie's destiny and his were linked, and, what was worse, he couldn't honestly say he minded.

IT WAS NEARLY MIDNIGHT by the time Lanie finished the household chores for Marlee. Tired, she crawled into bed, craving the oblivion of a dreamless sleep.

As she slipped between the cool sheets, she consciously blocked out all the confusion the day had brought. With her eyes closed, and her body relaxed, her thoughts drifted to Gabriel. She wanted to let go and believe that she could count on someone besides herself, but something continued to hold her back. Maybe it was her survival instincts, honed to perfection after years of disappointment and heartbreak.

She shifted, burrowing deeper into the soft mattress, and allowed the gray mists of sleep to close in around her.

Clouds of darkness gave way slowly to a sea of green and an ever expanding field of grass and sage. She recognized this place. She'd camped here during her travels. But not everything was the same. Ahead, between the cluster of tall pines, stood a beautiful Pueblo-style home. A low adobe wall encircled it. It was her dream home, one she had created in her fantasies and had held on to throughout the years. Whenever troubles had assailed her, she'd run here in her mind, and had found peace.

But this time she was not alone. To her delight, she saw Gabriel ahead. He was shirtless, chopping wood. He stopped as she approached. His smile was as intoxicating as ever.

"I've been waiting for you, my woman."

She allowed herself to be swept into his arms, glad he was part of her dream. It was as if he belonged there, and always had.

She nestled against him, and his arms tightened around her. "The robin's eggs hatched."

She looked up and saw a robin feeding her hatchlings. Contentment filled every part of her. Peace, belonging, a sense of rightness—they were all here for her in her dream.

"Maybe *we* should think of a family. We could start working on it right now," Gabriel whispered in her ear.

In her dream, she laughed, feeling a tinge of sadness at knowing that none of this was real. This was the only place where it was okay to let go, to let things follow their own course. "And if it doesn't happen the first time, we'll just keep trying, over and over again."

He laughed. "Count on it," he said, lowering his mouth to hers.

Gabriel's kiss was pure passion. His tongue penetrated her parted lips, stroking her with the patient expertise of a man who knew how to pleasure his woman.

Suddenly a high-pitched sound ripped apart the fabric of that world. The images melted away, and she felt herself spinning downward. With a gasp, she woke in her bed and turned off the alarm on the nightstand.

Lanie could still feel the warmth of Gabriel's kiss on her lips. It took a moment for her heart to stop hammering. With a long sigh, she tossed back the covers. It was time to get ready for work. Wishing dreams could last longer, Lanie got up and dressed. Slacks and a wool pullover would keep her warm, and they were a lot safer than the searing fires of the soul. No matter how beautiful the fantasy, she simply knew too much about people to ever trust anyone with her heart. And with her track record, she didn't want to risk anyone trusting *her*, either.

Lanie went to the kitchen and found it empty. Stillness filled the house. Marlee was probably still asleep. A look outside confirmed that Gabriel was already at work.

After fixing some instant oatmeal, she walked about with her cereal bowl and looked around. How odd that, despite all the little trinkets that made Marlee's home so pleasant, there were no photographs anywhere. Then again, knowing what she did about Four Winds and its residents, Lanie thought perhaps that was to be expected.

Checking the clock on the wall, Lanie rinsed out her cereal bowl and placed it on the drain rack. It was time to get going.

The crisp morning air made her walk a pleasant one. She'd always enjoyed mornings and the feel of a new day filled with promise and possibilities. It was a clean slate waiting to be written on.

She arrived at Alma's a short time later. The little bell

sounded as she walked inside, but Alma was nowhere in sight.

"Lanie, is that you?" Alma called out.

"Yes, it's me."

"I'm in the back. You're just in time."

Lanie hurried through the shop and saw Alma trying to move an antique rolltop desk that looked as if it weighed more than both of them combined. "Whoa! Hang on. I'll give you a hand."

Lanie took one corner and, coordinating with Alma, pushed it across the room. "What next?" she asked, hoping no more moving was on the agenda.

"I have to clear this side of the room as much as possible, including taking down the blinds. I'll be taking photos of all the smaller items we'll be advertising in the catalog, like the snuff boxes, storage boxes and such, and the lighting's got to be just right."

Lanie stared at the two massive bookcases that stood against the wall. *"Everything?"*

"Those bookcases will have to be moved out into the hall, but don't worry, it isn't as hard as it appears. Once the books are off the shelves, they're quite manageable."

Working alongside Alma, Lanie stored the vintage books inside small cardboard boxes. Alma was almost twice Lanie's age, but she seemed to have limitless energy. As Lanie cleared the shelf closest to her, she glanced at the titles. "You sure do have a lot of books on Native American art." She picked up one ragged volume that seemed to be falling apart and handled it carefully. "This one looks so old!"

"It's been out of print for a century or so." Alma smiled. "That one's going to an antiquarian book dealer in California."

Lanie remembered Rosa telling her that Alma was an expert. Now she understood why. "Do you keep some of these for your own use?"

"Of course. I've got an extensive library on the antiques I'm likely to come across and handle here."

Lanie leafed through the book carefully, studying hand-drawn sketches of Southwestern pottery. Maybe one of these books would have some information about her bowl.

Alma touched Lanie lightly on the arm. "You're welcome to borrow whatever you want, but right now I need you to help me move the books."

Lanie placed the book in a box and gave her boss a sheepish smile. "Sorry. I couldn't resist a peek."

"If you're interested in Indian artifacts, I can show you some of my own pieces. I have a feeling that little bowl of yours has whetted your appetite."

Lanie shook her head. "I'm afraid my life-style lends itself more to new car seats than to fine antiques."

"I understand." Alma brought out two floodlight stands, a tripod and a large camera case from the closet. "This equipment is the best I can afford. Catalogs are the heart of my business, so I need top-of-the-line photo gear—the modern to set off the old, as it were." As she hung up a pale blue background cloth on a sturdy old table, the doorbell sounded.

"I'll get that," Alma said. "Go on clearing the shelves."

Lanie heard Alma talking to someone in the next room as she continued to pack up the books. She'd filled two more boxes and had started on a third when she noticed a book that had fallen behind a bookcase. She reached down and managed to slowly free it.

It was a leather-bound manual for buyers of Indian arts and crafts, printed around the turn of the century. It fell open naturally to a section in the last quarter of the book, as if to the favorite passage of a much loved novel.

In the center of the page, Lanie saw a sketch of a bowl much like her own. The markings were similar, though not identical. The brief description at the bottom of the sketch made a shiver run up her spine.

The bowl pictured had been one of the two fashioned by a Navajo skinwalker. The second one had been listed as lost. The one pictured was purported to have been used to hold the ashes that a Navajo skinwalker needed to fashion a crude drawing of the man he intended to kill. The similarity to her own bowl and the mention of the other artifact unsettled her. It was obvious Alma had seen this sometime in the past, since the book opened to the passage automatically. Had she kept it hidden, then forgotten about it?

So engrossed was she in the book, that Lanie never heard Alma come in.

Alma cleared her throat loud enough to get Lanie's attention, then smiled when Lanie jumped. "It seems I can't keep you away from the books. Looks like I've hired a future antiquarian-book dealer."

"Sorry. I found this wedged behind the bookcase. It must have fallen there, but when I took it out, I couldn't resist looking inside. I found a sketch of a bowl much like mine."

Alma took it from her hands and looked at the cover. "I wondered where that had disappeared to. I had been looking through it for information and spotted that passage, but then I got busy with something else and set the book down. It must have fallen back there." She closed the book carefully, then placed it on the table she'd be using as a photo backdrop. "Unfortunately this book is quite misleading, because the anthropologist who wrote it didn't check out his facts. The book was written during a time when Indians were sick and tired of having anthropologists dissecting everything they did or said, and quite frankly, some made up things to shock or confuse the gullible white man. Most of the anthropologists knew that was happening and checked out their information with independent sources, but this guy didn't. His work is notoriously inaccurate.''

Lanie was unsure whether to be relieved or disappointed. As she thought back to what she'd read, and realized how willing she'd been to accept the story, she suddenly felt very foolish.

Alma smiled at her gently, misinterpreting Lanie's reaction. ''I'm sorry. I can see you were hoping your bowl would turn out to be a priceless artifact, but honestly, that seldom happens.''

Lanie started to point out that it had to be of some value, since so many others were apparently intent on having it, but changed her mind. It made no sense to dispute the issue when there was nothing to gain except alienating her new employer. At the moment, the last thing she needed was to lose her job.

Hearing the phone ring, Alma rolled her eyes. ''It's always like this when I take on a big project. Normally it's as quiet as a graveyard in here. Keep working, I'll be right back.''

Alma still hadn't returned by the time Lanie finished packing the last of the books. Rather than wait, she slid the empty bookcase out into the hall by herself. Lanie had just started moving the boxes filled with books when Alma came back.

''You should have told me,'' Alma said, a stern look on her face.

''You mean before I moved anything?'' Lanie looked at Alma in surprise. The woman's gaze was fixed and hard, and a muscle at the corner of her mouth twitched quickly.

''No, about this...'' She slapped what appeared to be a thin newsletter with the back of her hand. ''You should have told me all the problems you were having with the bowl, the break-ins, all that trouble....'' She shook her head. ''This is our newspaper, the *Last Word*. Ted Burns, the young man who works for me occasionally, just dropped a copy by, and it's all in here. Your bowl, and you by association, are now at the center of some very nasty business. And after people read this article, things are bound to get worse.''

Chapter Seven

Lanie took the paper from Alma's hand, and scanned the lead story. As she read the account, her temper began to boil. "This is really slanted, Alma. Truly. Yes, the events are basically correct, but the reporter makes a *lot* of assumptions. For one thing, he figures I'm going to be staying here for the rest of my life. That's just not true! As I've told you, *and everyone else,* I'm going to be back on the road the moment my car's fixed and I can pay for the repairs!"

Alma blinked owlishly but said nothing.

"And 'my home' wasn't broken into. It was the boardinghouse. And the thugs that jumped the Blackhorse brothers...well, there's no telling what that was about. I'm quite sure Gabriel and Lucas have a few enemies of their own."

"That's true enough," Alma admitted. "But this sort of thing seldom, if ever, happens in our town. It seems that the stories about the peddler always bringing trouble are coming true. What I don't understand is how that bowl of yours fits in." Alma pondered it for a moment. "Of course! The rumor mill attributed Mr. Simmons's good luck, getting that windfall and all, after finding the body, to the peddler. Maybe people figure that you're getting your bad luck in the beginning, like Simmons did, and soon the tide will turn. They hope the bowl is magic, and that it'll provide its owner with all kinds of wonderful things."

"The only magic my bowl has is its uncanny ability to attract trouble, believe me." Lanie followed Alma to the front of the store and accepted a cup of tea from her.

"If people's imaginations get too fired up, there'll be even more trouble. You can bank on it," Alma said. "If you'd like, I could help you put a stop to the rumors. I can take a look at the bowl and give you an honest appraisal. Facts will defuse some of the wishful thinking going around. People value my opinion about antiques around here, though perhaps not as much as they did my sister Emily's opinion."

Alma paused to gaze around the shop, and tears formed in her eyes. "You see, this shop was Emily's dream come true, not mine. I would have been content to work for a dealer, but Em wanted her own shop. She passed away about a year and a half ago. Sometimes I think the shop itself mourns her. It's as if a spark has been extinguished."

Lanie knew about deaths, how they wrenched out a part of your heart and crushed it. Memories of her days as a teacher crowded her mind. Roy, a student, so full of life and always eager to face his problems square on, had taken such a wrong turn. But his biggest mistake had been trusting her. Lanie's heart twisted inside her, and she fought back a tear of her own.

"Now I've made you sad," Alma noted. "I'm sorry. We were talking about your bowl, not Emily. Let's get back to that. I'll tell you what. Bring it to me tomorrow, and I'll have a look at it. I'll research it thoroughly and give it a firm price range. Then I'll make sure Ralph prints the story, even if I have to bake him some of my special apple pie. He's been after me to bake him another ever since I fixed him one for his last birthday. What do you say?"

"Sounds great to me." Lanie hoped Alma's plan would

take care of the problem, but if it didn't, she certainly had nothing to lose.

Lanie moved to the second bookcase and started to work on it as Alma opened the back door. "It's starting to get stuffy in here."

Lanie placed the books in the remaining cardboard boxes, then stood back. "Let's move the second bookcase. It's ready."

"We'll never get it into the hall—it's too cluttered in here. Let's move some of these cartons over by the door. They'll prop it open, and that'll get them out of our way," Alma said.

Once the task was accomplished, Alma pushed the bookcase into the hall as Lanie led the way, guiding it. They were placing it against a wall when a crash sounded in the back room.

Alma rushed back and Lanie followed, picking her way around the bookshelves. Lanie stepped into the room in time to see Alma straining with the doorknob, trying to pull the door open. Somebody was on the other side, trying equally hard to close it again.

"Help me, Lanie. It's a thief!" Alma yelled.

Just then, whoever was outside let go, and Alma fell back against Lanie. As they both tumbled to the floor, Lanie only got a glimpse of a figure running away outside, carrying something under his arm.

Alma groaned and Lanie was beside her in a breath. "Don't move. I'll call...do they have 911 in Four Winds?"

"No need, I'm all right. Good thing he didn't get my camera. It's still in the case. He only just had time to grab the book I had on the table next to it." Alma sat up slowly. "Looks like I skinned my elbow," she said, bending her arm and wincing.

"Did you see who it was?" Lanie asked.

Alma shook her head. "Some of the boys at the high

school don't like me. I won't hire them, even part-time, because they're too rough with my merchandise. I turned two of them away just a few days ago. They're probably still angry.'' She glanced at the books scattered all over the floor. "They didn't really want those, you know. They're just making trouble for me. I'll probably find the missing book in the trash a few days from now. I mean, really, what use would they have for a vintage book? They're only interested in TV and video games.''

Lanie helped her up, wishing Alma would have stayed where she was until someone checked her over.

"I know, you're thinking old women have old bones, but that just doesn't apply to me. I've always had a strong constitution.'' She waved away Lanie's help. "I can stand on my own, thank you very much.''

"I'm going to call the sheriff, though. That kid shouldn't get away with this.''

Alma shrugged. "I'll call Sheriff Blackhorse myself, but there's not going to be much he can do about this. I have a good idea who it could have been, but I didn't see the boy's face, just his back.''

Lanie gathered up the scattered books while Alma used the phone in the other room. She still wasn't convinced Alma was okay; she'd taken quite a tumble. Once again, Four Winds was showing that it had another side that existed just below its surface. Perhaps the adults were content here, but the kids weren't that different from the way they were anywhere else.

Gabriel responded a few minutes after Alma had placed the call. Lanie's heart skipped a beat as he strode into the room. He was all confidence and raw power. Every fiber in her body came to life, awakened by a yearning so strong it nearly took her breath away.

His gaze traveled briefly over Lanie, then he went to Alma. "I've only got some community first aid, but if you

need help, I can make sure we get some county EMTs
here.''

"No need, Sheriff," Alma said flatly.

"All right. Then tell me what happened." His voice was
low yet commanding.

Lanie saw concern flash across his eyes as he heard
Alma's account. Listening, Lanie began to think that perhaps she'd been wrong in her earlier assessment about the
kids here in Four Winds. It wasn't that they were a source
of trouble the residents didn't acknowledge, but rather that
some hidden balance had shifted since the peddler's arrival
and the kids weren't acting typically.

Lanie expelled her breath in a rush. She was really starting to lose it. Now *she* was searching for esoteric explanations when the facts were plain enough.

"I'd like to go and put a Band-Aid on my elbow, Sheriff. The scrape is rubbing against my blouse."

"Go ahead." As Alma left the room, Gabriel turned to
join Lanie. "Did you see anything that could help me
identify the thief?"

"It all happened in a flash. I didn't see much of anything, except that he was wearing jeans and a blue nylon
jacket."

"That sounds like half the boys in town. Blue is one of
the school colors. I sure wish she'd told me before today
that the high-school kids were giving her a hard time. I'd
have put a stop to it in a flash." Gabriel shook his head,
then continued. "Alma said that there were books in the
box he scattered, and that he took one of the books with
him. Can you add anything to that?"

She led him into the back room, and as she glanced at
the table, suddenly realized which book was missing. "I
know the book he took. Alma had just set it down on the
table. It was a valuable edition about Native American
pottery with hand sketches. It even had something about
my bowl. But why did he bother to grab that? Seems to

me, he should have tried harder to take the camera, which would have been easier to pawn."

"It is odd that he took a book that had information about the bowl. What did it have to say, anyway?"

She told him, sticking to the facts, then added, "But Alma warned me that although the book itself is a collector's item because of its age, it's not an accurate reference book."

Gabriel noted the expensive camera case and picked it up to verify the gear was still inside. Things were definitely getting interesting. "She's never had a break-in or trouble of any sort. Now someone steals a book with information about the bowl."

"I hope you're not linking the two. This wasn't an attempt to do research. There are other ways of accomplishing that."

Gabriel studied the back door, then opened it and looked outside, lost in thought. "How long was the boy in the shop before you two heard him knock the box onto the floor?"

She stared at the door, eyebrows knitted together. "It couldn't have been more than a minute or two. We were in the hall, not that far away, and kids scaring up trouble generally don't use the stealth of accomplished thieves."

He took a close look at the books that were in the tipped-over box, then picked the container up by the bottom. "I'll bring this back, but I need to see if I can lift any prints from either the books or the box itself."

As Gabriel carried the box to his car, Lanie returned to the front room. Alma was there waiting.

"That was a bad fall you took, Alma. Why don't you take it easy for the rest of today?" Lanie suggested.

Gabriel came back into the shop. "I second that suggestion, and if either of you see any kids hanging around, call me."

"No problem, Sheriff," Alma replied, walking to the back of the store slowly.

Gabriel took Lanie aside. "I'm going to be asking some questions at the high school. If the kids there have a problem with Alma or anyone else, I want to know about it. In the meantime, if Alma has any problems, medical or otherwise, call me."

After Gabriel had left the shop, Alma sat down in the chair by the window and watched as Lanie dusted the collection of antique storage boxes.

"Alma, there's something I can't figure out. It's about that antique book I saw you put on the table. Why on earth do you think the kid picked up that particular volume to steal?"

"I don't think he was aiming for it, if that's what you mean. He grabbed it because he thought I was using it, or simply because it was handy. It's the kind of thing a kid would do just to be annoying."

"Maybe," she answered, unconvinced. "Well, it could have been worse. At least your photo equipment is safe, so you won't miss out on producing your catalog."

Lanie worked hard all day, mostly trying to make sure that Alma didn't overdo it as she worked on the catalog. Though she was dog tired by quitting time, she hung around, reluctant to leave Alma alone.

Lanie dusted all the crosses in the window display and then shook out the Navajo rugs. She was searching for something else to do when she turned to see Alma working on the account books. "Would you like me to stay and fix dinner for you? It would be no trouble at all."

Alma smiled at her. "You're afraid of leaving me alone, aren't you?" Not waiting for an answer, she continued. "I'm safe enough, and I know how to take care of myself. I have some antique firearms in the store, and they all work. My father showed Emily and me how to shoot. Besides, I'm never alone here."

Lanie glanced around. The shop was empty except for them. "I don't understand."

"Emily and I worked in this store for many years. This was her great love, and I think a part of her will always be here. Sometimes I swear I can see her standing there, telling me how she wants the window display done. She was such a fussbudget! Everything had to be done exactly right."

"Memories can be a wonderful comfort, but you still need to eat," Lanie insisted in a soft voice.

"I will. I'll order something from Sally's, and her son, Peter, will bring it over. Nobody goes hungry in this town, dear, not unless they're dieting."

"I *have* noticed that Four Winds doesn't have any run-down neighborhoods."

"Some folks are better off than others in terms of how much money they have in the bank, but nobody's poor. Simmons was struggling, then after he lived here a short time, his luck turned around."

Lanie finished picking up, then glanced around one more time. "Are you sure there's nothing else I can do for you tonight?"

"Positive, dear."

"Well, in that case, I'll be on my way."

"Don't forget to bring the pottery bowl tomorrow. I'd like to put people's fantasies about it to rest as soon as possible—for your sake."

Lanie walked back to the boardinghouse, nodding to shopkeepers and residents who were in their yards or on their way home. It felt good to be part of their community, if only for a while. It had been a long time since she'd felt connected to anything.

Lanie arrived at the boardinghouse within ten minutes. She was tired, but there were chores to do for Marlee. As she stepped in the door, she saw Marlee carrying a big laundry basket, favoring her leg as if in great pain.

"What on earth are you doing?" Lanie took the basket from her, then smiled and added, "Trying to give Lucas a reason to come back?"

Marlee smiled back. "I like Lucas, that's true enough, but what woman around here doesn't? The Blackhorse brothers could coax a pulse from a stone."

She wasn't sure about the other Blackhorse brothers, but something about Gabriel definitely set her blood on fire. "Gabriel is...special."

"See that? You're not immune. You just chose a different brother."

"Not that it matters. I certainly wouldn't try to start something with Gabriel." Seeing the incredulous look on Marlee's face, she continued down the hall. "I better get busy."

Lanie carried the basket of sheets and pillowcases to the laundry room, Marlee's words still ringing in her ears. She hadn't chosen Gabriel. Events had brought them together. But she could choose what would happen now, and she intended to do her best to avoid him.

She measured soap powder and added it to the washer, pondering her own feelings. Her biggest problem, she told herself firmly, was she'd been on the road too long. That's why she felt so torn between her attraction to Gabriel and this town, and the need to take off as soon as possible.

Then abruptly she felt a change in the room. Though it was as quiet as it had been, her skin prickled and a disturbing warmth ribboned through her. She could feel Gabriel nearby, though she couldn't hear or see him. The air itself had become charged and held a tense edge that continued to build with each breath she took.

"Hello, Gabriel," she said without turning around.

"You see how attuned we are to each other?" he whispered. "Your heart sensed me."

She turned to face him. He was wearing only sweatpants, which hung low on his waist. His bronzed chest was powerfully muscular, and the sheen that accentuated those muscles suggested he'd been working out. She tried to think of something to say, but her mind was exploding with sensations too raw for rational thought. Sparks of fire and life coursed through her.

"You look beautiful. Your cheeks are flushed, and your eyes are sparkling."

"I look dusty and tired," she managed to say, her voice hoarse.

"Not to me."

Desire filled her. She yielded to it as Gabriel reached for her hand and pulled her to him. She could feel his heart pounding beneath her palm.

Gabriel tilted her head upward. As he covered her mouth with his own, erotic currents ribboned through her body. The tenderness of his kiss was practically her undoing. He held her as if she were precious to him, and that mattered to her because it meant that what was happening was far more than a physical response.

His arms tightened, as if he'd read her unspoken thoughts. Nothing in her life had ever prepared her for the yearnings that welled up inside her. He wanted her as much as she did him, and here in his arms, nothing else seemed to matter.

"Lanie?" Marlee called from the other end of hall. "I need your help."

Reality came rushing back. Lanie stepped out of his embrace slowly, torn between the magic she'd found in Gabriel's arms and the need to escape the emotions she'd found there.

"Lanie, could you give me a hand?" Marlee called out again.

Marlee's second call gave her the impetus she needed. "I've got to go."

As she hurried away, she felt more alone than she'd ever been. Hating herself for allowing her defenses to be stripped that way, she swallowed back the lump in her throat and promised herself it would not happen again.

Lanie found Marlee in the hall, struggling to stand by pulling herself up against the hall table. Lanie rushed toward her. "What happened?"

"Oh, it's just plain dumb. Alma stopped by for a moment to see if there was anything I wanted to include in her catalog. She's had her eye on the antiques here for a long time. I turned her down again, and she left. When I started down the hall to go to bed, I caught my foot on the rug and tripped. I couldn't get back up because this dumb cast is keeping me so off balance."

Lanie helped Marlee stand up. "I'm really sorry I didn't get here right away."

Marlee stood and immediately let go of Lanie's arm. "Hey, are *you* okay? Your face looks really flushed. Did I scare you?"

"Yes. When I saw you on the floor…"

Marlee narrowed her eyes. "It's more than that." She smiled slowly. "Gabriel." She laughed, seeing the expression on Lanie's face. "You need more help than I do."

As Marlee ambled unsteadily down the hall, Lanie sighed. Maybe Marlee was right; she did need help. Exasperated with herself, she selected the most physically taxing job Marlee had on her list of chores, and headed for the garage.

A table that had seen better days two or three decades ago needed sanding and refinishing. It was a job Marlee had wanted to do herself, but she wasn't up to the long stretches of standing the sanding required.

Lanie rolled up her sleeves and started the work, determined not to let Gabriel slip into her thoughts. Yet the more she tried, the more he crept into her mind. Beneath everything else was an image of him.

As the sheet of sandpaper in her hand became worn

smooth, Lanie discarded it and glanced around for another. The two paper bags closest to her were filled with cans of stain, but no sandpaper. Seeing a third sack on a shelf by the wall, Lanie went over and pulled it down to look inside.

As she brought down the bag, a neatly folded piece of paper stuck beneath the sack fluttered out and fell to the floor. Lanie crouched down to pick it up.

In muted shock, she stared at the page from Alma's stolen book, the one describing the skinwalker bowl.

Chapter Eight

Lanie stared at the folded book page in her hand. Had Marlee been behind the theft at Alma's shop? Surely the page was from the same book. The chances of a coincidence were pretty remote. Since it was Marlee's garage, she would have been in the best position to stick it there, but Lanie couldn't figure out why anyone would tear a page from a valuable book, then hide it inside a garage. Alma would have cringed at the thought, to be sure.

Lanie searched the contents of the sack. There were small cans of paint and varnish and several unused sheets of sandpaper, but no other pages, much less the book itself. After looking around the garage, Lanie also came up empty-handed.

Either Marlee had foolishly left the page where Lanie might find it, or somebody else had put it there to implicate Marlee. She shook her head, amazed at her find. The question now was what to do about it. She thought of asking Marlee about the page, but that seemed ill-advised at best. There was no way anyone could prove that the page had come from the stolen book, unless the book itself was recovered. And she was employed by Marlee in exchange for lodging. If Marlee wasn't guilty of anything, questioning her on something so sensitive would only create another problem.

Hearing footsteps, she turned around.

Gabriel walked into the garage. "I need to talk to you," he said, then stopped, studying her expression. "What's wrong?"

She hesitated.

"Did you find something that interested you?" He moved around her and glanced at the single page that she had unfolded and left next to the sack on the table.

"Where did you find this?"

She pointed. "Stuck under a sack, up there."

"Is this what you'd mentioned reading in Alma's stolen book?" Seeing her nod, he continued. "When we recover the book, it'll be interesting to see if there's a page missing." He took the sheet, picking it up by the edges. "I'll take this and ask Marlee about it in my own way later. Don't mention finding this page here to anyone, all right?"

"Sure. But why would Marlee hide something so damning here? She knew I'd have to get more sandpaper to finish the job she gave me."

"She may not have had anything to do with this. Marlee's house has been around a long time." He pointed to a spinning wheel at the far end of the room and a hand plow set up on one of the shelves. "All those things were part of the stuff already here, and Marlee seldom moves them around. They've been in the same place as long as I can remember. Someone may have figured this was an ideal hiding place. They probably got rid of the book—it was damning evidence—but this page wasn't something the thief was ready to discard."

"Why doesn't Marlee sell some of these antiques? I know Alma would love to market them. They aren't doing anyone any good just sitting here."

"Marlee has her own way of looking at things. She doesn't consider this house hers, for one. She has no deed, so she considers herself a caretaker for life. Have her tell you sometime how she came to stay here." He leaned against the doorframe and regarded her thoughtfully for several long moments. "There's something else you and I have to talk about," he added, his voice low and deep.

Sensual awareness made her pulse race and her blood sizzle. She took a step back, trying to hold on to her will-power. The lack of control she showed whenever she was around Gabriel was so unlike her.

He watched her widen the gap between them, but made no move to stop her. "Neither of us wants to start a relationship, but it's happening anyway. What we feel for each other has gone way past what a one-night stand might satisfy."

"The time is wrong for me," she answered. "I'm not ready to settle down anywhere. I…just can't."

"I know. That's why we're going to have to back off. I know you plan to leave once your car is fixed and you've met your obligations here," he said sadly, then reached out and caressed her face with his palm.

She felt the tenderness in his touch, and for that one moment she glimpsed what it would be like to be treasured by a man like Gabriel. When he stepped away and returned to the house, she felt desolate.

Lanie stared at the unfinished table. She had no heart for restoration now. She turned off the light and walked back over to the house.

Inside the silent confines of her room, Lanie opened the dresser drawer and traced the surface of the bowl with her index finger. Its cool smoothness comforted her, and she felt the tension wash out of her body. It was time to go to bed.

Unable to work up any energy for neatness, she allowed her clothes to fall onto the floor and crawled between the sheets. Sleep seemed to overtake her almost immediately, but instead of oblivion, she found herself back at her dream home. Once again, she saw Gabriel there, waiting. He stood shirtless by the door of their home.

"You've come to me again," he murmured, "my beautiful woman."

"It's just a dream," she told herself.

"No, it's more than that. You and I are both called here. If it's a dream, then it's one we both share." He took her gently into his arms.

She knew reality from fantasy, but within her there was still that little girl who yearned for the fantasy to be made real. Surely, in this magical place, there was no need for caution.

"Let your heart guide you," he coaxed gently. "Let me show you what is meant to be."

His whisper, moist and warm, danced along the column of her neck. He held her in his arms, letting her know him, arousing her as he was aroused.

She ran her hands over him, pulling his clothing away, amazed that this wonderful dream could convey such intricacies of texture to the touch. Desire guided and ruled her, and she made no move to stop him as he led her out into the sunshine and undressed her there, kneeling as he did. Inch by inch, he tasted her flesh, his mouth loving her in ways that left her trembling. He was a persuasive lover who knew how to make her open her body and her soul to him.

"Our lives were in preparation for this," he said, his voice jagged now and thick with passion.

Lanie clung to Gabriel, overwhelmed by feelings too intoxicating to resist. When at last he rose to his feet, and they stood face-to-face, he kissed her deeply, then entered her, reaching to the very center of her being. Each movement that rocked her body, each thrust, became a testimony to their mutual surrender.

He pulled away long enough to hold her gaze, and Lanie saw pure fire in his eyes. "I am the man meant for you," he said fiercely.

As their bodies flowed into each other, she felt elevated

by the surrender. It was surrender, yes, but it was also a mutual victory, a triumph for their hearts. This mystical experience had bonded them in a way reality would never be able to destroy.

"Remember," he whispered as dark clouds took the scene from her mind.

LANIE WOKE UP SLOWLY, tangled in the sheets. The dream lingered vividly in her mind, like the memory of a real event. She shifted, muscles straining with a telltale ache she hadn't felt in years. It was the physical weariness that came from a night of vigorous lovemaking.

Lanie shook her head gently. Her dreams were becoming impossibly real. Maybe it was the effects of Four Winds and all the strangeness here. The intrigues and mysteries the town kept hidden probably distorted people's sense of reality after a while.

She dressed quickly, wanting to get out of her room. Remembering her promise to Alma, she wrapped up the bowl using a scarf and some paper for protective padding, then placed it in her tote bag.

As she stepped out into the hall, she saw Gabriel. His eyes shimmered with the smoke of an inner fire. She felt her skin warm and her heart begin to pound against her sides.

"Good morning." His gaze captured hers and held it. "Some say dreams have magic. Do you remember yours?"

"Yes." She felt a shiver run up her spine. He couldn't know; it was impossible. Yet that intense look, the hunger in his eyes, all told a different story.

As thunder shook the walls of the house, rattling the windowpanes, she averted her gaze. The last request he'd made before she'd awakened from the dream suddenly came back to her. "Remember," he'd said.

But it had only been a dream. She clung to that as she

walked with him down the hall. "Do you remember *your* dreams?" she asked.

"Always."

With vivid images rushing into her mind, she practically ran to the kitchen. Marlee looked up as Lanie charged into the room, giving her a startled look. Lanie forced a smile and took an oatmeal-honey breakfast bar from a dish Marlee had placed on the table. "Can I help you with anything before I leave?" Lanie asked.

"No, that won't be necessary. I'm going to be working on the bookkeeping, so I expect it's going to be quiet and totally boring today," Marlee said, smiling.

Another loud peal of thunder reverberated in the air. It was immediately followed by an oppressive silence. "Lousy weather," Lanie said with a shudder. "Do you have an umbrella I can borrow, Marlee?"

"Sure. I keep one in the hall closet. Help yourself, but you probably won't need it. There'll be plenty of clouds, thunder and lots of wind, but don't hold your breath waiting for the rain."

Just as she finished the statement, the skies suddenly opened up and torrents of rain came down. Marlee looked at Lanie sheepishly. "So much for my reputation as a weather prophet. I should have known these strange morning clouds would bring a surprise. It could be a real gully washer. But don't be surprised, though, if you see folks peering out their windows just to watch it rain. It's always an event here."

Gabriel was zipping up his coat, standing by the door as Lanie came into the living room. "It looks nasty out there. Why don't you let me—"

The ringing phone interrupted him. Marlee picked up the receiver and, after a moment, called to Lanie. "It's Alma. She wants to give you a ride to her shop."

Before she could answer, Gabriel put his hand on her

arm. "I can save her the trouble of having to come here in the downpour."

She nodded, her skin melting under the touch of his hand. Her knees nearly buckled as she remembered the way he'd caressed her in her dream. "I'll tell Alma," she managed to respond.

After assuring Alma she'd bring the bowl along with her today, Lanie hung up.

Gabriel was waiting for her by the door as she returned. "I'll be going to my office for about an hour this morning," he said as Lanie buttoned her jacket. "Then I'll be traveling back and forth along the highway. I want to see if anyone's seen the peddler or knows anything about him."

"You're still on that?"

He smiled slowly. "People tell me I'm like a pit bull when it comes to police work."

Marlee came from the kitchen to look out the front window. "I can't say I envy either one of you having to go out in the middle of this downpour."

"I hated days like this when I was a teacher and had duty outside in the morning or at lunch. It could sure get cold fast in the rain, standing around watching kids and making sure they stayed out of trouble."

At the mention of Lanie's past, Marlee nodded curtly and walked back to the kitchen. Lanie shook her head slowly. Her teaching days were over, and she shouldn't have mentioned it, but Marlee's reaction seemed odd. Maybe Marlee had been worried that Lanie would take the opportunity to ask about her past.

"You ready? We better get going," Gabriel said.

After a fast dash to the Jeep, they were under way. The rain intensified considerably as they went down Main Street. The street seemed more like a muddy sea than the cobblestoned road she knew lay beneath.

Gabriel drove slowly. "We normally don't get this kind

of rain except in summer, and I can't figure out why we're getting it now.''

''Well, it's been a dry year. New Mexico can use the rain.''

''Yeah, but it's a weird twist of fate. I was planning to spend my morning driving around, looking and asking questions. Now I don't think I'm going to be able to get out of town. There's bound to be problems with the mud and the roads. Cobblestone is very slippery when wet.''

''Tracking down the peddler can't be that critical. One day won't hurt.''

''It could. Someone called me and told me they'd seen a man matching the description of the peddler camping over near the county line. That's why I was planning to head over that way. This rainstorm couldn't have picked a more rotten time to start.''

She shuddered, feeling as if an ice cube had suddenly been pressed to the small of her back. ''Now you're going to blame the weather on the peddler?''

''No, but I can tell you there are plenty who would,'' Gabriel replied.

Lanie watched the clouds covering the sky like black swatches of cloth. The sun was completely obscured. The rain had suddenly stopped, and at the moment, the air was still and quiet. Restless, she shifted in her seat and allowed the silence to stretch out.

They were almost at Alma's when, suddenly, a large paint barrel rolled off a highway-department truck parked next to the feed store. It bounced sideways off the curb and headed directly toward the Jeep.

Gabriel swerved sharply. ''Hang on!''

The muddy cobblestone made traction impossible. The barrel struck the front bumper and bounced off the hood, blinding Gabriel by splattering yellow paint all over the windshield.

They spun around and slammed sideways into the mail-box outside the post office.

Gabriel muttered a curse. "Are you okay?"

"Yes, I'm a bit shaken, but the seat belt worked. I'm fine." She glanced up and saw the yellow paint being washed away in streaks as the rain suddenly began again.

"Stay here," he snapped, his gaze on the highway-department driver coming from the feed store, newspaper on top of his head.

"Sheriff, are you okay?"

"Those paint barrels," Gabriel yelled over the down-pour, "who tied them down?"

"I did, and they were secure."

"Wrong. You're lucky there wasn't anyone else around. Someone could have been killed."

"Sheriff, I've done this dozens of times. I just don't understand how it could have happened!"

They checked the Jeep for damage, then moved away, arguing as the truck driver brought out his driver's license. Lanie opened her purse carefully, afraid her bowl had been broken. With relief, she saw that it was undamaged. Placing it back inside, then huddling in her jacket, she opened the Jeep door and raced toward Alma's.

As she hurried across the street, she wondered what Gabriel would have said had he known she'd been carrying the bowl with her this morning. She was almost sure he would have thought of attributing their bad luck to it.

She had another theory, however, one that held more appeal with each passing minute. Maybe it wasn't her bowl that was at fault, but rather the conflagration Gabriel and she made every time they were together.

As soon as Lanie ducked inside the door of the Golden Days Antique Shop, Alma rushed over.

"I was just about to come out! I saw the accident. I bet you Jeremy, that shiftless moron, did his usual semicompetent job. He's been working at the highway department too long, if you ask me. Someone should have fired him long before now.'' Alma brought out a chair and handed Lanie a towel. ''And of all the days for me to ask you to bring the bowl! Was it broken?''

''It survived intact. I checked it,'' Lanie said.

Alma nodded. ''Thank goodness the sheriff's reflexes are so good. Otherwise, that could have become a major accident.'' She took the towel from Lanie's hand and offered her some hot tea. ''Oh, my, I just thought of something. If anyone knew you had the bowl with you just now, it's going to add a lot more fuel to that fire!''

''Nobody knew I had it, and I think we should keep it that way.''

''Good idea.''

Lanie sipped her tea, trying to sort through her thoughts about the accident. She shouldn't have wandered off. Gabriel would probably need a statement from her. But it had been cold in the car, and after all, he knew where to find her.

''I've got the camera stand ready,'' Alma said, interrupting her thoughts. ''I thought I'd take several photos of the bowl so I could have those handy while I researched it.''

Lanie reached into her tote bag and gently brought it out. ''I'll place the bowl on the camera stand. I know you'd be very careful with it, but if there's anything to this curse, I don't want you to share the bad luck.''

Alma's gaze was filled with understanding. ''Please don't worry. I'll take my photos without even touching it, if that makes you feel better. But don't let this curse business throw you. It's usually people's beliefs that create the most problems.''

Lanie went to the back room and saw the blue background sheet Alma had draped over one wall then across the table, creating a seamless backdrop. Floodlights stood on both sides of the table in front of the backdrop and were diffused to take away harsh shadows. It was a simple setup, but she had no doubt it was an effective one.

Lanie placed the bowl in the center of the table. As Alma focused the camera, the doorbell sounded. "Can you find out who it is?" Alma asked without glancing up.

Lanie looked down at the bowl, reluctant to let it out of her sight, then after a pause, nodded, chiding herself for being so nervous about it. Nothing would happen to it here. Alma certainly wasn't about to run off with it, abandoning her store.

Lanie started to leave the room when a young man suddenly entered, nearly colliding with her. "Oops! Sorry, ma'am." He brushed back his oily blond hair with one hand and smiled.

Alma glanced up. "Oh, hi, Ted. Glad you stopped by. This is Lanie Mathews, my new assistant." Alma shifted her gaze to Lanie. "This is Ted Burns, the young man I told you works for me occasionally."

Lanie allowed her gaze to take him in, silently assessing him. He was about twenty years old, she figured, and over six feet tall. He had the laid-back style of a kid who didn't have a care in the world.

As if uncomfortable under her gaze, he turned to Alma. "I was on my way to Santa Fe today and I thought I'd come by and see if there was anything you needed from there."

"You can drop off some books I was planning to ship to John Sullivan's bookstore there." She gestured toward the far wall. "They're in that box." She snapped another photograph, but this time the flash didn't recharge. "Blast! Lanie, can you go next door to Rosa's and get me some double-A batteries for the flash? It'll just take you a second. In the meantime, I can get a packing slip ready so that Ted can get John's signature when he makes the delivery."

Lanie brushed aside her reluctance to leave the bowl.

Common sense told her it would be safe, even though she hated the thought of leaving it.

"If you're in the least bit worried, take the bowl," Alma said, as if reading her mind. "But believe me, it's safer here in my store than in your purse as you walk around."

The logic behind her words was hard to dispute. Lanie couldn't think of any way to gracefully take the bowl now, not without jeopardizing her new employer's goodwill. "Okay. I'll be back soon."

Lanie hurried over to Rosa's grocery store, returning with the batteries only a short time later. Though she didn't want it to be obvious, her gaze immediately strayed to the bowl. It was exactly where she'd placed it. Alma and Ted were talking near the back door.

"You make sure he signs for it, not his assistant, okay?"

"Sure. I'll take care of it for you."

After he left, Alma loaded the batteries into her camera. "Ted is sure a nice kid, don't you think?"

"He seems very nice. I gather his other job takes a lot of his time, and that's why he doesn't work here full-time."

"It's more than that, though I'm not sure he'd ever admit it openly." Alma paused as she checked the camera settings and readjusted a light. "I know Ted very well, mostly because I know exactly what it's like to walk in his shoes. He has goals and dreams of his own he wants to make come true, but his father is such a driving force here in this town nobody ever sees Ted as anything except Bob Burns's son. Being in someone else's shadow is a real tough load to carry, believe me. I've tried to help him, and we've had long talks about this, but he's got his work cut out for him if he really wants to be his own man someday."

He's lucky to have you for a friend." Lanie said gently. "It sounds as though he needs one." She sighed. "Gabriel should be coming by soon, I expect. He's going to want my statement on the accident report.''

"Maybe, maybe not," Alma said. "Things aren't settled in big-city fashion around here. If Jeremy's at fault, the paperwork will be handled by the highway department. Eventually a check will be mailed. People don't get excited about things like that around here. This town can't support a full-time lawyer.''

Alma continued to work. "By the way, I did some research on some genuine skinwalker bowls last night. If you check the volume I left out by the counter, I think you'll find that none of the markings on your bowl match the ones there. Even the style is different. I'm just not convinced this piece of yours is genuine.''

Lanie went to the counter in the front room and picked up the book. Opening it to the place Alma had marked, she studied the photographs as she walked back to the other room. The one bowl pictured was said to have been the property of a skinwalker. "You're right," Lanie called out. "This one doesn't look like mine at all. The one pictured here looks like an ordinary bowl.''

"That's my point," Alma said. "Yours is too eye-catching. A skinwalker would want to keep his identity a secret. He wouldn't have things that would easily advertise who and what he was. Witches of any culture thrive on secrecy. My considered opinion is that you've probably got yourself an old bowl, but it's not necessarily valuable or the property of a skinwalker. However, without testing the pigments, dating the clay and so on, I can't say for certain.''

"So it could be valuable, or not," Lanie said with a sigh.

"If I had to bet, I'd say it's a just a pretty little bowl, made eye-catching so it would be easy to sell.''

Lanie bundled the bowl up again and placed it inside

her tote bag. "Well, expensive or cheap, it doesn't matter. It was a gift to me, and I still like it."

"Though you suspect it's cursed?"

"I'm not sure what I think anymore. That's the honest truth." Lanie stared at her bag for a moment, lost in thought. Maybe the answer would be to pitch it out the window once she was back on the road. But she'd never do that. She wasn't the kind of person who would purposely destroy something so beautiful.

"Shall we get started on today's work? As usual, everything is backlogged. Ever since Emily's passing, I never quite seem to catch up. Emily's dream sometimes becomes my nightmare." Alma asked, interrupting Lanie's thoughts. "But wait. I wasn't thinking. You were just in an accident. If you're not up to this today, I'll understand, of course."

"I'm fine. I can get started as quickly as you'd like. What's on the agenda?" Lanie asked, glad to be able to focus on something besides the bowl.

"Since it's stopped raining, how about going to the library for me? Our town library has a vanity table that's around one hundred years old. It's back in the librarian's quarters. The town council has agreed to sell it in order to raise capital. I've agreed to take it on consignment, but I need to have photos to show it off."

"I'm not sure how good I am with a camera...."

"This one's really easy to use." Alma placed a small 35 mm camera in her hands and gave her a few directions. "When you get there, ask at the reference desk and someone will guide you to the back where the vanity table is being kept."

Lanie headed down the street. The clouds were finally breaking, and an anemic-looking sun was starting to peer through. As she went past the site of their accident, she saw that only the barest trace of paint had settled in the joints of the cobblestones. The truck with the paint barrels was gone, and so was Gabriel's Jeep. Everything was as it had been, yet from inside Alma's store, she'd heard no cars being moved or people cleaning up. It was as if elves had come out and cleaned while the men handled the negotiations. She smiled at the image. Anywhere else, she would have thought it was fantasy, but here in Four Winds, anything seemed possible.

Lanie was across the street from Charley's garage when she decided on the spur of the moment to go to see how the repairs on her car were going. She was at the corner, ready to cross the street, when she spotted her car going by. Shocked, she stared at it for a moment, trying to make sure it really was her car. The dented rear bumper left no doubt.

Perhaps Charley had been wrong and there hadn't been as much work needed as he'd initially thought. Seeing him circle the block, she waited, looking forward to the possibility of a smaller bill.

Charley looked surprised to see her as he pulled inside the garage and saw her waiting. "I know what you're thinking," he said, his voice grave, "that I was wrong about the repair time. But I replaced the ignition system and took it out for a test drive, wanting to hear how she sounded under a load. I barely made it back. Something is wrong with the valves—I could hear it clearly."

"I had hoped that if it was running..."

Charley shook his head. "Ask around. I'm an honest man. If you take this car with you now, you won't get up the first hill you meet."

She looked directly into his eyes but found she couldn't read him. She was certain of one thing, however. One way or another, Charley would prove himself right. She wouldn't get far in her car if she took it now. Of course, it was a moot point. Even if the car had been okay, she still couldn't have paid for the repairs yet. Until Alma paid her, all she had left in her wallet was a little less than fifty bucks.

"Take my advice, miss. Enjoy your stay in Four Winds. You've got a good job working for Miss Alma, and you're helping Marlee. Our town will grow on you, and maybe by the time I'm finished, you won't even want to leave."

For a moment, she couldn't shake the feeling that Charley was part of someone's plan to keep her here in Four Winds. Brushing the thought aside as crazy paranoia, she left the garage and continued her walk to the library.

Lanie crossed at the end of the street and decided to take a shortcut across the southwest garden bordering the library. Halfway across, she noticed a large well, almost completely hidden by a pile of tumbleweeds. She peered around them to look at the circle of stones set in mortar. It looked almost identical to one that had plagued her nightmares as a child.

Her skin grew cold and clammy as memories of her life at one of the group homes came rushing back. It had been the best of all the foster homes she'd stayed at, but certainly no picnic. The older kids had teased the younger ones unmercifully, spinning hideous tales about the well beside the barn. Gathering her courage, she'd approached it once, but one of the older boys, seeing what she was doing, had grabbed her from behind and forced her head down into the blackness. She remembered the terror of falling, the numbing cold and screaming herself hoarse because of the spiders she could feel but not see as they crawled all over her body.

But she'd been just a child then. She was a grown woman now, quite capable of stomping a few spiders into oblivion if she so chose. Yet despite the logic of the thought, Lanie couldn't help the shiver that ran up her spine as she stood near the well.

This was ridiculous. She was made of sterner stuff. She

forced herself to inch forward, then, taking a deep breath and gripping the side, leaned over and looked down.

Suddenly she heard footsteps behind her. She turned her head in time to catch a flash of a stocking cap just before someone grabbed her in a choke hold. He held her in a viselike grip, forcing her head down and cutting off the air from her lungs.

"I want the bowl. Where did you stash it?" His voice sounded deadly, though it was whisper soft.

"Let go!" she gasped. She stomped down on his instep, and as his choke hold eased slightly, she screamed for help.

Twisting around, Lanie grabbed at his ski mask, hoping to scratch his eyes and force him to let her go. The cloth tore, and she heard him curse, but then, in a lightning move, he grabbed her legs and lifted her over the stone wall, sending her tumbling into the darkness of the well.

Chapter Nine

Lanie landed with a soft thump. For a moment, terror obliterated all thought. Childhood fears, coupled with the reality she now faced, paralyzed her. She tried to scream, but no sound came out of her mouth. Her body was shaking so hard, her teeth were chattering.

She took a deep breath, trying not to panic, and discovered that the air was fresh, not stuffy. As she looked up, she realized that she wasn't in the rotting pit that had filled her childhood nightmares. Sand, which must have blown in over the decades, had half filled the well and cushioned her fall.

She stood up slowly. The sand flooring was soft enough for her feet to sink in up to her ankles. There was enough light for her to see that there were no snakes hiding there, nor was it teeming with spiders. It was too cold even for them. One section of the bottom was damp and compacted from the recent rains, but no puddle remained. A small tumbleweed was her only companion.

Lanie tried to climb out, but the sand was so soft, it broke away from her weight before she could find a toehold. She yelled for help, but after a few minutes, she stopped. Her throat was sore, but obviously no one had heard her. The side street had been deserted before and undoubtedly still was.

As the wind began to pick up, the temperature inside the well began to drop. She cupped her hands and blew into them, trying to warm them up. Anger filled her as she thought of the man who'd tried to mug her. At least he'd found out she was no easy target. But he was probably someplace warm now, hoping she'd freeze to death in the cold.

Horror movies about women trapped and alone filled her mind, but she pushed them back. She couldn't afford to panic now. Sooner or later, someone would walk by, and then she'd call out. Until that happened, she'd save her voice and energy.

She reached for her tote bag and checked the bowl inside. Once again, it had somehow survived intact. She placed her hands around it, surprised at how warm the pottery felt. Heat seemed to radiate up her arms, filling her body with a pleasant warmth.

Then she heard someone whistling. Lanie quickly tucked the bowl back into her bag and began yelling for help. A minute later, a head appeared above in the light. She recognized the newspaperman, Ralph Montoya.

"How in the...?"

"Please, Ralph, just go get a ladder or a rope or something. I've been stuck down here long enough. I'll be glad to explain when I get out, okay?"

"Sure, sure. Are you hurt? Lucas is gone, but I can call the sheriff and have him radio the county's EMTs."

"I'm not hurt, just please get me out!" To her own chagrin, a touch of fear tainted her voice.

Ralph nodded quickly. "Hang tight. I'll be right back."

The minutes after he left seemed the longest. Seconds stretched out into their own imitations of eternity. She knew there was no reason to be impatient now that rescue was assured, but she wanted out, and she wanted out *now!*

Lanie took several deep breaths, hoping to calm herself, but nothing helped. Her body thrummed. When she heard a strange rustling beneath the tumbleweed in the darkest shadows, all her old fears came rushing to the surface. She could feel the scream building at the back of her throat. Then she felt the breeze and saw the tumbleweed's tendrils rubbing against the side of the well. She sighed with relief.

"I'm here," Ralph yelled out at last. "I'm going to lower a ladder down to you, so try to keep out of the way so I don't hit you with it."

The way her luck had been running, that's exactly what would happen. "I'm ready."

Lanie climbed out in a hurry, and as she stepped back outside the stone wall, her knees almost buckled with relief.

"Boy, I should follow you around," Ralph said. "You've managed to make news again. Some of our oldest citizens have never had their names in the paper. You seem to be destined for notoriety."

She started to argue that she was only a temporary resident, but suddenly it didn't seem to matter so much. She was out of the well. She'd forgive him this time.

"I'd really prefer if you didn't report this, at least not right away. Like you said, I'm already the focus of enough attention around here."

"Well, I can't promise to ignore something like this, but I won't sensationalize it. How's that?"

"Better, but I really need you to hold on to the story, please, at least until I can talk to Gabriel and..." She saw the way his eyes rose the second she mentioned Gabriel's name, and instantly regretted having done so.

"*How* exactly did you fall in?"

Lanie shrugged. "I've had a really hard day, and I'm just too rattled to talk about it right now."

"Of course! Let me buy you something to eat. Sally's diner is just down the street, and her food can fix up anyone. As a matter of fact, that's where I was headed."

She wasn't hungry, just cold. "I *could* use something warm."

"Sally makes the best chili stew this side of the border. It'll be my treat, and no questions, I promise."

"I'm all covered with dirt. I must look like a mess," she said, brushing herself off.

"Sally won't mind."

Lanie wasn't sure if he was trying to ingratiate himself or not, but it worked. "I accept. Just point me in the right direction."

As they walked down the road, she could feel the questions in his gaze and in the way he studied her. Ralph was no fool. He had probably guessed that she hadn't fallen in of her own accord.

"What time is it?" she asked, more to take his mind off his suspicions and speculations than anything else.

"It's twelve-thirty," he said, checking his watch. "I was on my way to Sally's to pick up lunch. Come to think of it, I'm not going to be able to have lunch with you after all. I have to get back to the office. I have only one other worker there, and I promised her the afternoon off to go visit a relative. I intended to pick up a bagged lunch."

"That's no problem. If you want to hurry on ahead, I can find Sally's on my own."

"I'm not in that big a hurry. I still have to pick up my lunch, so I'll buy you a bowl of chili and then be on my way. Believe me, that stew of hers, with a couple of her homemade tortillas, will take the chill right out of your bones."

They arrived at Sally's a few minutes later. Several diners were already there, but Ralph was able to find an unoccupied booth in the corner. "You'll be okay here. I'll take care of ordering for you while I'm picking up my lunch."

Lanie watched him pick up his carryout at the cash register, surprised he hadn't been more hard-nosed about what had happened. It was instinct for a newspaperman not to let go of a possible story, so his departure threw her. Lanie stared at the exit for several moments, lost in thought.

"Hey, are you okay?" Sally said, coming up to the table. "Ralph said something about you having an accident."

"It was nothing, just a little mishap," she muttered. "I could use something warm, though. I'm cold all the way through."

Sally nodded. "Your green chili is coming right up."

It surprised her that Ralph hadn't divulged more details to Sally, but at least that was consistent with a reporter's desire to keep a story to himself until he was ready to break it. As her gaze drifted around the room, she saw the clock on the wall. Alma would be worried.

She walked to the phone booth, looked up the number and dialed the shop. Not wanting to alarm her, Lanie told Alma that she'd fallen down and needed to change clothes. Alma, after finding out Lanie was okay, assured her good-naturedly that the library would still be there in another few hours, and encouraged her to have lunch first.

Lanie returned to the table and saw Sally seated there in the booth. "Mind if I take a load off my feet for a few minutes? It's time for my break."

"Sure. Company would be nice."

"Don't worry. I won't ask you any questions about your accident. I can see that you'd rather put that out of your mind."

She nodded, but didn't reply.

Sally gestured toward the plate she'd just set down for Lanie. "That green-chili stew is my own recipe, and the specialty of the house. It'll warm you right up."

"You love cooking, don't you?"

She nodded. "It gives me a lot of pleasure to fix hearty meals people keep coming back for. Before I owned my own place, I used to cook for neighbors, for Peter's school functions, for just about anyone who'd enjoy it.''

''So this is your little piece of heaven,'' Lanie observed with a casual gesture that encompassed the room.

Sally smiled. ''Yes. Seems crazy, doesn't it? It isn't a reservations-required restaurant or anything, but that wasn't the type of place I wanted. I'd like for my diner to remain exactly what it is, a place people don't have to dress up to come to. A home away from home, where someone else fixes the meals.''

''This stuff is wonderful. Better than a brandy,'' Lanie said after several spoonfuls of the spicy and hot chili stew.

''Sure it is. A brandy doesn't warm you up, it just makes you feel that way while you actually lose more heat, I've been told. That stew of mine gives you fuel to burn.''

Though she hadn't been hungry, Lanie found that her appetite had been awakened. She consumed the food greedily as Sally chatted away.

''I don't know how you see us here in Four Winds,'' Sally said, ''but it's the best place on earth, as far as I'm concerned. It's a place for happy endings, if you're willing to work at them. You won't lack a helping hand if you reach out for one, either. And if you want to go it alone, people will let you be. Privacy is a big thing with all of us.''

''I've noticed,'' Lanie said with a wry smile.

Sally laughed. ''But is that a bad thing? We all have private lives that we want to keep that way. Here you get a chance to do just that. There are dues to be paid in every person's life, but once those are out of the way, you know you belong.''

''Dues? What do you mean?''

''Everyone who comes to Four Winds is facing one kind of trouble or another, or they wouldn't have left where they were. It differs for all of us. But it comes down to the same thing. There's always something that needs to be resolved before we can really find ourselves. That's the first step toward finding your dream and making it come true.''

Sally's answer had intrigued her more than ever, but she knew that to pry would mean Sally would clam up completely, just as she'd done before. Lanie had to let her go at her own pace.

"Of course, there will always be complications that arise," Sally added with a small sigh. "I don't know of any place on earth that can protect you from life's little problems."

"Neither do I, but if you hear of one, don't keep it to yourself," Lanie joked.

Sally laughed. "Heck, if I could find one, I'd zip over there with my son, Pete. That boy is making me crazy."

"Growing pains?"

"I guess so, but I sure do wish he'd show more responsibility. He's been running around with his friends instead of coming in after school to help me here at the diner. I count on him, and he's been letting me down a lot lately."

"The independent stage. It's rough for kids *and* parents."

"I know he wants to be his own person, but he certainly isn't going to find himself by hanging around with that lazy Ted Burns. He's the mayor's only son, and he's spoiled rotten. My son has to work for his allowance. I've tried to teach him some solid values, and believe me, it's tough getting the message across when he sees Ted free to do anything he wants."

"At some point, you have to trust him to find his own way. Too much interference can drive him in the opposite direction."

"You sound like you know a lot about kids," Sally said cautiously.

"Not enough. I've made my share of mistakes. But I was a teacher once."

Sally reached out and patted her hand. "We've all made mistakes at one time or another. I'm a world-class champ at it. But if you're a teacher, why don't you go over to the high school and interview for a job there? They need staff desperately."

"I don't teach anymore."

Sally nodded and, to Lanie's relief, didn't pry. "Well, I better get back to work. If you need anything, give a yell."

Lanie stood up. "I'm finished, so I'd better get going, too. I've got to find Gabriel, then change clothes before I go to the library. I've got a job to do there for Alma."

Lanie used the front door on her way out. She'd avoid shortcuts or side streets from now on. She was hurrying to Gabriel's office when she turned the corner and ran straight into him.

Lanie staggered back a step, but Gabriel reached out quickly and steadied her.

Gabriel's grip was strong. He looked down, noting how dusty her clothes were. "Where the hell have you been! I've been worried about you! Are you okay?"

"Yes, fine. I just had lunch...."

The concern on his face turned to gladness, and with one fluid motion he drew her into the shadows and pulled her against him. His grip was fierce and possessive. It felt wonderful.

"I've been searching all over the place for you," he murmured, his voice raw.

Before she could answer, his mouth found hers, caressing and seducing. The sweet fires spreading through her made her light-headed. She clung to him desperately, needing his strength to stand as his tongue slipped into her slowly, in a rhythm as primitive as the dawn of time.

Lanie surrendered to the exquisite pleasure that sizzled

through her body. She felt loved and cherished, just as she had in her dream. From the edges of her mind, logic screamed that she was no longer dreaming. Yet at that wonderful moment, she wanted to be swept away, and needed to give as much as she was taking.

As her heart roared above common sense, she pressed herself into his kiss. Gabriel's response, that jagged intake of breath, the way he tightened his hold, all added to the fire in her. He was like a wild desert wind, raging and shifting everything in its path, molding it to its will.

Just as the last bit of her willpower melted, she heard a car going by. The driver honked. Gabriel eased his hold, then with a groan, moved away from her. "We're in the middle of town, yet in another minute, I would have done a lot more than kiss you."

"In another minute, I would have helped you." She drew in a breath, trying to come to her senses. "I really don't know what's happening to me. Sometimes when I'm around you I hardly recognize myself."

"You're not alone in that, woman. A Navajo man is taught to live his life by certain rules. Harmony is only a word to many, yet to us, it is the basis of our strength. To be spiritually at peace, to walk in beauty, a man has to achieve a certain balance. No excesses. All in moderation. But when I'm around you, the last thing on my mind is moderation."

"If it's any consolation, I spent many years as a teacher. Control is, was, a big part of my job. I'm used to taking responsibility for my own thoughts and actions. Only none of those habits seem to work when you're near." Lanie leaned back against the cold wall. It gave her something to think about besides the desire to step back into Gabriel's arms. "The worst part is that I've heard all about the famous, or infamous, Blackhorse brothers, who can have their pick of women, and probably have."

"I'm going to tell you something, because I want you

to know exactly how I feel," Gabriel said, his voice low
and even. "I've known other women in my life, in every
way a man can know a woman. But it was mostly their
sex that aroused me, not who they were. Then I met you.
Everything I felt was different right from the start. I can't
explain it, it's not at all like me, but it is the truth."

"It's happening too fast. I don't want this."

"Don't you?" he murmured. "Some say Four Winds
reads the heart's deepest secrets, then finds a way to make
them come true."

"You don't really believe that," she countered quietly.

"No, but I have no better explanation. I'm not a man
prone to idealism, or romantic nonsense. I know sex for
what it is. But what I feel for you goes beyond that. Sometimes when I hold you, it's as if I've found a vital piece
of myself."

"I feel that way, too," Lanie breathed, though her heart
had lodged in her throat. "And sometimes that scares me
to death."

"It shouldn't be that way," he said slowly. "If what's
happening between us is meant to be, it'll unfold in its
own time. In the meantime, we have work to do together.
What we're facing could be a battle for our lives."

She nodded. "Which brings me to the reason I was on
my way to find you." As she explained, her words came
out in a torrent. In a spur-of-the-moment decision, she also
told him about her childhood fears and why she'd approached the well.

"I admire your courage, woman."

The simple words made her spirits soar. "Thanks. That
means a lot to me, coming from you."

"Let's go back to that well now. We may yet be able
to find some tracks or other evidence."

"By the way, why were you looking for me?"

He took a deep breath. "The accident in my Jeep this morning was no accident. Someone deliberately rolled that barrel into our path."

Chapter Ten

The news that the "accident" had really been a deliberate attempt on their lives filled Lanie with bone-chilling dread. "Are you certain?"

"The ropes holding the paint barrels had been cut with a knife."

"But were they after you or me, and why?"

"I don't know, except my gut instinct tells me it has something to do with the bowl."

"I had it with me this morning," she admitted.

Gabriel's eyes narrowed. "They couldn't have known that, or they wouldn't have risked the bowl." He stared at the ground for a moment. "Or maybe the accident was meant only to unnerve us."

"Well, it worked. Between that and the incident at the well, I'm going to be looking behind me all the time."

As they approached the well, Gabriel studied the area. "You say that Ralph brought you the ladder?"

"Yes. He was on his way to Sally's for lunch. I guess he decided to take a shortcut, too."

Gabriel crouched down. "I've always been glad our side streets were graveled—that is, until now." Gabriel searched methodically for footprints. "There are only a few tracks here that are clear, but they're right around the edge of the well where Ralph probably stood as he lowered the ladder. One set came from your flats, and the other two are clearly from athletic shoes. One pair, I figure, is about a size nine, which would fit Ralph. Then there's the other set, which appears to be slightly smaller. But it's hard to tell. The scuffle, and then your rescue, wiped out most of the evidence."

"Well, if you expect me to be sorry for fighting or for being rescued, you're nuts. I did my best at the time. I was worried about escaping, not preserving evidence."

"Understandable, but just be patient. I'll find answers."

"Let's hope it'll be in time. The way things are going, we may end up dead before long."

His eyes darkened and shone with the intensity of a fierce desert storm. "No one will harm you again. If you're in trouble, I'll sense it, and I will find you. I can't explain it, but I know I will be there to protect you."

The conviction of his words sent vibrations right to her soul. She didn't know nearly as much about Gabriel as she would have liked, but she felt safe when he was around. The problem was, she couldn't be with Gabriel all the time. They both had jobs to do. "I've got to go back to the boardinghouse and change. I'm already late for an appointment at the library."

He nodded. "That was the first place I looked after I went by Alma's. She told me you'd be there. When I didn't find you, I knew you were in trouble." Without being aware of it, his hand strayed absently to the medicine pouch that hung from his belt. "It was more than the obvious fact that people don't get lost in a town the size of Four Winds. I actually *knew* you were in trouble. You know what I mean, don't you?"

She nodded, unable to trust her voice. She knew. It was all part of what was between them, the way she'd sensed his presence in the laundry room without ever having heard or seen him. And then there were her dreams. But she wasn't ready to talk to him about those yet.

"Then believe me, you won't face anything alone." He led Lanie back to his patrol car, then dropped her off at Marlee's. "I wouldn't discuss any of what's happened with her."

"I won't. I'm not really sure I trust her, you know."

"Maybe that's for the best, at least for now."

A HALF HOUR LATER, Lanie finally arrived at the library. The small bowl was safely back among her sweaters inside the dresser in her room. She wouldn't carry it with her again, or leave it in plain sight.

As she entered the small adobe building, it seemed to welcome her. The stillness here was comforting. The library, obviously somebody's former home, seemed like an oasis of serenity. There were whitewashed adobe walls, the thick, original kind one seldom saw anymore. Dark pine shelves, stacked ceiling high with books, filled each room. A ladder affixed to a wooden-and-brass rail that encircled each of the rooms was provided for patrons who wanted books from the top shelves.

Crossing to the center of the house, she located the reference desk. The telltale click of her shoes against the brick flooring announced her presence as she traversed the room.

Lanie had expected the librarian to be as quaint and charming as the library itself. Nothing prepared her for the burly man who came out of the shadows cast by two oversize bookshelves.

Lanie took a step back, startled, and eyed him with suspicion.

He smiled, but somehow that didn't make him seem any friendlier. With his massive build, he resembled a hot-water heater with a head. His arms looked powerful enough to lift the ceiling-high shelf of books behind him.

"I'm Jake Fields, the librarian," he introduced himself in a gravelly voice. "Can I help you find something?"

It took her a moment, but she managed a smile. "Sorry, you startled me when you came out from behind the shelves."

He gave her a rueful smile. "And I'm sure I wasn't what you were expecting, either. It's beyond me why so many people picture librarians as frail, gray-haired females."

His voice was brusque, but his expression was one of weary patience. She wasn't quite sure what to make of him. "I'm Lanie Mathews. Alma sent me to take photos of the vanity table."

He shook her hand, and her own disappeared inside his beefy mitt. "I'm glad. I'm looking forward to selling it. This library needs more books and less fancy trappings. That's why I pressured the town council into letting me sell the table from the librarian's quarters to raise funds. I certainly don't need it." He led the way through to a back storage room, then gestured to an intricately carved oak piece.

"I don't know much about antiques, but that's beautiful." Lanie took several shots from different angles. Once she was finished, she returned the camera to her bag. "Thanks. If you have any questions, just call Alma at the shop."

By the time she walked back into Alma's shop, Lanie realized news of her fall had spread. She could see the concern on Alma's face and wondered how she'd found out.

"Are you okay?" Alma asked, rushing toward Lanie. "I heard from Rosa that you fell into the old well. Is that true? Jerry, at the post office, told her about it."

There was no telling exactly how the news had spread, except that one way or another it must have come from Ralph or the person who'd pushed her in. The story would be impossible to track, though.

"Are you okay?" Alma repeated.

"Yes, I'm fine, but honestly, the last thing I need is to become the talk of the town again. Can you downplay this if you hear anyone discussing it?"

She shook her head. "It gets worse, I'm afraid," Alma said, giving her an apologetic look.

"What do you mean?"

"Before I knew of the accident, I called Ralph to tell him that you had brought the bowl for me to examine this morning. I was trying to debunk the stories about its being valuable. Only, after what happened with the paint barrels and the accident at the well, you and the bowl are a hot topic of conversation. In case you're interested, people are saying that when the tide finally changes, and it starts bringing you *good* luck, you're going to end up with everything you've ever wanted."

"*If* I survive," Lanie muttered.

"I had a call from Mike Madison. He's a big-time dealer from Santa Fe who works with private collectors. He also learned about the bowl and wants to travel here to see it. If it's genuine and can be dated and identified, he'd like to buy it. He says he can make you a very generous offer."

"Do you know him?"

"Of him is more like it. I can tell you, though, that he's as good as his word. Problem is, I really don't think the bowl will stand up to the scrutiny a serious collector will give it."

"It doesn't matter. I'm not ready to part with it, anyway." Lanie had a feeling there was more to the bowl than she'd originally thought. She remembered the pulsing warmth that had radiated from the bowl into her body when she'd been chilled to the bone inside that well. And soon after, she'd been rescued.

"You certainly aren't going to start believing it has mystical properties, are you?" Alma stared at her. "I mean, I've heard stranger things, but I figured you to be the practical type.''

"I'm not sure about anything nowadays," she confessed. "I used to know my own mind at least, but ever since I arrived in Four Winds, my life's been crazy.''

"It's that way for all of us at first. Then we find ourselves and begin new lives.''

"Was it that way for you?''

Alma hesitated. "This store was always Emily's obsession. I never really thought we'd make a go of it here, and the first year we barely made it financially. But we'd used all of our money to produce the catalog, so we had to stick it out. I really hated the store that year. The way we'd locked ourselves in was almost like being caught in a trap. Emily didn't agree, of course, but then this store was the culmination of everything she wanted. Just as I thought we'd have to move on or go completely bankrupt, orders started coming in.''

"Are you happy here?''

"I suppose. Sometimes I wish I'd married when I was younger, though. I would have had a family of my own by now, and something besides the store in my life. Then again, the way families are today, maybe things wouldn't have been any different.''

The loneliness in Alma's words touched her deeply. Maybe it took someone well acquainted with that emotion to understand the cost it exacted. Alma had obviously lost her lifetime companion when her sister had died.

After the death of her student, Lanie had lost her ability to teach, to do the work that had given her life purpose. If anyone could understand and sympathize with Alma, she could.

IT WAS CLOSE TO FIVE when Lanie helped close up the shop. "Do you want me to stay and write catalog copy with you? I normally do chores for Marlee in the evenings, but I'm sure she won't mind if I'm a bit late."

"No, thanks," Alma said, continuing to study the reference manual before her. "Good night," she added absently.

Lanie walked back to the boardinghouse, making sure she stayed on the main path all the way. She'd taken all the picturesque side trips she ever intended to take in Four Winds.

A short time later, she arrived at the boardinghouse. Marlee was standing near the window, a tense look on her face. Lanie stopped in midstep and glanced at the tall, thin man in the room with her.

"This gentleman's been waiting for you," Marlee said. "I'll be in the kitchen if you need me," she added, excusing herself.

Lanie watched her, suspecting that Marlee had done too much today, since she was favoring her leg more than usual. "What can I do for you?" she asked, turning her attention quickly to the stranger.

"My name's Mike Madison," he said, shaking her hand. "I've heard that you recently acquired a very unusual bowl."

"I'm not sure what you mean by 'unusual,'" she said, "but it was a gift someone gave me, one that I value."

He nodded slowly. "May we sit down?"

She gestured for him to have a seat on the sofa, then sat across from him on a chair. Madison seemed to exude that old-money style that was synonymous with class and breeding. It could have been an affectation, but she didn't think so. He was probably used to success and undaunted by obstacles. "What's your interest in the bowl?"

"First I'd like to examine it. If it fits the requirements my buyer has given me, then I'm prepared to make you an offer right now."

"I'm sorry you've come all this way. It isn't for sale."

"Would you mind if I took a look anyway?" Madison pressed. "If it interests me, perhaps the peddler who gave it to you could find me another comparable one."

So he knew how she'd acquired it. "I understand he's very hard to find."

"I'm a resourceful man."

Lanie considered his request. It couldn't do any harm, and it wouldn't hurt to have the goodwill and interest of a big-time dealer, in case she ever *did* decide to sell it. "I'll let you view the bowl, but please don't handle it. It's really not for sale, and I don't want to risk any damage to it."

He nodded. "Very well."

She went to her room and returned a moment later with the bowl. Lanie lowered it carefully onto the coffee table before him, but remained close by.

Madison crouched down and studied it from all angles. "Without specific tests, I can't say for certain, but I'm willing to trust my experience. I'd say this is the genuine article, all right."

"A skinwalker's bowl?"

"That I can't say. But the markings and the weathered edges make it a rather interesting piece of antique pottery, at the very least." He stood up slowly. "I can tell you that I'd be extremely interested in buying it, should you ever change your mind about selling."

"You said you were prepared to make an immediate offer. But how can you do that without authenticating it first?"

"I've been in this business for a very long time. I'm willing to gamble. *Are* you interested in selling?"

Just then, Lanie heard the screen door open. Gabriel came in wearing a denim shirt and jeans. The medicine pouch hung from his belt, but his badge was nowhere to be seen. Giving her a nod, he sat in Marlee's chair by the window and began to read the newspaper.

Lanie stared at him, annoyed. She couldn't shake the feeling that he was deliberately eavesdropping.

"I understand you like to travel," Madison said. "I could make sure you have a top-notch vehicle, suited to cross-country travel, in exchange for the bowl. You could be on the road by the day after tomorrow."

Lanie realized that he'd done his homework. He knew about her broken-down car and probably a great deal more. She glanced at Gabriel out of the corner of her eye. The paper was in front of his face, but she could tell he was watching, waiting for her response.

Irritated, she turned her attention to the antique dealer. "Would you also be willing to add some expense money to that deal?"

He wrote down a figure on a piece of paper and handed it to her. "How's this? You understand that, between the vehicle and the cash, that's the price I'd pay for an authenticated piece. I'm taking quite a chance."

She looked into his eyes. She doubted that this man ever took any real risks. He was darned sure that it was genuine, just as sure as Alma had been that it wasn't. Her curiosity was piqued. Now she was really interested to see how far the price could be pushed.

She handed him back the sheet of paper on which was written the figure. "I appreciate your interest, but no."

Madison stood. "All right. Here's my final offer. There's no vehicle with this. It'll be strictly a cash transaction." He wrote a new number on the sheet. "And if you accept, we'll seal the deal in a few hours. All I need to do is find a bank."

Gabriel crossed the room, still carrying the newspaper, and bumped into the man hard. "Sorry! I wasn't looking where I was going."

She scarcely glanced at Gabriel, stunned by the high figure written on the paper before her. The sum would support her for a very long time.

"I'm prepared to give you ten percent right now, in cash." Madison reached into his back pocket. Suddenly his expression changed. His confidence vanished, and in its place was shock, then anger. "My wallet, it's gone."

He glanced around, obviously looking for Gabriel. "How long have you known the gentleman who was just in here?" He peered into the next room, the kitchen, searching.

"I can assure you he's incapable of stealing anything. Where else have you been today?" She helped him check the sofa where he'd been sitting, then look around the room, but they found nothing.

"I'm going to call the sheriff and file a report. May I use the telephone?"

She gestured to the end table, deciding not to tell him Gabriel was the sheriff. "Help yourself."

As she picked up her bowl, Lanie glanced around for Gabriel. She had no doubt he'd picked the man's pocket, though she was just as certain he had no intention of keeping the wallet. His reasons, however, escaped her. Perhaps he'd been worried that she would yield to temptation and sell the bowl, despite all his warnings. That was the only thing that made sense. Yet what bothered her most was that, until now, she would not have believed Gabriel capable of pulling such a stunt.

A smile tugged at the corners of her mouth. Not that she'd ever thought him saintly. She thought of confronting him, though. She knew she'd never be able to intimidate or bluff him into admitting anything. If he did, it would be only on his own terms, and because he chose to. And undoubtedly he would insist that he'd only had her best interests at heart. Her smile faded. That argument reminded her too much of her experiences at the countless foster homes she'd lived in as a girl. For as far back as she could remember, when people claimed to do things for her own good, that seldom turned out to be true. Those who professed to care for her had been the least trustworthy of all.

Chapter Eleven

After searching the house for Gabriel, Lanie walked out the front door and glanced at the parking area. His police vehicle was nowhere to be seen.

Lanie went back inside and saw Mike Madison leafing through the pages of the small county directory.

Madison spoke quickly into the phone, then hung up. "I spoke to the sheriff, and he has assured me that I will get my wallet back. I'm prepared to finalize the deal I started to make you. Though I can't offer you an immediate ten percent, I can have the full amount electronically transferred first thing tomorrow morning."

Lanie wondered what he would have done had he known that Gabriel *was* the sheriff. Shaking her head, she responded, "No, Mr. Madison. Your offer is very tempting, but on second thought, I just don't think I can sell it. The bowl was a gift, but for all I know, it could belong to the Navajo people. I need to gather more information before I make up my mind."

"My offer may not be as high a week from now, I warn you. The peddler may have other bowls like it, and I do intend to find him."

She nodded. "That's a risk I have to take."

She bid Madison goodbye and watched as he drove off in a late-model luxury car. His willingness to offer such a large sum of money, for an item that hadn't been authenticated, raised many questions in her mind.

Lanie had the distinct feeling that he knew far more about her bowl than he'd admitted. But what? She still knew precious little about it herself, except that from the moment she'd touched the bowl, it had called out to her.

Gabriel drove up a moment later. Lanie was waiting for him as he strode into the living room.

"Okay, I want to know what that nonsense was all about," she demanded.

"What nonsense?"

"Don't insult my intelligence." She kept her voice low, wanting to keep their conversation private. "You picked that man's pocket. Why?"

"To protect you," he answered. "First of all, I didn't think you should sell the bowl. Although I admit that I don't want you to leave town for personal reasons, there's another consideration here. If the legend *is* true, it may be dangerous for you to part with the bowl. Remember Lucas said it's supposed to be linked to you, its owner. Until we can establish exactly how, for you to sell it could be dangerous."

Though his claim of doing it for her own good had struck a nerve, she decided to let it pass. She'd seen evidence of the link between herself and the bowl. She was still upset with Gabriel, but there was no denying that his reasons were sound.

"A man who is any kind of man protects those he cares about," he murmured. His gaze was tender and infinitely patient. "Love frightens you," he observed, lifting her hand and pressing a kiss to the center of her palm. "But my love asks nothing from you in return."

"Neither of us is a child. We have pasts and lessons we've learned there."

"I understand better than you realize. Relationships mean sharing what's inside, in our hearts and in our minds, but what's hidden there usually does little to show us in a favorable light."

"So we remain alone, protecting all the demons we harbor inside ourselves," Lanie finished for him. She gazed into Gabriel's eyes and saw a mirror of herself, her fears, her needs. "We're kindred spirits in that way."

"Yes, I believe we are," he answered.

He walked to the window and stared outside for a long time. When he finally turned around, his expression was hooded. "Would you like me to tell you where Mr. Madison went after he left here?" he said, shifting back to business.

"You followed him?"

He nodded. "He went directly to the mayor's house. He and Bob Burns obviously know each other. I managed to get close enough to the house to see them arguing, but I couldn't make out their words, because the window was closed."

"Madison told me he was acting on behalf of a client. I suppose that client could be the mayor."

"I intend to check it out." He reached for her hand and held it in his. "I know you're worried. Many things are happening all at once. But you have to trust me, if not as a man who cares for you, then as the sheriff. I will stand between you and whatever danger you'll have to face because of the bowl."

She didn't resist when he pulled her into his arms; indeed, she leaned toward him. Lanie wasn't sure what compelled her to initiate the kiss. Maybe she needed to let him know that she was strong and quite capable of taking care of herself, that her strength matched his.

She had intended to keep the kiss soft, but the dark, deep taste of him muddled up her thinking. As she pressed herself into him, she felt his arms tighten around her. She heard the throaty sound that came from the depths of his being as he drank in her taste until it became part of him.

Lanie shivered, then feeling the fires rising, gathered the shredded remnants of her willpower and stepped back. "If we keep straying too close to the fire, sooner or later we'll get burned," she managed to say breathlessly.

"Some things are worth the risk," he answered quietly, then tearing his gaze from hers, walked out the door. Lanie watched Gabriel as he went to his vehicle. The stakes were higher than she'd ever dreamed. There was no doubt in her mind that her path and Gabriel's were woven together somehow. Their destination, however, remained as uncertain as ever.

GABRIEL DROVE to his brother's first-aid station at the edge of town. Lucas had called him on the cellular and asked him to come. His trip back to the rez had been only partially successful, but he refused to give Gabriel any details over the phone. Sometimes Lucas could be a pain in the neck, or lower.

Gabriel parked at the rear of the building and went up to the kitchen door. Lucas stood by the fridge, soda in hand.

"What's up?" Gabriel greeted. "You're back a heck of a lot sooner than I expected."

"Searching the rez for Dad and Josh is a lost cause. I asked around at the trading post, trying to get a lead as to where they were. I even did some hiking back into some of the areas, but you know as well as I do that unless you know where to look, an elephant—an apt comparison to Josh, by the way—could lose itself on the rez."

"Okay, so you failed. What's the good news?"

"I didn't fail—I just haven't succeeded yet," Lucas said. "As you know, I can't stay away from Four Winds for long—I'm needed here. So I've sent some of our cousins out looking for them. They'll contact us via telephone if they make any progress. In the meantime, I've found our uncle. He's visiting friends less than forty miles from here. They live in the mountains, but since the snows haven't started, you should be able to get to him without any problems.''

"Uncle has always prided himself on his knowledge of our ancestors. Let's hope he remembers all the details.''

"He won't know as much as Dad, I'll bet, but he's our only shot right now. Take the bowl and go talk to him tonight. Tomorrow he's flying to Washington to talk to the congressman about the gaming issues facing the tribe.''

"I'll go see if Lanie can get away. She'll have to come along to handle the bowl.''

Lucas looked at his brother, a shrewd expression on his face. "What's holding you back with this woman? Your feelings for her run deep—I can see that.''

"There are…complications. She's not exactly eager to get involved with me. When I look into her eyes, I see protective barriers there. Something bad happened to her.''

"I could say the same thing about you, brother. Only you don't often look within.''

"I already know what's there, that's why.''

"You two will have to learn to trust each other,'' Lucas said. "There's more at stake here than your own personal wishes.''

"It's that knowledge that scares me the most. I want to protect her, but I'm not sure that, in the long run, my efforts will be enough.''

LANIE GLANCED at the wall clock, then back at Gabriel. He stood before her, his face as expressive as that of a stone monolith.

"You want me to take my bowl to heaven knows where this late at night? You realize that so far it has created havoc each and every time I've had it with me. I can't prove that those instances were all connected, but I do know the bowl is like a magnet for crooks. They come out of the woodwork for the chance to get their hands on it.''

"I can't argue with that."

"But you still want to go now?"

"It's tonight or not at all. My uncle won't be around tomorrow."

"You've been to this place before?"

"No, and from what I can tell, it's going to be rough going. I won't be surprised if we have to hike the last few hundred yards."

"At night, through a forest, carrying the bowl," she reiterated.

"If I could take it myself without endangering you, I would, but I can't even touch it."

"Why not?"

He took a deep breath and admitted how it had burned his hand the one time he had tried. "I had it analyzed and I got the report late this afternoon. There's nothing corrosive in its composition."

She felt the blood drain from her face. "Why didn't you tell me about the burn before?"

"I thought it could have been an allergy or something like that. But there's no logical way to explain the burn or the pain I felt. I nearly dropped it," he admitted.

She remembered the pleasant warmth that had radiated through her in the well. It hadn't been threatening—in fact, just the opposite.

"What about the rest? Is it authentic and was it made with ashes?"

"There was so much carbon in its composition, they were able to use a radioactive dating technique. It's estimated to be anywhere from fifty to two hundred years old. The technique isn't that precise. They can't confirm the carbon came from ashes, either, but it could have."

"We'll go talk to your uncle. I think you're right. If he knows anything that can shed some light on what's been going on around here, it's high time we found out."

THEY REACHED the steep dirt track heading into the ponderosa pine forest at half past ten. "We're in the right place. It fits Lucas's description," Gabriel said.

She drew her tote bag closer to her, holding it as if trying to protect the bowl from an unseen enemy. The gesture had been done unconsciously, but as she followed Gabriel's gaze, she became aware of it.

"I just want to make sure it's safe," she said. "I can't let it end up in pieces, not until I'm sure the legend won't call for me to share its fate."

"I have a particular talent that I've developed as a cop. I can sense danger miles away. Right now, my gut tells me we're safe, so don't worry."

He gestured ahead, pursing his lips, Navajo style. "Here's the biggest problem we're facing now. That road looks iffy at best from recent rains. It should be passable with a four-wheel-drive vehicle, but I can't guarantee anything in the dark like this. We could lose a tire on the rocks. The safer course is not to risk a flat and to hike in. But it's going to be rough going, and it's at least three miles from here."

"Have you got a spare tire?"

"One."

She took a deep breath, then let it out again. "Let's drive until we have a flat tire. If that happens, we'll walk the rest of the way."

"Good compromise."

They drove slowly, the thick cloud layer making the bumpy track ahead appear and disappear as the Jeep was tossed from side to side, hiding the path from their headlights. About halfway in, they punctured a tire.

Lanie stood behind Gabriel, holding a flashlight as he worked to change the flat. As she bent down to retrieve a bolt, she caught a flicker of movement out of the corner of her eye.

"I think we're in trouble," she said, edging closer to him.

He reached inside his jacket, his hand stopping to rest on the butt of his gun. "What did you see?"

"There." She aimed the flashlight at an area thick with scrub oak. "There's something in there."

"Something or someone?"

"I don't know."

"Wait here." He took the flashlight and crept forward, hardly making a sound. Suddenly a creature came out of the shadows. The coyote was old, and looked as if it had seen lean times.

"Don't shoot it," she said, moving closer to Gabriel.

"I wasn't going to. Coyote is the trickster in our legends. When he appears, it is said that nothing will be as you expect."

The animal stared at them for a moment, its eyes glowing in the glare of the flashlight, then moved off. "Poor thing, it looked like it needed a good brushing, not to mention a few meals."

"There's game around. He'll be all right," Gabriel assured her.

As they returned to the car, she insinuated her hand inside her tote, lightly brushing her fingertips against the surface of the bowl. It felt pleasantly warm. "Do you consider the coyote's appearance an omen?"

"Let's say I'd rather see him as just another creature who hunts at night."

Despite their earlier agreement not to risk another flat now that their spare had been used, they opted to drive on. The rocky ground had given way to a wide meadow ahead.

Lanie peered through the darkness. "There's a light just across the meadow between those trees. I can't see it now, but when we turned with the curve of the road, I caught a flicker."

He shifted in his seat. "I see it."

They arrived three minutes later in front of a small, rectangular log cabin. Lanie started to get out, but Gabriel reached over and stopped her. "We wait here until they invite us inside. It's customary."

She sat back and waited. Minutes seemed to tick by. "Can't you honk the horn or something?"

"They know we're here. You can hear this Jeep coming miles away. Be patient."

No sooner had he finished speaking than an elderly man came to the door and waved an invitation.

"Finally!" Lanie said, relieved. "I didn't want to just sit out here in the cold and dark."

"Some women wouldn't have considered that a hardship as long as I was there with them," he said, grinning.

"You must have been more entertaining then," she teased.

"Remind me to show you my better side sometime," he murmured, his voice deep and velvety smooth.

A delicious shiver traveled over her, leaving her tingling. "I'll be sure and take you up on that someday."

He cocked an eyebrow and gave her a half smile that made her pulse race. She vowed to learn to keep her mouth shut one of these days.

"When you meet my uncle, don't offer to shake his hand. Navajos, the old ones in particular, keep close to our customs, and those include the dislike of touching strangers," Gabriel warned.

Lanie approached the door and got her first clear view of Gabriel's uncle. His face was scored with deep lines, yet the overall impression she got was of strength rather than age. Maybe it was his eyes, and the way they shone with a fire one didn't expect from someone of such an advanced age. Or perhaps it was his confident bearing. One thing was for certain: this wasn't a man anyone would ever dismiss easily.

"Uncle," Gabriel greeted. "Do you know why we're here?"

He nodded and waved for them to come inside. There were three hand-carved wooden chairs set in front of the fireplace. "Word reached me." He looked at Lanie with undisguised interest. "Will you show me the bowl?"

Lanie brought it out and started to hand it to him, but the man jumped to his feet and stepped back abruptly.

"No. No one must handle it except you. Just hold it out for me." He studied it for several long minutes. Finally, after a tense silence, he glanced up at them. "Do you feel it?"

Gabriel's eyebrows knitted together. "Feel what, Uncle?" Uneasy, his hand went to the medicine pouch that hung from his belt.

The elderly man looked at Lanie and smiled slowly. "*You* feel it," he observed.

"The bowl's usually warm to the touch, but here it's cold, almost like a piece of ice."

He nodded. "It doesn't like my presence."

"Do you recognize the bowl?" Lanie asked.

He leaned back against the wall as if suddenly weary. "That bowl has an evil past. It was created by an enemy of our clan and the Navajo people, many years ago."

His gaze shifted to Gabriel. "Flinthawk, our ancestor, was the medicine man who was called upon to do battle against the bowl's maker, the most powerful witch our people have ever known. And it is the flint-hawk fetish you carry in your medicine pouch, a gift handed down through the generations, that will protect you against that evil now. It is the strongest medicine your ancestor could leave for the future guardians of Four Winds."

"Family tradition makes me the bearer of the medicine bundle, that's true, but so far it hasn't brought me any answers. I need to know what, if anything, can or should be done now," Gabriel said.

"The medicine bundle won't provide you with answers. Its function is to strengthen you when you need it. Make no mistake about this. Your courage will be tested, and your lives will be at risk. Many will want the bowl and will try to take it from you. But it is said that for the bowl to accept a new owner, the current one must die." He met Lanie's gaze. "You will be in danger not only from those who believe in the magic, but from those who value the historical artifact and want to consider themselves the owner of such an object."

"The peddler passed it on to me. Does that means he's dead?" Lanie asked.

"No. The peddler was only a kind of messenger. He carried the bowl until the bowl chose its destined owner. But mark my words. That bowl was created for evil and will corrupt all it touches. It's up to you to end its legacy. My brother, or perhaps his youngest son, or the *hataalii* teaching him, will be able to tell you how to do that, according to our ways. I can do no more for you. But you have been warned. The longer you keep it, the more the danger will encompass you. I feel this as clearly as the cold wind that blows through the cracks in the door."

"It seems a shame to destroy an artifact with so much history," Lanie said.

"It has to be done. Nothing good will come from preserving it." His expression was grim as he met Lanie's gaze. "Listen carefully to me now. When you reach home, hide that bowl someplace only you know, where you're certain it'll be safe. But make sure it's near you." He went to the door and held it open for them. "Now go, please. That bowl must not remain under this roof any longer."

Lanie walked outside, her hands slipping inside her tote bag. Despite the colder forest temperature, the bowl now felt warm to the touch again.

"I don't understand *any* of this. All I've learned about this bowl contradicts every belief I've ever had. Yet I'm

certain that ignoring the warnings I've been given as su-
perstition is a mistake that will put me in even more danger than I'm in already."

"So you're going to take my uncle's advice, and hide
it when I get back?"

"Yes, I'm already trying to figure out the best place to
keep it. Let's go home. I've got work to do."

As they drove back, Gabriel glanced at the clock on the
dashboard. "I'd like to make a stop before we go back to
the boardinghouse."

"Where?"

"The library. It's closed at this hour, but I may be able
to persuade Jake Fields to open the back door. I'd like to
see how far back the microfiche of the town newspaper
goes. Maybe there is something about the bowl there."

"That's a great idea. But Jake may not appreciate it if
he's already in bed."

"He won't have to go far. He lives on the premises. It's
part of the deal he has with the town. When Jake came to
Four Winds a few years back, everyone thought he was
an ex-serviceman drifting and looking for trouble. We
were partially wrong. He was an ex-ranger, but what came
as a surprise was his college degree in library science. The
high-school teachers had always complained that we didn't
have a properly run library in town, so he was just what
Four Winds needed."

"People talk about Four Winds as if it has a living,
breathing soul. It can be unnerving, you know."

He grinned. "Four Winds, in its own way, is as alive
as the people who live there. It does have a spirit all its
own."

"Had anyone told me that when I first arrived, I would
have thought they were nuts. Now I don't know. Do you
realize how disconcerting that is? We all grow up taking
certain things for granted. You expect the sky to be blue
and the grass green for the foreseeable future. But if some

morning you woke up to find the sky green and the grass blue, then the guideposts you'd lived by would be demolished. That could be a person's undoing.''

He nodded thoughtfully. ''Many say that Four Winds always tears you down at first, so it can build you all over again.''

''Like boot camp,'' she said with a thin smile. ''Do you believe that?''

''I believe that it's been true for some, but it wasn't that way for me. Four Winds has always been home to me. I came back because I needed to find myself again, and I knew I could do that here.''

''I've always wondered what 'home' would feel like. It must be wonderful to have a place where you know you'll always belong,'' she said softly. ''I've never had that. Uncertainty is the only constant I've ever experienced in my life.''

''What do you mean?''

She took a deep breath, then let it out again. She wasn't sure how much to tell him. Then he reached for her hand, covering it with his own. Her resistance melted away. ''My mother wasn't married. She barely made ends meet and couldn't afford a child, so when I was four I ended up in foster care. My mother disappeared without ever signing the papers needed, so I wasn't eligible for adoption, either, until much later. I grew up in a succession of foster homes. I'd see other kids at school, kids with real homes, and wish with all my heart that someone would want me. But that never happened.

''Holidays were the worst,'' she continued. ''There were always invitations during Christmas and Easter from people who meant well, but what those stays did was give me a close-up of the very things I wanted and never would have. I learned back then that when you hope too hard for something, your heart can break. The only dreams I would have a chance of making come true were those that depended on no one outside myself, and even then, only if I was willing to fight with everything in me to make them happen.'' She squared her shoulders and looked at him proudly. ''Those weren't bad lessons.''

He said nothing for several minutes. ''I can't even imagine being without a family,'' he said at last. ''We had our differences, of course. My father is a traditionalist, my mother was a Christian.'' He slowed down as they entered Four Winds. ''That's why all three of us have biblical names. But no matter how we fought among ourselves, we knew that when the chips were down we had backup.''

He parked behind the library and gestured at the lit window on the south side of the building. ''He's up. Now let's see if he'll open the door for us. He's got a mind of his own and enough of the ranger mentality to be a stickler about schedules.''

Gabriel knocked and identified himself. Silence greeted him. Gabriel knocked again even more firmly.

''I heard you the first time,'' Jake called out. ''But unless this is a law-enforcement emergency, we have posted hours and you're outside those limits.''

''It's not an emergency, but I'd be grateful if you'd let us do a search in special collections.''

Lanie leaned closer to the door. ''It's Lanie here, too, Jake, and I desperately need some information on my bowl. Won't you help me out?''

''Why didn't you tell me that's what you wanted?'' Jake opened the door. ''I've been looking into that subject myself. I've heard the stories about the peddler, and it made me curious.''

He led them to a small, windowless room, probably a former pantry. ''I've only found one reference to a bowl like the one people have said you have. It was in a journal kept by one of the original mayors of Four Winds. In it, he chronicled turn-of-the-century events in our region.''

He set up a viewer. ''I've had this transferred to microfiche. Take a look at the bottom of the page. As you see, when Dusty Calhoun decided to move back east with his family," Jake said, "he sold off everything he owned. He was this area's largest landowner, so it became almost the biggest event of 1900. The entry finished by listing some of the more interesting estate pieces. One was a small Indian bowl reputed to have belonged to a skinwalker. But there wasn't any more of a description, so there's no telling if it's the same one."

"Will you keep looking for information? Maybe there's another journal somewhere," Gabriel suggested.

"You bet, I'll stay on it. I like doing research. But why the rush all of a sudden?"

"Too many things have been happening to me, Jake," Lanie said. "I can't go into them now, but believe me that the sooner I get answers the better off everyone will be."

"We'll leave this research to you now. It's time for all of us to get some sleep," Gabriel said.

Lanie and Gabriel left the library and drove to Marlee's. As they walked across the yard to the door, Gabriel glanced up at the sky. "Wouldn't you know it? Now that we don't need the extra light, the clouds have dissipated."

"I'm glad. I need a calm, beautiful night to lift my spirits right now."

Gabriel leaned back against the wooden edging of the portal. "It's so quiet right now. This time of year, not even the insects come out. I like that total stillness. I think that's what I missed most when I lived in L.A."

"Why did you go to such a large city after growing up in Four Winds? Didn't you know how rough it would be?"

"I went for precisely that reason. I needed to find out what I was made of. Know what I mean?"

"Sure. In my own way, I had things to prove, too. After college I wanted to earn my own place in the world. I started as a castoff, but I had no intention of letting that label define what I became."

"I don't understand something, Lanie. Having a real home is something that's important to you. You could have that here in Four Winds if you wanted. Why is it that you're so set on leaving?"

"As I told you, I've discovered that there are things that are not meant to be ours. To reach for them brings only disappointment." She knew all about love, and the high price it carried. It was the one lesson she'd learned in the foster homes she'd stayed in. Every time she'd formed attachments, she wound up with a broken heart. She'd had to relearn that lesson as a teacher, and that almost finished her. She would never repeat the mistake again.

"Fear is a good thing. It brings caution, but sometimes fear can be a bad enemy. It prevents us from taking what is freely given, because we don't quite trust our good fortune."

Lanie looked up and saw desire flickering in Gabriel's eyes. "What is ever given freely?" she whispered, her voice taut.

"Let me show you." Long fingers wound through her hair, cradling her head as he lowered his lips, taking her mouth with his own.

Wonderful sensations rippled through her as she allowed herself to bask in the wonder of loving and being loved in return.

It was chemistry. It was heaven. His maleness, his heat, all enveloped her seductively. She wanted him. Her tongue darted over his, mating with him, then drawing away.

She didn't want the kiss to stop, but her finely honed instinct for survival roared into play. She drew back into herself, finding strength there, and stepped back.

"I'm not ready for this," she said, her breathing ragged. "I don't really know you—do you realize that?"

"What your heart tells you is more important than anything else." He gazed into her eyes, then smiled gently. "But a woman like you deserves more from a man like me." He glanced out onto the deserted street. "I need to take a walk. Will you come with me? I'll show you a side of Four Winds you'll seldom see."

Moonbeams dappled the ground, forming complex kaleidoscopic shapes as they strolled down Main Street. Tree branches bent down as if trying to shelter them as they walked. Everything was covered in a muted silvery glow that was as beautiful as it was comforting.

"Four Winds is much like the kind of town I envisioned settling down in when I left college," Lanie admitted, pulling her jacket tightly around herself.

"Why didn't you find a hometown for yourself?" He placed his arm around her shoulders, keeping her near his side.

He was strong, both physically and spiritually. Yet his touch was remarkably gentle. "I was offered a job in the city, teaching in one of the toughest high schools around. I was so full of idealism then. I wanted to touch lives, to make a mark on the world, to reach those kids other people gave up on."

"What happened?"

"I had to learn to accept reality. Teaching is one of the most important jobs around, but it's also very badly funded. I did my best for the kids, but with staff cutbacks and many of the teachers having to take second jobs, there was just so much that could be done."

"But something else happened, something you never expected, didn't it?" he observed.

She nodded. "I was doing my level best, but..."

Suddenly Gabriel stopped in midstride and stared at the reflection of the street in the store window.

"Is something wrong?" A chill ran up her spine.

"We're being watched. There's a car about fifteen yards

behind us. The headlights are off, but it's there and it has been following us."

She hugged her bag closer to her. "I should have left the bowl back at Marlee's."

"Don't worry about that now. Let's start walking, but keep your pace normal. When we get to the end of this street, I'm going to pull you into the shadows as if I'm going to steal a kiss. Then, when we're out of sight, I want you to duck down fast and stay there. I'm going to run back and see who's following us."

Gabriel pulled her closer, his arm still resting over her shoulders. That weight was her only comfort as fear tightened its grip on her, choking the air from her lungs.

"They're after the bowl," she said. "I just know it."

"Don't jump to conclusions. Let me handle this."

A moment later, in a smooth move that appeared playful, he pulled her into the shadows. A breath later, he was gone. Lanie pressed her back against the cold adobe wall, watching the street from behind cover. She couldn't see Gabriel, but she could see the dark outline of the vehicle as it stopped behind a tall block wall.

Gabriel came out into the open briefly, obviously searching for the car. From his vantage point, she knew he wouldn't spot the vehicle. Fear slammed into her. Unless he saw it before reaching the intersection, he'd be the one in trouble. He'd come out right in front of it.

Lanie ran out of the shadows just as Gabriel approached the wall where the car waited. Suddenly the vehicle's headlights came on. Lanie shouted a warning, running toward him. As the car accelerated, Lanie reached the street. Gabriel wouldn't escape in time. Neither of them could outrun a car.

Cutting behind him and positioning herself between Gabriel and the speeding car, she held out the bowl in her hands. It was no talisman, but it was their one hope. If she was right, the driver would not risk destroying it.

Chapter Twelve

Blinded by the headlights, she focused on the bowl. She heard the squeal of tires, then felt the rush of cold air as the car swerved and shot past her.

Relief made her weak. Lanie fell to her knees, the bowl still in her hands.

Gabriel reached her in seconds and pulled her into his arms. "Why did you get in the way? I could have dodged that car!"

Lanie shook her head, her gaze on him, then on the bowl. "They wanted this. I took the chance they wouldn't risk destroying it." She saw the fear in his eyes, and the testimony of his feelings, etched so plainly there, took her breath away.

His voice shook with fierce need. "I don't want to lose you. Don't ever do anything like that again."

"You would have done it for me."

"Yes." His whispered answer was so intense, it made a shiver race through her.

Lanie rested her head on his shoulder. They were a part of each other in a way that was as undeniable as it was inexplicable. Suddenly she felt full of hope. Providing they learned to work together, they'd survive whatever lay ahead.

As GABRIEL WALKED back to the boardinghouse with her, he cursed himself for ever having suggested they go for a walk. Nothing was simple for them, nor would it be again, until the matter with the accursed bowl was settled.

He thought of how she'd risked her life to save his. He knew now that her feelings for him were as deep as his were for her. A strong woman like Lanie did not surrender her heart easily. But he hadn't been fair to her. That knowledge knifed at his gut. No matter what the consequences, he would not hold anything back from her anymore. He needed to show her the side of himself he'd kept hidden. She deserved to know.

"I have to go back out there," he said once they were inside the boardinghouse. "I have to gather whatever evidence I can about that vehicle." He paused. "But tomorrow we need to talk man to woman."

"Yes," she whispered, her voice tremulous.

It was amazing how a little thing like the sound of her voice could turn his blood to fire. He wanted to take her to his room right now and make her his in the most primitive way of all. Yet beneath the intense passion he felt for her was another emotion equally startling. He needed to protect her, from himself if need be, at all costs.

"I'll be back," he said.

He walked away from her quickly, at home within the darkness and shadows of night that hid their own secrets.

LANIE STRIPPED OFF her clothes and got ready for bed. She'd hidden the bowl in the back of the linen closet in the bathroom. For now, it would be safe there. Marlee had put her in charge of putting away the laundry and placing clean linens on the beds and fresh towels in the bathrooms.

She turned the lights off and crawled into bed, hoping she wouldn't dream tonight. Those wonderfully erotic dreams disturbed her, raising more questions than she was prepared to answer.

Lanie settled deeper under the covers, inviting the oblivion of sleep. She had just started to drift off when a scratching sound at her door, followed by a click, woke her abruptly.

She sat up slowly and saw the door begin to open. Lanie reached for the empty vase on her nightstand. It wasn't much of a weapon, but it would have to do.

She scarcely breathed as the intruder stepped into her room, a shadowy figure who moved fluidly and silently. Lanie prepared to throw the vase when suddenly she heard the front door slam.

The man shot out of her room and ran down the hall. Lanie caught a glimpse of his ski mask in the muted light.

"Stop!" Lanie screamed for help as she took off after him.

Gabriel rushed out of the kitchen and into the living room at the sound of Lanie's voice, but before he could reach the hall, the man bolted out the front door and into the night. Without hesitation, Gabriel rushed after him.

GABRIEL RETURNED a short time later and joined Marlee and Lanie in the living room. "He got away," he said, obviously disgusted with himself.

"Did you see who it was?" Marlee asked.

"No."

As his gaze seared over Lanie, she realized that she was dressed only in a T-shirt that almost, but not quite, covered to her knees.

"I like your mouse's ears," he said.

The comment threw her, and as she glanced down she realized that the ears fell over her breasts. She felt her face grow hot. "I need to get a robe on," she muttered, dashing back to her room.

Marlee followed her. "I guess we all better start locking our doors."

"I do that anyway. It's a habit," she said, fastening the belt of the robe securely.

Gabriel crouched by Lanie's door, examining the doorknob. "Is it possible you could have forgotten to lock it tonight?"

"No." Locks were a luxury for her and one she enjoyed using. Privacy was something she'd seldom had as a kid growing up in foster homes. Before she'd gone on the road, her home had been equipped with all kinds of them, ensuring her privacy. Here in Marlee's, she was sometimes reminded of her days in foster care, because it was a home shared by strangers thrust together by circumstances. The lock on her door had been imperative, a reminder that she'd earned the right to control her environment and future.

Gabriel studied it closely. "I've got bad news. There are no signs of forced entry."

"He *was* in my room!" Lanie protested.

"I only have one spare key. It's on a hook in the kitchen."

He glanced at Marlee. "You always keep the front door unlocked during the day, so it wouldn't have been difficult for someone to sneak in and take it, or even borrow it long enough to make a copy. The keys are marked clearly."

Marlee reached up, covering her heart with her hand. "Everything really is changing here. Four Winds has never been a town where locks were needed."

"It is now," Gabriel said. "Until things return to normal, you're going to have to start using the locks."

"But what if the person still has the key?" She drew in a sharp breath. "I better call Darren Wilson right now. I know it's late, or early now, I guess, but he owes me a favor. I put him up here for weeks without any charge when he first came to town."

"Doesn't he run the feed store?" Lanie asked.

"Yes, but he used to be the town's locksmith before he

opened the store. There wasn't enough business for a lock-smith, but there was need for a feed store." Marlee made her way slowly down the hall.

"When Darren gets here, ask him to make sure your lock only has one key. Under the circumstances, I don't think Marlee will mind," Gabriel said before leaving her room.

Wondering if she'd ever feel safe again, Lanie sat down on the edge of the bed, her fingers curled tightly around the terry-cloth folds of her bathrobe.

TWO HOURS LATER, the new lock was in place and the only key was securely in her hand. The dead bolt was sturdy, and she was certain it would keep anyone out. Lanie checked the bowl inside the linen closet, then returned to her room.

As she slipped off her robe, she heard a faint knock on her door.

"It's me," she heard Gabriel whisper.

Lanie slipped her robe back on, unlocked the door and invited him inside. "Did you find out anything useful?"

"No, I'm sorry," he said, reaching for her hand and brushing her knuckles against his lips.

The warmth of his kiss raced up her arm, then down her body with devastating effects. She felt dizzy and wonderful, all crazy inside.

"It's time we talked," Gabriel murmured, his voice like a smooth, velvety wine. He sat on the edge of the bed, then pulled her down until she sat beside him. "The feelings between us are strong. I can feel your reaction to me whenever I touch you. And you know my reaction, as well." He unbuttoned his shirt, took her hand and placed it against his heart. "There's a fire inside me. Every time my heart beats, it calls out to yours."

Her throat closed, and she could barely draw in a breath. "I'd say we want the same thing."

Gabriel drew her to him, his kiss hard and possessive. He heard her whimper, and the desire that clawed at him was as sudden as it was fierce. He wanted to push her back onto the bed and make love to her, slowly, tenderly, until there was nothing and no one in her mind but him.

He swore, pulling back away from her. "I won't seduce you. When we make love, I want you to make love to *me*, not an illusion."

"You are no illusion."

"But the way you see me, as opposed to what I am, may be so far removed from each other that, in essence, I am an illusion. I've seen it before. Women are sometimes swept away by the mystique of my heritage. They spin fantasies about Indian warriors and forget that we are just men." He stood and turned to face her. "I am capable of many things, but not of seeing the light of reality shatter the softness in your eyes when you look at me. Do you dare see *me* as I am?"

Words lodged in her throat. She took a deep breath and forced herself to speak. "You're worried about your past, but I'm not the innocent you may think I am. You asked me once why I was on the road, what I was running from. The answer is easy. I'm running from myself."

Gabriel nodded. "I felt that when we met, and I hoped that you'd someday trust me with your story."

She walked across the room, moving away from him, needing to draw strength from herself alone. "You know I was a teacher. One day a kid came to me after school. He was having a lot of trouble with one of the gangs. They were trying to recruit him, but he kept putting them off. He knew that once you were in, it was nearly impossible to get out. I couldn't spend as much time with him as he wanted me to that day, because I had a staff meeting to attend and grades to turn in the next morning. So I told him to hang tough, and that he should talk to one of the counselors, a man who was working with the local police in a gang-prevention program.

"I could tell he was hesitant, scared, so I set up an appointment for him to meet with the counselor the next day. The boy agreed, but he never kept the appointment. Two days later, I heard he'd been killed in a drive-by shooting while walking home." It wrenched her heart to remember. She stared out the window at some indeterminate spot in the darkness beyond her room, and tried to push back the hurt.

"It wasn't your fault. The blame lies with those members of the gang who pulled the triggers." He raised his hand as she turned around and started to protest. "But I do understand guilt, and how it stays with you, eating at your soul, destroying you a little bit at a time."

Lanie forced herself to meet his gaze. The look in his eyes reflected empathy, not judgment. "You have your own scars, Gabriel. It sounds as though you know the terrible cost of a mistake, too."

He nodded slowly. "When I was a cop in L.A., I became involved in an armed confrontation involving hostages. I negotiated with the robber and managed to get him to release several people. But then everything fell apart. He saw a member of the SWAT team near the door. He panicked, and so did the remaining woman hostage. She broke free and ran. I jumped in the way, trying to shield the woman, just as the man fired. Two of his bullets struck my bulletproof vest, but the third bullet hit the woman. SWAT members grabbed the perp, but the woman died right there on that sidewalk.

"I was decorated for that incident, but I didn't feel like a hero. All I could remember was the terror in that woman's eyes."

"I could tell you what I've told myself, that you're only human, that everyone fails sometimes and that you have to let go of the past." She forced back the lump in her throat. "But, you see, I know they're only words, and it's up to each of us to work it out."

"We *are* two of a kind." He wrapped his arms around her.

Desire ribboned through her as he kissed her, his tongue dancing with hers. They needed each other. His love for her was as dark and savage as the night, and her body ached with the need to find peace in his arms. Only love could soothe her scarred heart.

Gabriel picked her up, cradling her in his arms, and carried her down the hall. "I want to make love to you in my room, on my bed. If you leave me someday, then I'll still see you there in my mind when the nights are cold and I'm alone."

Lanie had never seen his room, but everything there wore his stamp. There were two striking sculptures of a rodeo rider and a wild bronc. A red-and-black Navajo rug covered the floor by the bed. On the dresser, along with a few personal effects, were two turquoise bear fetishes. The room spoke of his past and his present, and exuded an unmistakable masculinity that engulfed her senses, filling her as he himself would very soon.

"This is where I'll make love to you, my woman," he said, placing her gently on his own bed. "I've seen you here many times in my mind. But tonight there will be no dreams, just flesh against flesh."

Lanie would have promised him anything, but he hadn't burdened her with his own promises, nor had he spoken of love. He had trusted her with himself. And now she would do the same. No words were needed. Neither of them could guarantee tomorrow; it wasn't theirs to give.

He lay beside her and, pulling her robe apart, rained kisses down her body. She cried out his name, pulling him closer to her. Shudder after shudder racked her body. His mouth was so hot and so wet, his love sweet and savage.

Fires danced along her spine as he found the center of her femininity and loved her slowly there.

When she could give no more, he held her, stroking her gently, soothing and calming her before the fires grew hot again. "*Sawe*, my sweetheart, I need this time with you. I want to become a part of you. Not to conquer you, although I do want your surrender, but to make you remember me always, no matter what the future holds."

Lanie had thought he hadn't offered her love because he hadn't said the words. But the cherished hope he'd just revealed to her spoke of a love as strong as the noonday sun.

He used his mouth to incite her again while he stripped off his own shirt and pants. Years of loneliness vanished as he slid his hand beneath her and eased deep inside her. Each stroke became a step toward mutual surrender. Pleasure rocked and held them. When she came apart, arching toward him, he drove into her hard. With a final cry of surrender and triumph, he exploded inside her.

As if from a great distance, she heard him murmur, "Mine."

Her sleep was peaceful that night. There were no dreams…perhaps because they'd already been made real.

GABRIEL WATCHED Lanie sleep as the sun rose outside his window. She looked peaceful now; all the fears that had clouded her mind appeared to be gone.

He glanced at the clock on his nightstand. He would have given anything to be able to linger in bed with her, but it was time for him to go.

He took a quick shower, dried himself, then with a towel around his waist, went back into the room. He saw her eyes open as the door squeaked on its hinges.

"Good morning," she greeted him with a sleepy smile. "Where are you off to?"

"I need to talk to Lucas before he leaves to make his rounds."

He watched her sit up, holding the sheet against herself in a futile gesture of modesty. To show her that they needed no more secrets, he pulled his towel off and walked naked to the drawer to retrieve some underwear and a clean pair of jeans.

He could feel her searing gaze on him as he moved. His body grew taut, and desire thundered through him. "Don't," he warned. "If you keep doing that, I'm almost certain I won't be catching up to my brother this morning."

"Would that be such a tragedy?" she asked.

He drew in a breath, the fire within him growing hotter. His manhood throbbed as he felt her gaze drifting over him intimately. When she dropped the sheet she held, revealing the soft swell of her breasts and her hardened nipples, his resolve faltered.

He took a step toward her, then suddenly a gust of wind slammed against the house. A tumbleweed hit the windowpane hard, and Lanie jumped.

"It's okay," he said, looking out. "It's just the wind. Our people say wind carries news, both good and bad." Gabriel stood immobile for several seconds, listening, alert to any whisper of danger. "We're all right for now," he said at last. "But I have to go."

"It's okay. I understand. We both have jobs to take care of," she said, her voice soft. She grasped the sheet and once more held it against herself like a protective shield.

She'd withdrawn into herself again; he was acutely aware of that. She'd feared love, and after last night she was more vulnerable than ever. They had not spoken of commitments, yet on some level, they both desperately needed them. But the truth was, he didn't have enough to offer her. Though she'd helped him, his feelings for her couldn't ease or heal the sorrow that encased her heart.

His chest ached with that knowledge as he turned away from her.

Gabriel finished dressing quickly, then walked to the door. "I'll catch up to you later," he said before turning to look at her once more.

As their gazes met, he knew that she'd read his thoughts and understood. Without any need for further words, he stepped out into the hall and closed the door behind him.

Dawn in New Mexico was a palate of rich earth tones, as if Mother Earth dressed in her finest to greet the sun. For a short time, with Lanie in his arms, he'd found peace, the outer world overwhelmed and conquered by an inner world of pure emotions. But it was a new day, and new realities waited to be challenged.

Lanie was his woman for now, at least, and the problems that had come from the peddler and the accursed bowl directly affected both of them, as well as his town. Somehow he would see this through, both as a man and as the sheriff of Four Winds.

He arrived at Lucas's a short time later. His brother's truck, in all its decrepit glory, was parked near the side door. Gabriel's guess was that Lucas had gotten in late last night and was still sound asleep.

Gabriel smiled. Good, he'd enjoy having some fun at his brother's expense. He opened the door and walked noiselessly through the house. Lucas, as usual, hadn't bothered with locks.

Gabriel went to his brother's room and almost laughed, seeing Lucas half-dressed, face down on the bed.

He banged hard on the wall by the headboard. "Police! Against the wall!"

Lucas jumped, slammed his head against the headboard, then seeing who it was, threw an empty soda can at him. "Police harassment. I'm pressing charges."

"Late night, Shadow?" Gabriel asked, sitting on the

edge of his brother's bed. "Or do you always smell like women's perfume?"

"That's incense, Fuzz." Lucas rolled out of bed, rubbing his neck with one hand.

"You're no fun this morning. You look like something that's been spoiled and reheated."

He gave Gabriel a disgusted look. "I suppose there's a reason for you to be here?"

"I need to know if there's any news about Dad's and Joshua's whereabouts."

"No, but the reason I was up until four this morning is because I decided to drive all the way to Naomi Blueyes's. Remember her?"

Gabriel nodded. "She's got to be close to one hundred years old. Is she still lucid?"

"Seems that way. She lives near the Hogback in the same hogan her family's always occupied. The tribe offered her better housing near Shiprock, with all the modern conveniences, but she refuses to move. Naomi says she has everything she needs. She might at that," he added.

"I know she's an herbalist, but what's she got to do with the bowl?"

"Her granddaughter, Nydia, is a cultural anthropologist. Works at the university. Mrs. Blueyes helped her contact people who don't talk to outsiders, so she doesn't get all the made-up stuff usually passed along to anthropologists. I figured Nydia might know something, and I'd heard she was there visiting."

"Did she know about the bowl?"

"Nydia told me of one story she came across while compiling Navajo legends for her doctoral thesis. She never used it, even though Rudolph Harvey, the *hataalii* Joshua is studying with, told it to her, because she was never able to substantiate it."

"I'm listening, and I want all the details."

"According to what Rudolph told her, the bowl was crafted by a very powerful skinwalker. When the skinwalker died, the magic object became contaminated by his *chindi*. The bowl is said to have great influence over its owner and it can quickly win over the weak willed. It can also affect others around it. However, if the *chindi* finds it can't control the owner of the bowl because that person is too strong, it will try to find a way to kill that person, though it can't do this directly.''

Gabriel stood up and paced. He hated mysticism. It was an intangible he couldn't fight openly. "I have to find Rudolph Harvey, the sooner the better." He told Lucas what their uncle had told them.

Lucas let out a low whistle. "It just keeps getting worse." He shook his head in exasperation. "Don't worry, Fuzz. I'll continue to look, and as word spreads on the rez, others will join the search, too. I'll do all in my power to help you and your woman."

This time Gabriel didn't argue with the designation. His woman, indeed. Lanie was part of him now. He would do anything, including give up his own life, to protect her.

FEELING LONELY now that Gabriel was gone, Lanie walked to her own room and sat on the bed. What had happened between them last night had changed her forever. She knew instinctively that there would never be another man for her, and even if she didn't stay in Four Winds, Gabriel would always be in her heart.

It was early, but feeling restless, she dressed, then glanced around for a hiding place for the bowl. She walked to the bathroom down the hall, bowl in her hand. The linen closet there seemed the perfect place to stash it. Before placing it behind the towels, Lanie held it for a moment longer, once again surprised by the silky smoothness of its sides and the way it seemed to radiate coolness or heat, depending on what she needed at the moment.

Right now it was pleasantly warm. Lanie rubbed her palms against it, enjoying its texture. Such a beautiful thing. How on earth could it cause so much trouble? Reluctantly she tucked it behind the towels. Beautiful things weren't much good to anyone if they had to be kept hidden.

As Lanie stepped back out into the hall, Marlee approached.

"Good morning, Lanie. I wonder if you can help me. I told Alma that she could have a look through the boxes of stuff in the garage. I'm tired of not having enough room to move around in there and, as it happens, I need some cash for taxes."

"How can I help you?"

"Alma's on her way over now. Will you help me sort through the boxes? There are some things I intend to keep, though most of what's in them can go to her for sale."

Lanie followed Marlee to the garage. Although Lanie wanted to ask her about the torn pages from Alma's stolen book, she held back as Gabriel had asked.

"There's another box here somewhere," Marlee said, looking around, then pointing to a high shelf. "There. Next to the one marked Christmas Ornaments. Can you bring it down for me? Only be careful when you pull it out. I had Gabriel wedge it in there so the ornaments would stay put."

Lanie took the stepladder from the corner and positioned it securely against the cabinets that lined the bottom. "Stay well back, just in case something topples down."

"I will."

As she wriggled the box free, it tipped out of her hands. She tried to catch the box in midair, but suddenly her feet slipped off the ladder.

Lanie fell to one side, landing hard. Stars exploded before her eyes, then gave way to a mushrooming darkness.

LANIE WASN'T SURE what happened, except that when she woke up, she was in her room and her head throbbed with such intensity she almost thought it would burst.

She sat up slowly, touching her temple where the pain was greatest. There was no blood, caked or otherwise, but blast, it really hurt!

Wanting some aspirin, Lanie started toward the bathroom. She was halfway to the door when her room seemed to tilt and shift out of focus. She grasped the side of the dresser and blinked hard. Something terrible was about to happen.

Her vision cleared slowly, and the sweet scent of blood that suddenly filled her nostrils almost made her gag. The walls turned into a bright and flowing river of crimson. Feeling something warm on her hand, she glanced down. Blood was oozing from the top of the dresser, practically drowning her hand. She jerked back, but her footing was suddenly uncertain. Looking down, Lanie discovered a rising river of blood where the floor had been.

Her own cry of terror woke her. There was no disorientation this time. She knew precisely where she was. Her eyes focused on Marlee's face. The garage floor was hard and cool.

"You scared me half to death, Lanie! Don't move! I'm going to get a cold compress for you, then I'm going to call Lucas and Gabriel."

"No, don't call anyone. I'm okay." Lanie sat up slowly. Nothing was out of focus, and her head didn't hurt nearly as much as it had in her dream. But the dream was still with her. She remembered every bit of it. "How long have I been out?"

"Not long—less than two minutes," Marlee answered.

A sudden realization startled her. Unconscious people didn't dream. Or did they? She wasn't sure of anything anymore. "I'm okay," she repeated, standing up.

Just then, they heard the doorbell and Alma calling out. Marlee glanced back toward the living room. "I'll let her in, then go get a cold compress for you."

Before Marlee could take more than a few steps, Alma breezed in. She stopped in midstride staring at the women before her. "What happened? Are you okay?"

Marlee gave Lanie a sheepish smile. "Oops. Looks like I forgot our new rule about locks and left the door open." She looked at Alma. "Will you stay with Lanie for a moment?"

Alma rushed over to where Lanie stood, insisting on supporting her by holding on to her arm. "My dear, what on earth happened? You're as white as a ghost."

Lanie explained succinctly. "But I'll be just fine. The cold compress Marlee's bringing will help a lot."

Marlee came in and handed her the cloth. "Can you walk okay?"

"Of course." Pressing the cool washcloth to her temple, Lanie went inside the living room, the women on both sides of her.

"Let me fix you some tea or something. You still look pale to me. Are you sure you don't want me to call Lucas?" Marlee asked, obviously concerned.

"Positive, but I would love some tea, the regular kind. No herbs that are going to knock my silly, okay? Been there, done that," Lanie added with a smile.

"You've got it. How about chamomile? It's one of my favorites."

"Fine."

As Marlee walked out, Alma gave Lanie a worried look. "If you're going to be okay, I'll go help Marlee. If she makes it too strong, it'll be just as bad."

"Go ahead."

Alone, Lanie's thoughts shifted to the bowl. She could feel something was wrong. The sudden, irresistible urge to check on it compelled her to go down the hall to the bathroom. Lanie closed the door behind her, then went to the linen closet and looked inside. A wave of fear, black and suffocating, slammed into her. Her bowl was gone.

Chapter Thirteen

Gabriel hurried inside, slamming the front door behind him. He'd been driving past the boardinghouse when something inside him had told him Lanie was in trouble. He wasn't sure how he knew with such certainty, but he wasn't going to question his instincts.

As he stepped across the living room, Lanie came around the hall corner, colliding with him.

"What the—?" As she started to collapse, he lifted her up and carried her to the couch.

Marlee and Alma came out of the kitchen, Alma holding a teapot and some cups on a tray. The moment Marlee saw what had happened, she turned and hurried to the phone. "I'm calling Lucas, and that's that."

"What happened?" Gabriel asked, his eyes on Lanie. The rosy, satisfied look that she'd had when he left her was completely gone. Her face was flushed, and her eyes had the hollow look of someone who hadn't slept in months.

"She took a fall," Alma answered.

"That's not it," Lanie interrupted, clutching Gabriel's hand. "I just went to the check on the bowl—I'd hidden it in the linen closet. But it's not there. It's gone."

"Did you tell anyone where it was?" Gabriel asked quickly.

"No, not a soul."

"When did you see it last?" Gabriel felt his stomach sink. The bowl and Lanie were linked. There was no telling what would happen now.

"Thirty minutes ago, tops."

Gabriel stood as Alma handed Lanie some tea. He couldn't quite shake the feeling that they had just taken another step toward their destiny. They'd made love, and the very next day the bowl had disappeared.

"There's one more thing," Lanie said, her voice whisper soft.

As Lanie told those around her about her dream, Gabriel felt his gut clench. He'd never heard of anyone dreaming while unconscious, though he wasn't willing to say that it was categorically impossible. He would have been more inclined to call what she'd experienced a vision. Still, it seemed strange that she'd have a vision like that the same morning the bowl disappeared.

"Before, my dreams were…softer, full of love."

He met her gaze. "As my dreams of you have been," he said, confirming what they'd both already known. Somehow their dreams were linked.

"But this one…" She closed her eyes, then opened them again. "Did you see it?"

"No, not this time."

Lanie stood up, but her knees were weak and she sank back onto the couch.

"Stay seated until Lucas gets here," Marlee said firmly.

Lanie remained on the couch, unwilling to trust her legs again. "This isn't from the fall," she said, her voice tremulous. "I wasn't feeling this woozy after I fell."

Gabriel speculated silently that perhaps her fall had coincided with the theft of the bowl. "Who was around when you had your accident?"

"Marlee, and Alma, who came right after I fell." Lanie looked at Alma, who nodded. "That's all."

"So only three people have been here today, including myself." Gabriel stated.

Marlee glanced up at Gabriel, shaking her head. "I've been leaving the front door locked like you told me to, but I forgot to lock it after I went out this morning to pick up the paper."

"So anyone could have come in," he finished.

One other thought nagged at the back of his mind. Was it possible Marlee had seen Lanie hiding the bowl and had devised a plan to get it? She was used to taking care of her guests, making sure everyone had fresh towels, and having Lanie's help hadn't changed that much. But in all fairness, anyone else could have sneaked in the open door and spied on Lanie while she'd hidden it, too. "Did either of you hear anything out of the ordinary this morning?" he asked, looking at Marlee and Lanie.

"I didn't, but I certainly wasn't listening," Marlee said.

"Neither was I," Lanie added.

Hearing his brother's truck, Gabriel stood and walked to the door. "Stay put," he said to Lanie. Gabriel jogged to meet Lucas outside, joining him at the curb. "We've got trouble."

"I know. Marlee called and said that Lanie had fallen off a stepladder." Lucas grabbed his medical bag from the seat beside him.

"That's only part of it. The bowl's gone, and it's possible it was stolen at about the same time she fell."

Lucas stopped halfway up the walk. "Do you have any leads?"

Gabriel stepped over to retrieve his investigation kit from the police unit. "I'm going to try and lift some prints, but I doubt that's going to give me anything conclusive." He was not going to tell his brother that, at the moment, despite her injury, Marlee was his prime suspect. He'd searched the garage a few days back for signs of the book that had been stolen from Alma's but hadn't found it.

When he'd spoken to Marlee about the pages found in the garage, she'd claimed not to know anything about it.

Of course, one thing did speak in her favor. It seemed more likely that she would have had a more rehearsed story had she been guilty of the theft at Alma's. But hearing that the bowl had disappeared from under her roof put a different slant on things.

Lucas went inside and sat beside Lanie. "There's only a small bump on your head," he said, checking her over. "Did you hit yourself anywhere else?"

"My shoulder. I think that helped break the fall."

As he felt her forehead, his expression grew concerned. "Have you been sick?"

"No."

He reached for a thermometer and placed it in her mouth. "You'll have to bear with me—I don't have the latest equipment."

He waited until it registered and the tone sounded, then checked the reading. "You're a degree and a half above normal. It's nothing to worry about, but I advise you to take it easy for the next few days."

"I've probably got a virus or something."

"Are you experiencing any other symptoms?"

"None, except I felt really sick to my stomach when I discovered the bowl was missing. I think that was probably just anger." She stared at her hands for a moment, gathering her thoughts. "I hate the idea that someone took the one thing of value I have. But I'm going to get it back. I have a feeling it's not far."

"Explain," Gabriel asked.

"I can't. It's just a feeling, that's all."

"Well, just to be on the safe side, I think you should let my brother do the detective work for a while," Lucas said.

Alma gave Lanie a sympathetic look. "It looks like Four Winds is really giving you an initiation!"

Lanie smiled. "That's one way to put it."

Gabriel picked up his investigation kit. "I'm going to dust the door on that linen closet for prints."

"I need to talk to you about another matter," Lucas said. "So if you don't mind, I'll come and watch you work."

As soon as they were alone, Lucas expelled a breath. "I didn't want to say anything in front of the women, but Lanie's fever worries me. She didn't notice it before, and there's nothing about the fall that can account for it."

"You think it's connected to the bowl?" Gabriel worked over the surface of the linen closet.

"Who knows? But if it *is* linked to the bowl, she'll get worse."

"I'll keep an eye on her."

"If she develops any more symptoms, or if the fever goes up, call me right away. Medically I can't do much, but I may be able to find a *hataalii* who can help us."

"I've managed to get a few prints off this," Gabriel said, "but they're probably Lanie's and Marlee's. I'll check them against the samples I took after the break-in." Gabriel stood up slowly. "By the way, I'd appreciate it if you'd ask your patients about the peddler. It's possible someone might have noticed where he goes when he leaves Four Winds."

"I've been doing that all along, but I'll keep trying."

"I sure wish I could shake this feeling that what's happening was predestined. I don't like being at the mercy of something I can't confront."

"There are many ways of fighting, as Joshua would say," Lucas answered.

"Yeah, but you and I have always been better with our fists. Let's face it, Shadow, this isn't my kind of battle." Gabriel shook his head.

"Don't be so sure. It may yet turn out to be right up your alley."

Lost in thought, Gabriel watched his brother walk out. Something told him that before long the final battle would begin, and it would take everything he had to stay alive and protect the woman he loved. He fingered the medicine pouch at his waist. Maybe fate had made the right choices. Lanie and he were both survivors, and that would be the one skill they'd need to call upon most.

LANIE SAT on the kitchen floor with Marlee while Alma sorted through the contents of dozens of large cardboard packing cases from the garage. "This wooden box with the cross was used to store family Bibles. I can get you a good price for this," Alma said.

"I'd sure appreciate that." Marlee turned to Lanie and smiled. "Your color is back. It must be Lucas's touch."

"Nah, he doesn't do that much for me."

"Well, Gabriel certainly does. He makes you all crazy inside," Marlee baited.

"I can handle it."

"You can? How often?" Marlee laughed at her own joke.

Alma flushed crimson. "All right ladies, I think that's enough of that."

Marlee smiled. "Sorry about that, ma'am."

"I certainly don't expect you two to be impervious to the boys. Those Blackhorse brothers could make the heart of any young lady miss a beat." She gave them a knowing smile. "But there are certain matters that really shouldn't be discussed out loud, and a man's anatomy certainly falls into that category."

"I stand corrected," Marlee said with an impish grin.

Hearing someone call out her name, Alma stood up. "Here's young Ted now. Earlier I'd asked him to stop by in case I needed his help hauling things back to the shop." After loading up both suitcases, Alma turned to Lanie.

"Don't come in to work today," Alma advised Lanie. "Just relax and take it easy."

"I'd rather work. Otherwise, I'll just dwell on what happened to my bowl."

Alma nodded. "I can understand how unsettling that is."

"I still can't figure out how the thief knew to look in the linen closet."

"We have no way of knowing how long the thief had to search," Marlee countered. "There aren't that many places to hide something in your room, and the closet is close by. This is my fault, and I blame myself."

"Let's just hope Gabriel finds it," Lanie said softly.

After Alma left, Lanie joined Marlee in the living room. "You started teasing about Gabriel just to make Alma uncomfortable," Lanie said sternly. "Why did you do that?"

Marlee gave her a sheepish smile. "She's so prim and proper, she bugs the heck out of me. She never has one hair out of place, even in a windstorm. Her hands are always perfectly manicured. I feel like a charwoman around her."

Lanie laughed. "She's really a nice lady, you know. If you'd give her a chance, you'd see that, too."

"People like her make me feel awkward. All of a sudden, I start looking at my teacups, searching for chipped rims. Did you see the way she stared at my cream server?"

"Well, I stared at it, too. Where on earth did you get a pig that pours from its snout? It's disgusting."

Marlee laughed, and Lanie joined her.

"If you don't need me for anything else, I'm going to go for a walk, then I'll be at Alma's shop. I need to keep busy, or I'll go crazy."

"Don't push yourself today. Remember what Lucas said."

Lanie said goodbye to Marlee, then stepped outside and

took several deep breaths. The freshness surrounded her in scents as wild and free as the forest around Four Winds. Piñons rose high in the air. She walked slowly, the cool temperature refreshing against her heated skin. She didn't have to check to know she was still running a slight fever.

Lanie stopped by the garage. Charley greeted her as she came inside. "I'm still waiting for some parts. I'm sorry for the delay, but we had to try several dealers to get you the best prices."

"I appreciate that." She was grateful for his efforts. Price mattered a lot. Even with saving everything she could from her salary at Alma's, it would take a while to get enough cash amassed to pay the bill.

As Lanie strolled down the street, she saw that some chickens from the feed store had managed to get loose. Two men and three women were running around, trying to round them up.

She was passing by the side street near Sally's diner when her skin prickled disturbingly. She turned around, but no one was there.

Lanie quickened her pace. She'd stop by Sally's, have something to eat, then continue over to Alma's. The wonderful scent of roasting chilis made her mouth water.

As she passed the alley with the trash cans by the side of Sally's diner, she heard a quick shuffling sound. Suddenly an arm snaked around her throat, jerking her backward into the shadows. There was no time to scream. Acting on instinct, she slammed her elbow into her assailant's midsection.

Normally that would have bought her enough time to make a run for it, but her adversary didn't let go or even ease his hold. He grabbed her hair and yanked her back into the shadows.

"No more games," he whispered, deliberately distorting his voice. "I want what you've got."

Lanie stepped down hard on his instep, then twisted,

trying to get free. As she did, she caught a glimpse of his face. It was covered with a ski mask.

She tried to reach for it, but the man was too quick. As they fought, Lanie saw Peter, Sally's son, looking out the kitchen window. It didn't appear as if he was going to help. He was probably terrified.

Lanie screamed, but her attacker clamped his hand over her mouth before the sound carried. In desperation, Lanie bit down hard and was rewarded by a cry of pain. Taking advantage of that moment, she jerked free and ran toward Sally's back door.

GABRIEL SAW Lanie dive in through the back door as if demons were after her. With an excuse-me glance to Clyde Barkley, the postmaster, with whom he'd been conversing, he rushed toward her.

He got enough of the story to burst out the back door, but by then, nobody was around. Gabriel searched the ground, saw enough to verify the scuffle, but found no trail he could follow. His best chance, he realized, was to question Lanie while her memory was fresh.

He rushed back inside and found Lanie huddled up defensively in a booth near the back. Rage still seethed inside him, but he pushed it back. One thing at a time.

Gabriel sat down beside Lanie and gently brushed her hair back from her face, searching for bruises. "What happened?" He was surprised that his voice sounded so controlled. Had he caught the man who'd attacked her, he would have torn him apart, badge notwithstanding.

Lanie told him what had happened, fighting back tears. The fear in her eyes knifed straight through him. "Did you see his face at any point?"

She shook her head. "He was wearing a ski mask. But Peter watched the whole ordeal."

"Sally's kid?"

She nodded. "I'm really not sure why, but it was creepy. He was just watching, his face completely blank."

"Don't tell Sally just yet. I've got an idea I want to follow through on."

"There's something I just don't understand. Why is anyone after me *now?* I don't have the bowl. It's been stolen from me."

"There are two possible explanations. The simplest is that there's more than one person after the bowl, and the one who just attacked you didn't know you didn't have it anymore. The second..." He tapped the table with one finger and avoided looking at her.

"Is that the new owners want me dead," she concluded.

"Well, if that is it, they're going to learn that I'm not an easy target."

"And you've got allies that will stand by you," he said, his hand covering hers. "Lucas is still trying to track down my brother and dad. Once we find them, we'll have answers." He looked around the diner. "Things will slow down here soon. When they do, I'm going to have a little talk with Sally. Then I'm going to question Peter. By the end of this afternoon, maybe I'll have a better idea of what's going on. For now, let me drive you back to Marlee's. Stay there until you hear from me. Tell Alma you won't be in—she'll understand."

"All right, but I don't like the idea of being forced by a criminal to change my plans."

"That's the least of your problems."

"True." She stood up and walked with him to the door. "We do have one factor in our favor. Since I'm still the owner of the bowl, maybe the knowledge will work against whoever has it now and give us the advantage."

WITH LANIE'S WORDS echoing in his ears, Gabriel dropped her off at the boardinghouse, then returned to the diner. Sally was cleaning up, the place quiet now.

"Mind if we have a talk?" Gabriel sat on a stool by the counter.

"About what happened to Lanie? You're sweet on her, Gabriel, aren't you?"

"That has nothing to do with this. I don't take it lightly when someone in my town gets mugged in broad daylight."

She continued wiping the counter, though more vigorously now. "This never used to happen here. What's happening to us? Is it that bowl of hers?"

"It's people who are doing the attacking, not an object," he argued. "Now, tell me about Peter. Has he been in trouble lately?"

"Trouble? How?" She stopped in midmotion and met his gaze. "My boy isn't perfect, but if you're suggesting he's responsible for what happened to Lanie..."

"I know he wasn't. He was watching through the window when she was attacked, though he never bothered to call for help or offer any."

She stared at him, her face so pale that the freckles on her nose looked like tiny spots of fire. "You're mistaken, Sheriff. Peter has been at home in bed for the last few days with the flu."

"Well, then, I think I'll go over there and have a talk with him."

"Not without me, you're not," Sally said, throwing the damp cloth she'd been cleaning the counter with down hard. "I'm going with you."

"There's no need. This isn't a formal questioning, though admittedly the time might come when I need to do that."

"Peter's my son, and I intend to be there," she said in a clipped tone.

Sally's home wasn't far. Gabriel could see her car right behind him as he glanced in the rearview mirror. After a five-minute drive, they arrived at a small housing area nes-

tled at the base of a hill. Each of the adobe homes held
the stamp of its owner. Sally's was painted in a sand color
with bright turquoise trim. At least ten-red chili *ristras*
hung from the wood-framed porch.

Gabriel parked by the side of the house, and a few seconds later Sally pulled in the driveway.

"Let's get this over with. I'm not in the habit of closing
down my business in the middle of the day."

"You didn't have to be here at all—you know that. I
told you, all I want to do is ask him a few questions."

Sally rubbed her hands against her pant legs nervously.

He recognized the signs of fear, but what he couldn't
figure out was what was bothering her so much.

"Sally, there's something wrong. Why don't you just
talk to me?"

"You think my boy is guilty of some crime and you
want me to trust you? I don't think so, Sheriff."

She looked as if she wanted to bolt. He had a feeling
that only one thing was keeping Sally there—the protective instinct a mother felt for her child. "Your boy's in
trouble. Why don't you let me help?"

For a moment, Gabriel thought she was about to come
clean, but then that hooded expression fell into place and
he knew he'd struck out. Whatever battle had been waging
inside her had not come out in his favor.

She led the way through the house to a room in the
back and she knocked lightly on the closed door. Loud
rock music came from inside. "It's Mom, Pete," she
shouted, trying to be heard over the din. "Sheriff Blackhorse is with me. He wants to talk to you."

The music was shut off. "Come in."

He saw Peter lying, fully clothed, on top of the covers.
The seventeen-year-old young man, easily as large as Gabriel, didn't look sick, regardless of what Sally had said.
Gabriel glanced furtively at Sally. She looked like a
woman whose life was coming apart at the seams. Her

eyes gleamed as she held back tears, refusing to let them spill down her cheeks. She stood rock still with her arms crossed in front of her tightly.

"So, what's happening, Pete?" He straddled the chair near the bed.

"Not much, Sheriff."

"Why don't you tell me about the scuffle you saw behind the diner?"

"Scuffle? I don't know what you're talking about. I've been here all day."

"What makes you think I meant today?" Gabriel baited, hoping to rattle him.

Pete looked him in the eye and smiled.

"You came today, so I assumed you meant today."

Cool customer. Gabriel let the silence stretch out. With some, that was an effective tool, but it didn't seem to bother Peter much.

"You have any other questions?" Peter asked calmly.

"You want me to leave now, do you, son?"

"That's up to you. But I do have some studying to do."

Gabriel stood and walked to the window. As he stared outside, letting time drag, he heard the floor creak in the adjacent room. He turned around and captured Peter's gaze. "Who's in there?"

"None of your business," Peter said calmly.

He waited, listening, but the sound did not come again. He saw the pinched look on Sally's face. She looked as if she was about to snap. "Why don't I take a look in there, just to make sure you folks don't have an intruder?"

He put his hand on the knob when Peter suddenly sat up. "I think you need a search warrant for that, don't you? Or permission?"

Gabriel looked at Sally. "You have an objection to my looking in there?"

"Yes. I'm going to have to insist that you respect my son's privacy, Sheriff."

Gabriel moved back from the door. "You're both hiding something, and let me assure you I'm not going to let up. I won't tolerate trouble in my town."

Suddenly the door swung open. Ted Burns, the mayor's son, stepped into the room. "There's no great mystery here, Sheriff. Pete's just trying to help me out. I'm supposed to be on my way up to the state capital on an errand for my dad. I didn't go."

Gabriel watched him speculatively. Though he was only twenty, he had the air of someone older. He was over six feet tall, a former star quarterback of the high school. He had mooched off his father since graduation.

Gabriel eyed the long scratch on Ted's neck with suspicion. "That looks like a nasty scratch," Gabriel prodded, wondering if Lanie had left it there during the scuffle. "How did you get it?"

"A stray cat. Found it in an alley, tried to pick it up, but got that as a thanks. You can never tell with strays."

Ted's face was expressionless, but there was a defensive tightening around his eyes. Gabriel had seen the same look on older criminals. The boy was trouble—he was certain of that—and he was taking Peter right along with him.

"I'd be careful about handling strays in the future," Gabriel said, his voice glacial. "They learn a lot about survival, and that means they sometimes hunt in packs. You get my drift?"

Ted smiled slowly, his eyes burning with a cold fire. "We all have our survival tricks, Sheriff. It's nature's way."

Gabriel's muscles knotted, but he kept his expression deceptively placid. "In the end, strength and experience are unbeatable. You'd do well to remember that."

Gabriel left the room and made his way to the door. His gut told him Ted was involved, but the reason escaped him. He certainly didn't need the money. His father was well-off. It was true that Bob Burns had tried to buy the bowl, but it seemed a stretch to believe he would have sent his son as a hit man.

As Gabriel drove back to the boardinghouse, he considered the matter, but answers eluded him. When he finally arrived, Gabriel parked and was on his way in as Lanie came out to meet him. Her cheeks were flushed, her eyes bright. He felt the fierce need to protect her, but there was nothing more he could do at the moment. Frustration tore at him.

"What happened? Did Peter tell you why he just stood there and let me be attacked?"

"He denied being there," Gabriel said, giving her the details.

"He's lying. He was there watching. Believe me," Lanie affirmed.

"I don't doubt your word. I also saw Ted, the mayor's son. He had one hell of a scratch on his face."

"I don't remember scratching the man who attacked me, not specifically anyway, but it's very likely I did. But Ted? Why would he do this? He could have taken the bowl from Alma the day I brought it to her shop so she could photograph it. He was there that morning, helping out. It doesn't really make sense for him to act now. Peter, of course, is another story."

"He's no leader," Gabriel said. "In fact, neither of those two is. The boys bear watching, but the answers lay beyond anything those two could ever concoct." He touched the side of her face in a caress. Her skin felt hot. "You've been taking aspirins for that fever?"

"Sure. It's no big deal. I can cope with this." She returned to the couch where she'd been sitting. "Here's a thought. What if Ted's learned that his father was interested in getting the bowl, and decided to beat him to the punch? Maybe he's trying to prove he's capable of doing something the elder Burns couldn't do."

"It's possible, but it doesn't seem likely. He'd never be

able to brag about something like that, you see, so it would defeat his purpose.''

Lanie remembered what Alma had told her about Ted having dreams of his own. ''Maybe money is more important to him and he plans on selling the bowl and then getting out of town.''

''It's possible, but that kid's been trying to prove himself in the eyes of too many people here since high school. He wants approbation from folks he's known all his life. He wouldn't get that if he left. And I just don't think he's got the patience to set a long-term goal, say, wait a few years and then come back as a rich man. He'd still be afraid of the questions. He's basically a coward. If he had any kind of backbone, he would have gone out on his own a long time ago. Guts just isn't one of Ted's strong points.'' He rubbed his jaw pensively. ''For now, don't let Alma know what we've discussed. If she's fond of Ted, she may decide to tell him right now. I want to play things my way.''

Gabriel paced around the room. He needed answers. Time was working against them. Lanie reminded him of a candle that was burning too bright and too fast. As he thought this, he was overcome with dread. He knew with a deep, abiding certainty that unless he turned events around, her wind breath would leave her body soon and she'd pass into the afterworld.

LANIE STOOD alone in her room, tired yet unwilling to go to bed. Angry with herself, she continued to pace. She needed to sleep. Yet the fear of having another horrific dream was keeping her from crawling into bed.

With a burst of determination, she pulled the covers back and crawled between the sheets. She closed her eyes and tried to think of something pleasant, something good.

She fell asleep with the image of Gabriel's face drifting

in her mind, as if he were her guardian angel, pushing back the darkness.

She wasn't sure how much time had passed before finding herself outside her fantasy home. Lanie walked inside slowly, and as she stepped over the threshold, the nightmarish vision unfolded. Blood was splattered everywhere, staining the whitewashed walls, running in rivulets down the brick floor. The color seemed to glow with unearthly force. She saw a child's rag doll on the floor and picked it up. The material disintegrated in her hands, the stuffing dissolving into a mass of red that oozed between her fingers. She screamed and dropped it onto the floor.

Although she wanted to run out of that cottage, something compelled her to move forward. As Lanie stepped into the bedroom, she saw a man lying on the floor. His face was hidden in the shadows, but the badge on his chest was covered in shimmering waves of red.

Sobbing, she ran from the house into a wooded area. Someone was calling out to her, a man, urging her to turn back. She didn't stop. Somehow she knew that to return would mean death.

Then she felt a sharp pain in her leg. It traveled upward, corkscrewing through her body. She staggered to the ground.

"Wake up, honey."

The words drifted to her as if from a great distance. Lanie opened her eyes slowly. Gabriel was shaking her gently. Disoriented, she looked around. "What... where...?"

"You were sleepwalking. I saw you coming out here, and followed. You fell over that branch," he said, gesturing behind him. "Come on. You need warmth and rest." He lifted her easily into his arms and carried her back from the yard into the house.

"I don't want to sleep anymore," she whispered, burying her head against his neck.

He took her to his room. "You're safe here. I'll watch over you." He laid her down on his bed.

She clung to him, unwilling to let him go as shudders shook her body. "There was a time when we shared dreams, didn't we?" she said.

"Yes. It was something we both knew after that first time, though we didn't speak of it then."

"I couldn't talk about it. It was difficult for me to even face that squarely," Lanie said. "I didn't understand how it could be possible, and it frightened me. Did it affect you like that, too?"

He shook his head. "I am Navajo. I was raised to accept many things the Anglo world sees as magic. But it was unsettling."

"These new...nightmares are different. I wouldn't wish these on you, ever."

"I'm too tired to dream, my *sawe*, my sweetheart. When I crawl into bed, I'm too tired to even think." He held her close, hoping she'd stop trembling, and brushed her forehead with a kiss. "It's okay. I'm here now."

Exhaustion took its toll, and this time, nestled in the warmth of his embrace, she didn't fight as gray clouds gathered and overtook her.

Gabriel continued to hold her. When Marlee came into the room with some warm tea, he shook his head. "She's asleep," he mouthed.

Marlee nodded and slipped back out noiselessly.

Gabriel kept her close to him. He wasn't sure of anything anymore. Dreams meant little to the Anglo world, but in his, they were forces to be feared. Some of his tribe believed that the evil seen there would take place unless a *hataalii* was called in to do a sing. Others, with good-luck songs of their own, would sprinkle pollen and sing the bad dreams away.

As he held her, feeling her softness melt into him, he began to sing softly, filling the darkness with his song.

Chapter Fourteen

Lanie woke up slowly, her cheek rested against Gabriel's bare chest. His arms were wrapped around her tightly. As she stirred, she saw he was already awake. "You've been sitting up holding me like this all night?"

He tried to nod, but winced as if in pain. "I think I need to stretch out a bit."

"You could have nudged me to one side. I wouldn't have minded," Lanie said with a thin smile. The warmth of his gaze traveled like a bolt of lightning through her, awakening her desire.

Gabriel stood up, wearing only loose-fitting jeans, and stretched his muscles like a powerful mountain lion. "I'll be okay."

"Come back to bed," she whispered, her voice thick with passion.

Their gazes met, and she saw that the fires within him burned as hot as they did inside her.

"There's no time, love," he said, buttoning a shirt and bending over to pull on socks and boots, "though I wish there was."

"Where are you off to?"

"I've been doing background checks on some of our residents, and I'd like to finish them up as soon as possible. It's an invasion of privacy I'm sure most of them would not forgive, but under the circumstances, I don't have a choice."

Lanie could feel the sense of urgency that drove him and knew she was part of the reason behind it. She hadn't been able to shake the fever. Now she was acutely aware of the dryness in her throat and the deep ache in her muscles. "I'm going to make a friendly stop by Ralph Montoya's before I go to work. I have the feeling that he knows something."

"You think he's involved in what's happened to you?"

She twirled a strand of hair around her index finger. "I don't know. What I do know is that he was in the right place at the wrong time at least once. I want to have a talk with him. It may turn out to be a waste of time, but then again, it may not."

"You're still running a fever. You shouldn't be pushing yourself."

"I've got to do something. I can't just stay on the sidelines."

Gabriel fastened his belt, adjusted his holster, then walked to the bed where she was sitting. "I care about you, woman." He tucked her hair behind her ear, then brushed a kiss over her eyes. "Look after yourself when I can't be by your side. I need you."

As he walked out of the room, Lanie threw back the covers and headed for the shower. As the warm water ran over her, she closed her eyes and remembered his caress. With a reluctant sigh, she released the mental image. It was time to solve other problems, not indulge in fantasies. She dried off and dressed quickly. Ten minutes later, she walked into the kitchen. Marlee was fixing some coffee.

"Morning, Lanie. Shall I get you some breakfast?"

Lanie shook her head. "A cold glass of milk and two aspirins is all I want." Lanie went to the refrigerator and poured herself a tall glass. The cold liquid felt good against her parched throat. She swallowed the aspirins in one gulp.

"I'm worried about you," Marlee said. "You've got to eat."

"I have enough in reserve," she answered, patting her buttocks. "You just don't notice it 'cause the jeans fit right."

"No, I don't notice it because it isn't there," Marlee said. "Here. Take some of these cocoa packets I've mixed up. My cocoa only puts you to sleep if you drink it when you're exhausted. During the day, it just relaxes you. You can have a cup with Alma during your morning break."

She knew how Marlee's cocoa could relax you. Chloroform was probably on a par with it. Not wanting to hurt her landlady's feelings, however, Lanie took the two packets. "Is there anything you need me to do before I leave?"

"No, not at the moment."

"Okay. In that case, I better get going. I've got a lot to do today."

Lanie walked down the street, her thoughts still on Gabriel. He'd held her all night, and that had shown more caring, more tenderness, than a million nights of lovemaking could have. Well, maybe.

She sighed as she approached Ralph Montoya's office. Issues of the *Last Word*, the town newspaper, lined the front window. Lanie stared at them pensively. Something bothered her about those, but she couldn't quite put her finger on it.

Seeing her at the window, Ralph waved, inviting her inside. "Come in, come in!" he greeted. "It's cold this morning. No sense in standing out there in this wind."

The cold had actually felt good against her skin, but he'd given her the opening she'd needed. "Good morning."

"Are you on your way to Alma's?"

She nodded. "I've still got plenty of time, though.

That's why I couldn't resist a peek in your window. You do a very good job with the newspaper."

He shrugged. "It isn't much of a paper. Let's face it, anywhere else it would be called a newsletter. But it's enough for me. I'm the reporter, printer and editor-in-chief. I make my own rules." He saved what was on the computer screen, and moved away from it.

"You remember that Gabriel asked me to do a search in regards to that bowl of yours?" he asked.

"Yes, of course. Did you find something?"

"Not on the bowl, no. I've looked for articles about thefts from archaeological sites and that sort of thing, but haven't found anything useful. I did come across something interesting, though. It's about one of the residents of Four Winds. Since I'm going to be out of town for the rest of the day, could you pass it on to the sheriff?"

"Sure. No problem."

He handed her a photocopy of a newspaper clipping. "That's our mayor, but without the mustache he wears nowadays. He went by William Burns, not Bob Burns, back when that was printed. Seems he was brought up on charges of embezzlement while working for a bank in southern Colorado."

Lanie stared at the photo, then read the story. "He was acquitted, it says."

"Yes, but what's interesting is that as mayor, he's also the chief money manager of Four Winds."

Lanie took a deep breath. Maybe it was time Gabriel looked at the town's finances. "Interesting."

"Look, in deference to fair play, tell no one else about this except Gabriel, okay? The man is entitled to his past, whatever it may have been."

She stared at the photo. As she started to fold up the clipping, she suddenly realized what had been niggling at the back of her mind. "I know what's been bothering me about the *Last Word*. There's never a photo in it. That's very unusual, wouldn't you say?''

"My camera broke, and I never bothered to replace it," he said, not meeting her eyes. "It doesn't bother anyone else, and people still buy the paper. Of course, it's the only one here."

"But…"

He hurried her to the door. "Look, I've really got to be going. I've got to go to the 4-H fair in the next county. Some of our kids have livestock in the show, and they get a kick out of seeing their names in the paper when their animals win something."

"I bet they'd love photos, too. Couldn't you borrow a camera? I'm sure Alma would be glad to loan you one." Lanie could see Ralph was almost ready to jump out of his skin. He was looking at her as if she had suddenly grown horns.

"I don't like to borrow things," he said curtly, then guided her out. "Have a nice day," he said, shutting the door firmly behind her and drawing down the shade.

Lanie smirked. Oh, that had gone well. She sure as heck had a gift for getting people in Four Winds to open up to her.

She walked over to the sheriff's office, and as she approached, Gabriel stepped out.

He looked preoccupied, but the moment he saw her, concern, and another, gentler emotion transformed his expression. "Hey, beautiful, are you looking for me?"

She nodded, a hint of a smile playing on her lips. "I've got something for you."

He grinned slowly. "Wouldn't you rather have a little more privacy?"

His voice was smoky, and she felt a delicious thrill run up her spine.

Hearing the sound of men's voices as they unloaded a truck outside the feed store brought her thoughts back in line. Lanie cleared her throat and reached inside her purse. "Here you go. An interesting tidbit from Ralph."

He glanced at the article. "This wasn't in my police files, probably because our mayor's changed his name. He's not the only one. This town is a maze of secrets."

"So, now what?"

"I'm going to have a talk with the mayor, I guess. Quarterly audits will take place in about another month. If he's dipped into the town's funds for personal reasons, he may be looking for a score that will help him replace what he's taken."

"You think that his son is working with him?"

"It could be, but that doesn't sound quite right to me. Ted's his only kid. My guess is our mayor would do anything to protect Ted by keeping him out of that."

"Well, good luck with the mayor. Meanwhile, I better get over to Alma's."

"See you later, and remember, I won't be far."

His words washed over Lanie, warming her as she walked inside Golden Days. What a strange sense of welcome the place always seemed to give her. It was cozy here. She took a long look at the pipe rack on the wall, the shelves of scent bottles and the santos and kachinas on the table across the room.

"I recognize that gleam," Alma said quietly. "I used to see it all the time in Emily's eyes. The antique business is winning you over."

Lanie considered Alma's words. Teaching had been the only vocation to truly capture her heart. Antiques, however, held her interest, and that was more than anything else had done since she'd left school.

"I love the things you've gathered here," Lanie admitted. "But I don't think I have a business heart. I'd want to keep all of them for myself," she added with a chuckle.

"Oh, that would change when it was time to buy groceries."

Lanie laughed. "Yep, I think you're right." Lanie followed Alma to the back room. "What would you like me to do today?"

"Will you go over to Bob Burns's and take some photos for me? He's decided to sell his chair. It's an unusual thing that uses longhorn cattle horns as the frame. It was crafted around the late 1890s, and I'm virtually certain I can sell it through my catalog."

She hesitated. What if Ted had been the one who'd attacked her? She considered the matter. Even if he had, he wouldn't do anything in his own home, or in broad daylight if she stayed out of isolated areas, which she certainly intended to do. "Should I take the 35 mm camera?"

"Yes, it's right there on the counter. Take shots from as many sides as possible, and I'll choose the best one." Alma gave her directions to the house, then added, "It's a pleasant walk. You go down Main, then past two really nice neighborhoods. There'll be people about if you get lost, but are you sure you're up to it? Your cheeks looked awfully flushed."

"I'm fine. A walk will do me a world of good. Everyone needs fresh air now and then."

The walk to the mayor's home took her almost fifteen minutes. Lanie glanced around as she approached, wondering if Gabriel was still there. His vehicle, however, was nowhere in sight. She walked up the landscaped driveway, surprised by the elegance of such an estate here in Four Winds.

The spacious veranda looked out to the east and was bathed in the shade of giant cottonwoods. Heavily carved wooden doors, typical of the old-style Spanish architecture, were inset into the adobe-lined courtyard wall. She rang the brass bell, then went through the private courtyard, and walked up to the front door.

Raucous laughter greeted her from inside the house. She

used the iron knocker, and at the sound, the noise within stopped abruptly. A breath later, Ted came to the door.

"Well, hi. How can I help you?"

Lanie forced herself to act completely unconcerned. "I came to photograph the antique chair your father is selling."

"He's not here right now, but I know about the chair he wants to unload. It's ugly as sin. I can show you where it is."

As she followed Ted Burns down a long corridor, she saw that several other young people were in the den, intent on a game of pool. Their presence reassured her. "I'm going to have to go," he said after ushering her into the study, "but feel free to stay as long as you want. The chair you want is against the corner."

"Thanks."

"If you need me, I'll be at the pool table."

While she worked, Lanie caught snippets of the kids' conversation in the adjacent room. They were talking about the bowl...and Lanie herself. She was contemplating moving closer so she could hear, when a young girl about seventeen or eighteen came in.

"You're the lady the peddler gave the bowl to, aren't you?"

Lanie nodded. "That's me, all right, Lanie Mathews. What's your name?"

"Annie O'Malley." She crinkled her nose in disgust, looking at the chair Lanie was photographing. "That's ugly. Miss Alma's going to have a tough time selling that. Your pottery bowl will probably go fast, though. Will she be selling it for you?"

"No, somebody stole it."

"The sheriff will get it back. I heard he's really interested in you." Annie smiled.

Lanie looked at Annie. The girl was pretty in her own way. She had flaming red hair and bright freckles that almost entirely covered her face. The New Mexican sun had to be hard on her. "News really travels around here. I've noticed I've become a topic of conversation. Why is that, do you think?"

"Well, you're the first woman that Sheriff Blackhorse has paid any serious attention to since he came back. You two thinking of getting married?"

"We have no plans for that." She wasn't crazy about being the topic of speculation, but at least the gossip here wasn't malicious. Maybe that was because the subject was Gabriel, and nobody wanted trouble with him.

"I've also heard that you've brought a truckload of trouble to a few kids around here."

"I don't understand."

"Pete's been sick, and Ted says you made things worse by getting Pete all upset, blaming him for things he didn't do."

Lanie started to put her camera away. "I didn't make trouble for Peter. I've never even spoken to him. If anything, I think he's brought his problems onto himself."

"Well, I know that Pete's been acting really weird lately."

"Weird, how?"

"He's not usually standoffish, at least not to me, but for the past week or so, he won't even talk to me on the phone. That's just not like him. I came here today with the guys, hoping he'd show up. But he's not around."

"Annie, are you coming?" Ted called out from down the hall. "We're taking off."

The girl turned around. "I've got to go. Bye."

Lanie watched Annie rush out. By the time she put the camera away in her purse, the big house was completely silent. A trickle of unease rippled through her.

She walked quickly to the front of the house. Ted was gone with his friends. There was no reason for her to be frightened, but she was anyway. Under different circumstances, she would have simply attributed it to a case of nerves, but she wasn't willing to discount her feelings so quickly anymore. Was it paranoia if someone really was after you?

She'd just reached the front door when it suddenly opened. Lanie jumped back and saw the mayor standing in front of her. She recognized him right away from the photo Ralph had shown her. He was balder now, and a bit heavier, but it was the same man.

"This is *my* home. How did you get in?" he demanded.

"Your son let me in," she said. "He and his friends—"

Bob Burns lifted a hand, interrupting her. "My son is here?"

"He *was* here. He let me in to take photos of that chair, but then went someplace with his friends."

"Ted…here," he said slowly, his voice holding a faraway quality. "And he had friends over. I'm glad to hear that. He hasn't invited anyone here for a long time." He glanced down at her bag. "You're all finished, then?"

"Yes, I am. I'm going back to Alma's now."

"Tell Alma I appreciate her efforts to sell my chair, and for agreeing to include it in her catalog at the last minute."

"I'll do that."

Lanie walked away, feeling the mayor's eyes on her back. It was surprising that he hadn't mentioned the bowl. By now, she was sure he knew it had been stolen. He'd shown interest in it once, through a buyer, so she would have expected a question or two about the progress of the investigation. Lost in thought, she hurried down the street.

Chapter Fifteen

The wind was cold against her as she walked back to Alma's. The warmth slowly left her body, and by the time she reached Sally's, she'd started to shiver. On impulse, she decided to duck in and grab something hot to drink. She desperately needed something to warm her up.

Lanie walked inside and saw Gabriel by the counter. Sally, across from him, had a very peculiar expression on her face. Her eyes seemed unnaturally bright against the pallor of her skin. She plucked at the edges of her apron, though from what Lanie could tell, there was nothing wrong with it to adjust.

As Lanie reached the counter, Sally turned away from Gabriel and approached her.

"What can I get you?" She bit off the words.

"Coffee to go," Lanie answered, figuring Sally was probably angry with her after the accusation she'd leveled at Peter.

Sally reached for a foam cup, filled it with steaming coffee, then capped it. "Here you go. That'll be sixty cents."

"I know how upset you must be, but I hope you know that I'd never lie about seeing Peter."

"You made a mistake, but that's created a lot of problems for me and my kid. This is a business establishment, and you're welcome to eat here, but don't expect any favors from me.''

As Sally strode away to the kitchen, Gabriel joined Lanie. "She's furious with both of us."

Lanie placed the coins on the counter and picked up the cup. "She's trying to protect her son. That's natural."

"You're right on both counts. I did a background check on Sally and I discovered that she, like our mayor, has been living here under an assumed name. I confronted her with it just now. That's why she's upset."

"Has she broken the law?"

"No. She pays her taxes under a company name, and the business is legitimate."

"Then why the assumed name?"

"Peter's father is a known felon, on the run from the law. He's tried twice to take the boy away from her, and the second time he was nearly successful. He took Peter and left the state. But Sally lucked out. Her ex ran into a roadblock, and one of the cops manning it recognized Peter."

"So she changed her name to make it harder for her ex to find her," she finished for him.

"That's it in a nutshell. I let her know that I knew all about her past. The idea was to prove to her that I wasn't her enemy. I assured her that if her husband tracked them to Four Winds, I'd protect her."

"She didn't appreciate the gesture?"

"Not quite. She told me Peter was her responsibility, and she could take care of herself and him. She was furious that I'd pried into her life. But there's more we're not seeing. Something's scaring her, and she won't open up to me."

"Peter's at the center of it, I'll bet. I heard that nobody's seen the boy for a while outside the house." She told him about her conversation with Annie.

As they walked down the street toward Alma's, Lanie's

gaze fell on the mail carrier. He looked about fifteen. The small mail bag was wider than his shoulders. "He's kinda young, don't you think?"

"That's Manuel Ortega. Believe it or not, he graduated high school last semester."

"He delivers mail to everyone in Four Winds?"

"He's our only mail carrier."

Lanie smiled slowly. "So he delivers all the mail, and everyone knows him."

"I see where you're headed with this," Gabriel said. "Not a bad idea. Come on, let's go talk to him."

Gabriel approached the young man and introduced him to Lanie. Curiosity shone in Manuel's eyes. "I've heard all about you, ma'am," he said to Lanie.

Gabriel took the mail carrier aside. "Manuel, I need your help with a police matter."

"Uh, okay, Sheriff, what can I do?" He shifted from side to side, adjusting the mail pouch.

"Tell me about Peter Jenkins. Is he usually home when you make your rounds?"

"He has been lately. I've heard his voice inside the house. I think he's got company."

"Did you recognize the voice of the other person?"

Manuel shook his head. "I wasn't paying that much attention, to be honest."

"Do you remember seeing any cars parked around Sally's house?"

He considered it for a moment. "You know, I don't normally notice cars. Dogs, well, that's a different matter. But there aren't any problem animals in that area."

"So, you have no idea who Peter's visitor is?" Gabriel asked.

Manuel took a deep breath. "Well, there was one time... But I kinda hate to say anything. I think they were just roughhousing."

"Tell me. I'll check it out."

"Recently, when I came up to the door, I saw Ted Burns scuffling with Peter. Ted grabbed him by the collar and threw him across the room. Peter fell hard, so I opened the screen door and went inside. I thought I'd better split them up. But when Ted saw me, he started laughing. He helped Peter back up to his feet, and they were okay with each other. The next day, I *was* paying attention, but they were just playing the radio and horsing around."

"Horsing around how? Tell me what you remember," Gabriel prodded.

"Peter was playing his guitar and Ted was singing along, way off-key, so I knew things were okay."

"Thanks, Manuel. I appreciate it."

"No problem."

Lanie stopped at the door to Alma's store. "There's something going on with those two boys. I feel it."

"I'm going to do a little digging. It's amazing what talking to a few neighbors can reveal."

Alma came up to the window and waved at Lanie from inside. A moment later, she joined them on the sidewalk. "Are you okay? You didn't have any more problems, did you?"

"No, not at all," Lanie assured. "I've got lots of shots of the chair, though I really don't think there's a flattering angle for that thing!"

Alma laughed. "Come on, let's go inside. It's freezing out here."

"I better be on my way," Gabriel said. "Have a nice day, ladies."

As they stepped inside the shop, Alma looked at Lanie. "I have a problem. I'd totally forgotten that I'd promised to try and market Ralph's old typewriter. It dates back to the early 1900s, and since he doesn't use it, he wants to sell it. Can you go over there for me now and take some photos?"

"Ralph mentioned that he was going out of town."

"His assistant should be there. I'm sure he'll let you take the photos."

"I'm on my way." Lanie gulped down her coffee, then picked up the camera and her bag.

As she walked down the street, a plan formed in her mind. She'd try to strike up a conversation with Ralph's assistant. Maybe she'd be able to get some answers from him.

When she arrived at the newspaper office, she was surprised to see Ralph there.

He eyed her with suspicion. "What are you doing *here?*"

"I came on behalf of Alma, to photograph your type-writer."

"Oh, that. Yes, I'd almost forgotten." He walked inside the storeroom, brought the old machine out and set it on a table near the window.

"Thanks." Lanie began taking photos, covering different angles. "I thought you were going to be out of town."

"I sent my part-time helper. I have other work here that must get done. And on that note, I better get to it."

She took a few more photos and then went back to the outer office. Ralph didn't even look up. If she could only get him to relax. That's when she remembered Marlee's cocoa. "It's so cold outside." She gestured at the skeletal cottonwood tree branches blowing against the side window.

"It's a bad day," he grumbled, then squinted as he studied her. "You look flushed, as if you've got a fever. Are you okay?"

"Yes, but I could use something warm to drink before going back out. I've got some cocoa packets in my purse. Will you have a cup with me?"

Ralph hesitated.

"I don't know what I've done to upset you, Ralph. You weren't so dead set against me when we first met."

"You ask too many questions that are, quite frankly, none of your business." He left his desk and took the packets of cocoa from her hand. "But I will sit down and have some cocoa with you. It's a cold, miserable day, and I forgot to buy more coffee. I need some caffeine—I haven't had a decent night's sleep in two days. I've been trying to finish up a book I've been working on."

"About what?"

"It's a novel about a newspaperman," he said briskly.

Lanie opened the packets and emptied them into two mugs Ralph had filled with hot water from the percolator. "If I ask too many questions, Ralph, it's just because I'm desperate. I'm not sure who my enemies are, and it's hard to fight what you can't see."

He said nothing, stirring his cocoa with a letter opener. He'd given her the spoon. Ralph must have enjoyed the cocoa, because he emptied his mug in three big swallows. Now, if only Marlee's cocoa worked on him the same way it had worked on her! She leaned back, barely sipping hers. "I have to find out *why* I'm a target before I can do something about it."

"*I'm* not after you," he said simply. "The bowl and the gossip about the peddler intrigued me, but that's the extent of my interest." His movements were slow as he walked to his desk.

Picking up the camera, she placed it on her lap and pretended to adjust one of the settings. "I just realized that I still have six more shots. Do you mind if I finish the roll by taking a few more photos of your typewriter?"

He waved toward the other room. "Help yourself."

Lanie deliberately took her time. Ten minutes later, she looked through the doorway and saw Ralph leaning back in his chair, asleep.

This was risky, but it was the perfect opportunity. She crept past him and went to the file cabinet by the wall. Lanie opened each drawer slowly, taking care to be as quiet as possible. When she opened the fourth drawer, however, a high-pitched squeak reverberated in the silence of the room.

She held her breath and glanced over at Ralph. He stirred, but did not waken.

Lanie knew she'd have to move faster. If the phone rang, there was no way he'd sleep through that. She finished searching the file cabinet quickly, but found nothing. As she looked around the room, afraid this had been a waste of time, she saw a small, two-shelf bookcase partially hidden behind a cart. The shelves held no books, only what appeared to be a scrapbook of some sort and some packets of computer and fax paper.

Lanie silently moved the cart, then pulled out the thick scrapbook. Realizing that she couldn't hear the sound of Ralph's steady breathing, she turned around uneasily, but saw he was still sound asleep. He'd shifted to his side, and his position gave her the creeps. Had he been awake, she would have been directly in his line of vision.

She watched him for several moments. Then, convinced that he was really asleep, she continued her sleuthing. Lanie sat on the floor and leafed through the scrapbook. Inside were the mementos of a distinguished newspaper-man. Awards and special stories with his byline chronicled a fine career. Then, toward the end, the focus shifted. First came the article about a battered young woman who couldn't remember who she was or how she'd been injured. Ralph had written several consecutive stories urging the community to help the police identify her. The woman's photograph was prominently featured on the front page.

Then Lanie saw the last story. The woman's assailant had read the newspaper accounts and, fearing for his own safety, tracked her to the hospital. Evading the guard, he'd gained access to her room and killed her.

The very last item was the killer's confession, claiming

Ralph's articles had forced him to take action. Below that was a small sidebar, announcing Ralph's resignation from the paper.

She stood up slowly and carefully placed everything back as it had been. Though the woman's death had not been directly his fault, Lanie now knew why Ralph never used photos in his articles. Ralph carried his own demons, born of that incident. But unfortunately none of this brought Gabriel and her any closer to solving their own mystery.

She picked up her bag, crept to the door silently, then walked out into the cold air. Catching a flicker of movement inside the office out of the corner of her eyes, Lanie turned her head. Ralph was standing by the bookshelf that held the scrapbook, and he was looking right at her. He gave her a nod, then went back to his chair.

Lanie stared at him in shock. He'd been sound asleep and couldn't have known for sure what she'd done. If he had, surely he would have stopped her or spoken up. Convincing herself that she had nothing to worry about, she returned to Alma's.

LANIE STOOD in the window display at Alma's store, dusting. Her fever didn't feel as if it had risen, but she still felt lousy and ached everywhere. She glanced at the ancient grandfather clock, which seemed to work perfectly. It was nearly two, but Alma had told Lanie to close early today. She had just stepped out of the display to put the Closed sign up when she saw Gabriel walking down the street coming toward the store. His loose-legged stride gave off an unspoken challenge, and she saw how the other men automatically stepped aside as they greeted him.

A moment later, the bell above the door jingled, and he came into the shop. ''I ran into Alma. She said she'd given you some time off since she wanted the afternoon alone to finish some catalog copy. Are you ready to call it a day? I figured I'd give you a ride home.''

"All I have to do now is lock up. Alma is out, running an errand someplace.''

His gaze swept the small room, filled floor to ceiling with antiques and collectibles. "You know, this place just doesn't seem the same since Miss Emily passed on. Alma seems to go through the motions, but she's not really investing much of herself into this business.''

"This was never her love. To her, it's just a way to make a living. If anything, I think she regrets letting Emily talk her into getting this place.''

"Could be.'' He looked around curiously as she locked up in back. "By the way, I ran into Ralph. He said you'd stopped by earlier.''

"That I did,'' she admitted, and recounted what had happened.

He smiled. "That old man's crafty. I'd bet you he never was asleep and deliberately allowed you to find the scrapbook.''

"But why? That doesn't make any sense.''

"Sure, it does. He wanted you to find your own answers, knowing darned well that you'd probably doubt his word if he just came out and told you.''

"That's a good point. I guess I'll never know for sure, though. I certainly can't bring it up without admitting what I did.''

"Which is probably what he's counting on, too. Having you learn about his past this way guarantees you won't ever bring it up again for discussion.'' He sat down while Lanie drew the shades. "How are you feeling?''

"Besides humbled?'' She shrugged. "I'll live.''

Lanie heard the door chime jingle and cursed herself for not having locked the door. Hoping the business wouldn't take long, she glanced at the young man who entered, then realized it was Manuel Ortega, the mail carrier.

He looked at her, then at Gabriel. "I...um...well, I was thinking about all the questions you asked me earlier, so I decided to investigate a bit."

Gabriel's eyes narrowed. "What exactly did you do?"

"I took a little more time than usual over at Sally's home today." He began to talk quickly. "When I came up the walk, I heard Ted and Peter arguing about something. Since I couldn't make out what, I went around the back hoping I could hear better from there. I sure got an earful. Ted and Peter were really going at it. Ted was saying that he'd brought his gun along just as insurance. Peter argued back, telling him that he didn't care what Ted called the gun, he wanted it out of his mom's house. Ted called him a wimp. Just then, Mrs. Miller, the next-door neighbor, saw me. I had to cover fast, so I told her I'd seen Mrs. Potter's kitten wandering loose, and I was trying to find it."

Gabriel nodded. "Good save. But don't ever do something like that again. I appreciate your help, but things could have gone very wrong, and there wasn't anyone there to back you up."

"Okay, Sheriff. But whenever you need help, you just let me know, hear?"

"You've got it."

Once Manuel left, Lanie looked at Gabriel. "The more I find out about those two boys, the less I trust them. An agile male took Alma's book, remember? The pages concerning the skinwalker bowl ended up in Marlee's garage, which is something that may have appealed to them. You know, hiding evidence right under our eyes. They could have also been the pair who jumped you and your brother."

"True. But would they be doing this on their own? I don't think so. I don't believe neither of those kids has the contacts to market a bowl like that. If they did steal it, it was for someone else," he said.

"I know you don't agree with my theory, but if the mayor is behind it, then at least it makes some sense," she said. "Ted could have been trying to prove something to himself, as well as to his dad. Maybe his father didn't hire him, but rather Ted acted on his own, and Burns is now working with his son in order to protect him." She expelled her breath slowly. "The problem is, like you, I can't see Ted working with him." She then related her brief earlier encounter with the mayor. "They are father and son, but they barely communicate."

"I think it's time for us to go have a talk with the mayor. I want him to understand a few things, including how the bowl has affected your life, physically and mentally. If his kid is involved in this with someone else, then Ted is clearly in over his head, whether he knows it or not. Just from a practical standpoint, Ted can't market that bowl alone, and if he's connected with some major player who wants to cover his tracks, Ted could end up dead."

They arrived at the mayor's spacious home ten minutes later. The lights were on in the den, but the rest of the house was dark.

Gabriel knocked, and moments later Bob Burns came to the door. "Come in. How about a drink, folks?"

Gabriel shook his head, and Lanie also declined.

"I guess I'm stuck drinking alone, then."

Lanie watched the mayor's unsteady gait and surmised he'd already had several drinks. It suddenly struck her that Bob Burns was a lonely, haunted man. He lived with an unpleasant past, an alienated son who was no longer a child and an uncertain future.

"Is your son around?" Gabriel asked.

"Is Ted in trouble?"

"That's not an answer," Gabriel said.

"I don't know where he is, Sheriff. I seldom do nowadays. Are you here to talk to him or to me?"

"To you, for now. I understand that you hired an intermediary to purchase the bowl Miss Mathews was given,'' he said without elaborating. ''Why were you interested in obtaining that particular artifact?''

''I felt it was a good investment, but because of my position here, I thought it was in my interest to use Mr. Madison as a go-between.''

''You were willing to offer me quite a lot of money,'' Lanie stated. ''Why were you so desperate to get it?''

The mayor met her gaze. ''I have money, Miss Mathews, but outside this town I'm nobody. If I had a treasure like that, I could loan it to universities and museums, and make a name for myself. I'd be respected and sought out in circles that currently show me no respect at all. But once that piece was authenticated, then everyone would bid on it and the price would reach levels that were beyond me. My one chance lay in acting quickly.''

''We believe your son is involved in the recent theft of the bowl. Would he have done that for you?'' Gabriel asked.

The mayor looked at him in surprise. ''You think Ted stole the bowl? That's ridiculous! My boy has no need for money, and he doesn't give a hoot about prestige. If you have evidence, I want to hear it.''

''I don't have any concrete proof, but believe me, I'm only trying to help Ted,'' Gabriel said. ''I think he's gotten himself involved in something that could cost him his life.''

''You mean someone might kill him if they, too, conclude he's got the bowl?''

''That's one possibility, but the bowl itself is also a danger,'' Lanie said.

Burns nodded slowly. ''I've heard bits and pieces of that legend recently. But surely you two don't believe all that.''

''I can assure you that the bowl brings trouble regardless of what your beliefs are," Gabriel said, avoiding a more direct answer.

The mayor looked at Lanie thoughtfully. "Ralph's kept me up to date on everything. You've been through hell. Some bozo is trying to make the legend seem real at your expense." His gaze stayed on her pensively. "But there's more to it, isn't there? It's taking a physical toll on you."

"Yes on both counts," Lanie replied.

He took a deep breath. "What would you have me do to protect my son?"

"Help us," Gabriel said. "We have to find the bowl, and if we work together, maybe we can keep everyone safe. Let me search Ted's room."

"You won't find anything there," the mayor said flatly.

"Let me search it, then," Gabriel insisted.

"All right, but I want to be right there with you."

"Agreed." Gabriel went out to his Jeep and retrieved a handful of evidence pouches, which he placed in his jacket pocket.

He joined the mayor and Lanie a minute later. Together, they went upstairs. Gabriel took the boy's room in at a glance. Then, following a hunch, he went directly to the trash.

Using his pen, Gabriel lifted a black ski mask from beneath an empty pizza box.

"The person who has attacked me twice wore a ski mask," Lanie said, and drew closer. "In the struggle right before I was tossed into the well, I ripped the area around the eyes." She pointed to the mask. "Like that."

"The men who jumped Lucas and me also were wearing ski masks," Gabriel added, glancing at the mayor.

He placed the mask inside an evidence pouch and continued his search wordlessly. Unable to locate the bowl or any other incriminating items, he turned to face the mayor. "This isn't conclusive," Gabriel informed him, "but Ted will have some serious questions to answer."

The mayor's face was as white as a sheet. "I don't understand any of this." He slumped down into the nearest chair.

"How has Ted been acting lately?" Gabriel asked.

Burns rubbed the back of his neck with his hand. "He's been in a very dark mood, losing his temper at the slightest provocation. But I can guarantee you it's not drugs. I've searched the house carefully for any evidence of that." Burns stood up. "I'd like you to leave now. Next time I see my son, I'll bring him in to talk to you, with an attorney."

"That's fine, but remember that at this point all I want is to ask him some questions," Gabriel said.

Lanie walked with Gabriel to the door. Hopefully Ted would be the key that would unlock the mystery.

GABRIEL DROVE AWAY from the mayor's home, silence stretching out between them. "I've got a plan that will get us inside Sally's house, where I think we'll find the mayor's son. But I'm going to need Sally's permission, and I'm not sure how to get that."

"I don't know how much help I can be. Sally's angry with me, too." Lanie's body went from hot to cold, and she shivered. She'd have to take more aspirins soon. "But maybe if I'm completely honest with her, she'll be more inclined to cooperate with us."

"You want to tell her how the bowl's been affecting your life?"

She nodded. "If I can convince her that my back is to the wall on this, maybe I'll get through to her. Of course, she may not believe that there's any truth in the legend."

"In case you haven't noticed, people around here don't discount things like that so easily. Besides, all she has to do is take a good look at you." His gaze was filled with tenderness and concern. "Are you sure you're up to this?"

Gabriel reached out to her and brushed his knuckles against her cheek.

Lanie felt a wonderful warmth course through her. He could stir her senses so easily! "I can do whatever I have to do," she said. "Don't worry."

"But I do. Can't help it."

She understood what was in Gabriel's heart, knowing she'd feel the same if he were threatened in any way, and smiled gently at him. "I'll be okay."

It was three-thirty by the time they walked inside Sally's diner. She was alone, sipping a cup of coffee. As they approached the counter, Lanie saw the pain in Sally's eyes. It sliced right through her.

Lanie forced herself to hold the woman's gaze. "Sally, you've got to listen to me," Lanie said, then quickly explained everything she knew about the bowl. "Look at me, Sally. You'll see I'm not lying. That bowl attracts evil, and Peter could be in real danger from other people who want it and will stop at nothing to get it."

"It's all true," Gabriel said, then he told Sally about the ski mask they'd found in Ted's room. "We know Ted's got some kind of hold on Peter. Let us help you. Don't let your fears endanger your son even more."

Sally's hands gripped the counter. "What can I do? Pete's my son. My *only* son," she added.

"Then fight for him. He can't handle this alone," Lanie said.

Sally leaned against the wall, one of her hands covering her face. "This all started when they heard about that bowl. Pete's not blameless, but he's not a bad boy. He's just made some bad choices."

"If he can't back out of this on his own, you've got to take action yourself," Gabriel pressed.

"You don't understand. Ted's gone crazy. He swore he'd shoot Pete and me if I told anyone or did anything to interfere. And there's someone else in this with Ted, though I don't really know who it is. Lately, usually after midnight, someone comes up to the house on foot. Ted's careful, so neither of them can be seen, but the voice I've heard belongs to a woman, or a girl. It puzzled me because, as far as I know, Ted doesn't have a girlfriend.''

"What we have to do first is get Peter safely away from Ted," Gabriel explained.

"How? Lately Ted doesn't let Pete out of his sight for more than a second or two."

"I've got a plan," Gabriel answered.

"I won't do anything to endanger Peter." Sally looked at them tearfully. "Neither of you have kids. You can't possibly know how afraid I am of losing him. If anything happened to my boy..."

"I do know what it's like to lose a kid to violence," Lanie said, her voice taut as memories came rushing back. "A boy died once because I didn't act when I needed to." She told Sally the whole tragic story.

When she was done, Sally looked at Lanie as if seeing her for the first time. "Now I know what you're running from." She turned to Gabriel. "Will Lanie be included in your plan?"

"She's an integral part of it."

"Then I'll place my trust in you, Sheriff, because of Lanie. She'll do her best to avoid having to live with a second mistake."

Gabriel looked from face to face. "We better get started, then."

"Where are we going?" Sally asked, locking the diner doors as they stepped out onto the sidewalk.

"To the boardinghouse, then to your home," Gabriel said. "To pull a successful con, we're going to need some preparation time."

Chapter Sixteen

Lanie looked at herself again in the car mirror. Gabriel was in the back seat, crouched below window level. Sally's blond wig didn't look completely out of place on Lanie, but her figure was fuller, her hips and bust more prominent than Sally's.

"I'm not sure about this. Will I really pass for Sally even from a distance?" Lanie asked.

"Follow Sally's pattern. Come in through the front door and make a loud noise when you slam it shut. Sally said the boys are always in Peter's room and don't come out to say hello. Once you're in, go to the kitchen, open the back door for me, then duck out of sight."

Lanie parked Sally's car on the left side of the small driveway, just the way Sally did, and took a deep breath. "Well, it's show time."

"If one of the boys does happen to come downstairs, go into the bathroom just off the kitchen and make retching noises. They'll leave you alone."

"Wonderful. I haven't practiced my retching noises since junior high."

"Oh? I didn't realize anyone *practiced* retching noises."

"You would be surprised what you learn in Catholic school."

Gabriel chuckled. "I stand corrected."

Lanie nervously opened the car door. "Here we go." Staring down at the pavement in case anyone was looking out the window, Lanie walked quickly to the front door. Sally's wig was a bit loose, and she prayed it wouldn't fall off or spin around on her head.

Lanie unlocked the front door and slammed it behind her, then walked across the living room quickly, following Sally's directions to the kitchen. She'd almost reached the doorway when Ted Burns came down the hall, holding an empty can of cola.

"Get me another one, Sal—" Eyes wide, he reached back and drew a small-caliber pistol from his waistband.

Lanie dove behind the couch just as Ted fired. Tufts of padding exploded outward, and a spring came bursting out of the back in the wake of a bullet.

Suddenly Peter came running into the room. "Stop it. She's my mother."

"Get out of here, Pete," Ted snapped. "This isn't your mother. Leave if you don't want to see what's going to happen to her."

"No, you're crazy. This stops right now!"

Lanie peered out and saw Peter launch himself at Ted. Then, with a thundering crash, the window on the other side of the room exploded inward. A figure that was nothing more than a blur hurdled into the room.

When Ted turned to shoot, Peter pushed him to one side. As the boys hit the floor, the gun went off. Peter's cry of pain tore through Lanie. She dove forward, covering Peter with her own body as Ted raised his pistol again.

"Drop it, Burns, now!" Gabriel ordered from behind the doorway, his pistol out and ready.

Ted fired two rounds, forcing Gabriel back. Grabbing something from the bookshelf, Ted dove through the broken window. Gabriel's single shot was a second too late.

After a quick glance to ensure that Peter and Lanie

weren't badly hit, Gabriel ran to the door and out after Ted. By the time he'd crossed the yard, Ted had disappeared into the woods.

"He's gone for now, but I'll get him," Gabriel said as he returned, breathless. "How are you two?"

"I'm okay," Lanie replied, "but Peter's been shot in the upper arm. I'll keep pressure on the wound, but he needs medical help."

"I'll radio my brother. Hang tight, Pete," he said.

"I'll be okay, Sheriff." The moment Gabriel left the room, Peter gave Lanie a mournful look. "But it hurts like hell."

"I bet it does, but Lucas will be here soon. He'll patch you up."

Peter nodded, sitting up, still clutching his upper arm. "You scared me half to death, you know. I thought you were my mother."

Lanie smiled. "And you saved my life."

"No, I just slowed Ted down enough for the sheriff to reach us. I knew he was out there. I'd seen him from my window."

Gabriel returned again. "Lucas was at the aid station and will be here in a few minutes. The state police are setting up roadblocks. If Ted tries to get out of the county, he's going to run right into their hands."

"By the way, what did he grab from the shelf?" Lanie asked. "Was it the bowl?"

Peter nodded. "It's making him crazy. That bowl is all he thinks about. He didn't steal it for himself, but now he's saying it's meant for him."

"Who did he steal it for?" Gabriel asked.

"Some woman who comes to meet with him at night. But once he had it, he refused to give it to her. He told me that he was going to make us both richer than we'd ever dreamed. Then he changed. He started saying that I was weak and couldn't handle anything, though I always managed to get whatever he needed done. I stole Alma's book and hid the page about the bowl in Marlee's garage just like he ordered me. Ted was sure it would throw you off if you ever did find it.

"But as the days went by, he just acted crazier and crazier," Peter continued. "Then he threatened my mom. When Mom stood up to him, he forced her to stay quiet by keeping me here and waving that gun of his around."

As Lucas came in, Lanie stepped aside. Lucas talked to the boy quietly, calming him down at the same time as he bandaged him up. Lucas was ready to transport him when Sally came rushing through the door, her head covered by a fuzzy winter hat.

"Pete!" Sally ran to her son and fell to her knees beside him. "Oh, honey, what have they done?" She stared accusingly at Gabriel and Lanie. "You said you'd keep him safe!"

"Mom, stop fussing," Peter said. "I'm okay."

"He's a hero, Sally," Lanie said, explaining how he'd deflected Ted's aim.

Sally's eyes brimmed over with tears as she held her son's face in her hands. "I'm so very proud of you."

"Yeah, well. Now will you stop fussing?"

Sally laughed and tossed Gabriel a set of keys. "I borrowed your Jeep. I didn't want to wait so far away, so I parked it just down the street."

"You shouldn't have, but I'm glad you brought it here," Gabriel admitted. "I have to go over and talk to Mayor Burns and let him know what happened."

"Why don't you help Peter into my truck, Sally?" Lucas asked. "I'll be there in a minute. He's going to have to go to the hospital."

As Sally led Peter out, Lucas took his brother and Lanie aside. "A cousin of ours tracked Joshua and Dad down. They've made camp just north of Cañoncito. Apparently Rudolph Harvey, the *hataalii,* is no longer living around

Mount Taylor. That's why I had such a hard time finding them. I'll make sure Bob Burns gets word, if you want to go talk to Dad and Joshua right away. It shouldn't take long. You can stay in radio contact with the state police, too, since you won't be hitting mountain territory.''

"I'll radio the state cops and ask them to stake out Burns's house, while I'm heading over to their camp."

"The *hataalii* wants to see the owner of the bowl, too." Lucas said, nodding to Lanie.

"Good, because there's no way I'm staying behind," Lanie said.

GABRIEL LOOKED OUT across a wide arroyo. The sandy floor was still discolored by the recent rains.

"The place Lucas mentioned is right over that low ridge," he said, pointing by pursing his lips, Navajo style. As he glanced back at Lanie, his gut tightened. She looked even worse than when they'd left, despite the fact that they'd stopped for food and water. Maybe it was lack of sleep, but he thought it more likely that her weakened state was due to being farther away from the bowl now than she'd ever been. Determination and fear wound tightly inside him. He would not lose this woman. They'd come too far together to let anything take her from him.

"I'm really eager to talk to the *hataalii*," she said, interrupting his thoughts, "though I'm surprised that he specifically asked to see me."

So was he. It was an unusual request, particularly since Lanie was not Navajo. "We'll be there shortly. Our questions will be answered then."

They climbed out of the arroyo and drove across an outcrop of sandstone. At long last, they saw a camp ahead. Two white canvas-wall tents, the type used by shepherds, had been pitched in the middle of a clearing.

Gabriel parked well away from several horses that were grazing on the meager grasses, then approached on foot.

An elderly man, wearing jeans, an old faded shirt and a white bandanna sat near a small camp fire. He waved at them to approach. As he did, his large turquoise-and-silver ring captured the fire's gleam, giving it an ethereal quality.

"Uncle, I'm here with the woman at your request," Gabriel said. "I understand my father and brother are also with you."

Suddenly Joshua came out of one of the tents, moving slowly and giving the impression of something that was being unfolded. He straightened his back, then with a grin, placed an arm on Gabriel's shoulder, resting his weight on it. "You were always too close to the ground, big brother."

"Easy there, Tree. I'm not made of stone." Joshua's size had earned him that nickname with his two older but smaller brothers.

Joshua laughed. "I hear you need to talk to us, Fuzz. I guess I better be careful. I don't want to snap you into two before you get a chance to ask your questions." He took his weight off Gabriel with exaggerated care.

"Nice to see you again, too, Tree." He turned to introduce his brother to Lanie, who was watching wide-eyed. He guessed that Josh was probably one of the largest men she'd ever seen. Gabriel's baby brother was six foot six, incredibly tall for a Navajo, and was built as sturdily as a gnarled oak. He worked at it, too, having lifted weights and kept himself in top physical shape for years.

"Hello," she whispered.

Joshua smiled disarmingly, used to people's reaction to his intimidating size. "Welcome," he said in a voice as gentle as the breeze.

Hearing other footsteps, Gabriel turned around and saw his father approaching from up the arroyo. His hair was gray now and touched the top of his broad shoulders. The familiar face, with all its stubbornness and pride, refreshed Gabriel's spirits.

"Hello, son," he greeted. As he looked at Lanie, a smile lit up his face. "I have heard about you. I'm glad to meet you face-to-face." He glanced at his eldest son, and Gabriel knew with that one look that his father approved of his choice. "We don't use names here, but you know who I am."

"The resemblance is there," she said quietly, looking at the eldest Blackhorse. "I would have known you anywhere."

"Sit down, please," the *hataalii* said. "We don't have much time."

Gabriel tried to shake his uneasiness. Many said that Rudolph Harvey knew things before they happened, but right now, his gut told him he really didn't want to know what lay ahead.

The healer looked at Lanie, his gaze deep and searching, then he focused on Gabriel. His expression was one of open concern. "Ask whatever you wish."

"Tell us how to fight what the bowl is doing to her," Gabriel said.

"First you must recover it. Then you must take it to where the skinwalker who crafted it was killed. The owner of the bowl," he said, nodding to Lanie, "must break it there. That will release the witch's *chindi*. You," he said, looking at Gabriel, "as the guardian, must bury the shards inside your medicine bag along with the flint-hawk fetish and sacred pollen."

"But if I'm linked to the bowl, then how can I break it without destroying myself?" Lanie asked.

"You are the only one who *can* destroy the bowl. If anyone else tries, they will die in the attempt. Since you are the rightful owner of the bowl, it is your responsibility. You will never be truly free as long as it exists. Do you understand?"

"Yes. Can you tell us where the skinwalker died, so we know where to take the bowl?" she asked.

"No. I don't have that information. That is something you must find out for yourselves."

The *hataalii*'s eyes were filled with sympathy. "You will face great odds, but you have each other. He is your guardian," he said, looking from Lanie to Gabriel. "That role has been his destiny all along."

"My guardian has a direct link to the bowl's past, so his role is understandable. But why was *I* chosen?"

Harvey stared at a piece of quartz in his hand for a long time, as if in a trance.

Gabriel captured Lanie's gaze, and shook his head, cautioning her wordlessly not to interrupt him. Harvey was a gifted crystal gazer. Normally that meant a finder of lost things and a diagnostician, but Harvey's gifts clearly exceeded that. Whatever he revealed to them now might save their lives in the not too distant future.

Harvey finally looked up, his gaze on Lanie. "Your past had its share of darkness, but that darkness never claimed a victory over the goodness in you." He drew in a long, clear breath. "An even greater darkness is now seeking to destroy that balance inside you. You have on your side the feelings between you and the guardian. Love is full of light and carries its own power. But you must embrace those feelings and allow them to fill your heart." His voice was strong, and his words rang with the spirit of truth.

Lanie looked at Gabriel and smiled. "Love charts its own course. It didn't need my permission to grow and deepen, but no matter what happens, I will never be sorry I met you."

Harvey smiled and nodded in approval. "Depend on your guardian as he will depend on you. In that partnership lies your survival. You need the flint hawk's protection, and the guardian needs you to destroy the bowl. The evil in that bowl will try to destroy you both—make no mistake about that. And neither of you can succeed without the other." He stood up. "Now you must go, and act quickly."

As Harvey walked off into the desert, Joshua stood beside his brother. "Don't worry. The healer will get back safely. He often goes away for several hours." Joshua looked at Gabriel. "When I heard about the trouble, I packed up, ready to leave, but I was told that I couldn't join you in this fight. All I'd do is make things more difficult for you."

The elder Blackhorse came to stand beside his sons. "I also would have left to come to your aid, but the *hataalii* assured me that I, too, would be more of a hindrance than a help. I'm no longer the lawman, the guardian of Four Winds."

"This duty falls to me," Gabriel acknowledged. "I will see it through."

AS THEY TRAVELED back to Four Winds, regret filled Lanie's voice. "I am going to hate destroying that bowl. When I was pushed into the well, it actually helped me survive."

"You *have* to destroy it. Look at what it's doing to you now. If you don't do as the *hataalii* says, it'll either own you or kill you."

As the moon slipped behind the clouds and she stared at the gathering darkness descending over them, Lanie fought a sick, growing fear. Although facing danger alone was scary, facing it with a loved one was terrifying. The possibility that Gabriel would be harmed or even lose his life in the battle that lay ahead filled her with suffocating dread.

The aches and pains corkscrewing through her body as a result of being separated from the bowl intensified...but they were nothing in comparison to the heartache she felt when she thought about losing Gabriel. She swallowed back tears, gathering her courage. They'd handle this together. One way or another, they'd protect each other and see this through.

LANIE WOKE UP shortly after dawn the next morning. She moved slowly, stretching carefully. Pain was her constant companion these days. She felt as old as a biblical patriarch. Uncomfortable, she got out of bed and dressed.

The house was still; nobody was up yet. Lanie walked to the living room and drew open the curtains. As light streamed into the room, she saw an envelope that had been slid underneath the door. It had her name on it. She gathered it up and tore it open. The note inside had been printed in block letters.

The bowl is yours if you convince the sheriff to clear the roadblocks and turn his souped-up four-wheel-drive vehicle over to me. If you don't, I'll start setting fires until all that's left of Four Winds are ashes and rubble. Go to the library this morning for a demonstration. If my terms are accepted, have the sheriff fire off three rounds into the air at the crossroads before the highway. More instructions will follow.

The letter *T* was scrawled at the bottom of the page. Lanie ran down the hall to wake Gabriel, but as she reached his door, he opened it.

"What's wrong?" he asked, buttoning his shirt.

"How...?"

"I don't know. I woke up early and I felt..." He stopped, trying to find the right words. "I felt your fear."

She held out the note. "This was slipped underneath the door."

He read it and then headed quickly down the hall. "Call

Jake Fields. Tell him to get out of the library building."
Gabriel ran for the door.

Lanie rushed to the phone just as a sleepy Marlee came
out of her bedroom. In between rings, she explained the
note. Finally, after the eighth ring, Jake answered, grum-
bling into the phone.

"Don't ask me to explain, just get out of the library
now!"

"Lady, I'm not going…"

"Someone's planning to burn it down."

"Why the heck didn't you say so?"

He didn't hang up. She heard the phone hit something,
then the noise of something being toppled over. "Jake?"

Not getting an answer, she rushed out the door and
jogged all the way down Main Street. She arrived breathlessly at the library several minutes later. Everything
looked fine. Maybe it was a hoax after all.

As she drew closer, she saw Gabriel dragging Jake out
of the building. Then suddenly, Jake pulled away, his arms
raised in a military fighting stance.

"Look here, Sheriff, I'm not—"

The earth shook, and the air reverberated with a breath-
taking blast that sent glass flying everywhere. Gabriel and
Jake were tossed away from the building like mannequins.
As they scrambled to their feet, fire erupted inside the
library.

The street had been empty, but quickly people started
arriving from nearby houses. Lanie looked for signs of the
fire department, then realized that she'd never heard anyone mention one. Maybe Four Winds didn't have fire protection, and that was why the threat had been so effective.

Lanie joined people dragging lengths of garden hose
from their yards, linking them together to spray small
streams of water at the burning structure. As her gaze
shifted to the ever expanding blaze inside the library, she
knew it was a hopeless battle. The others must have known

it, too, yet everyone kept working. Lanie realized then that the fighting spirit was alive and well in Four Winds. Even more important, she was now part of it.

Chapter Seventeen

Alma stood with Lanie beside the charred building. Smoke
still curled up from the embers, and some of the men were
still extinguishing hot spots with garden hoses.

"Our beautiful library...it's gone," Alma said. "I can't
believe it. I hope we have enough insurance to cover the
building and most of the contents. But some of the collections were irreplaceable."

Lanie glanced at Jake, who was helping Gabriel search
the ruins for the device that caused the fire. "That poor
man! Where will he live now? He's just lost all his possessions and his job!"

"Nobody ever loses their job in Four Winds. If anything, he'll be working twice as hard to build a new library. In the meantime, he'll more than likely move to
Marlee's."

Gabriel came over and took Lanie aside. "The town got
off lucky. That fire could have spread to Main Street if
the wind had kicked up. We don't have a fire department
here—we share with the next town, and theirs was already
on another call."

"Maybe the flint hawk is helping us now."

He nodded. "Yes, I believe it is. Jake and I escaped the
blast unharmed. But now it's my turn to buy us all some

time. I'm going to fire off those shots and let Ted think we're playing his game."

Lanie watched Gabriel leave. Fear for his safety lay like a cloud over her soul. With one last look at the ruined library, she turned and walked back to the shop with Alma. "May I have today off? I'd like to go back to Marlee's and help her prepare a room for Jake."

"I'll tell you what. Give me an hour, and help me with some catalog copy. It's got to be faxed in by ten this morning. After that, you can go back to Marlee's. That sound fair?"

"Sure."

Alma opened the door, went inside, then stopped in midstep. "What's this?" She picked up the small folded sheet of paper from the floor.

Lanie felt herself grow cold all over. It looked like the note she'd received back at Marlee's.

"Your name's on it," she said, handing it to Lanie. "Secret admirer?"

"Hardly."

She opened it with trembling hands. Ted's block printing caught her eye immediately. She dropped down in a chair and read the message.

If I hear the shots and my terms have been accepted, then come to the old abandoned barn just outside town. I want you both there and in plain view. No one else! To show my good faith, I'll come out into the open, unarmed. You get the bowl, and in exchange, I get the sheriff's Jeep and no roadblocks. This will be your last chance to get the bowl back.

"My dear, you look as if you've seen a ghost. What on earth does that note say?"

Lanie shook her head. "Believe me, Alma, it's better

you don't know." She stood up and hurried to the door. "I can't stay, I'm sorry."

Lanie walked out of the shop and rushed to the site of the fire. She had planned to ask for directions to the crossroads where she knew Gabriel would be, but as she approached, she saw him still there by his vehicle talking to some men.

Taking him aside, she handed him the note. As he read it, she watched his expression grow deadly.

"I'm tired of playing cat and mouse. Let's go now. I'll fire off the shots, then continue on to the meeting place."

Gabriel spent several moments on his radio. Once finished, they were on their way. The landscape was nothing more than a blur past Lanie's window. She was sure she'd never ridden in a car going that fast before. It was both exhilarating and frightening. Yet what seemed the most ironic was that she was having that experience because of the happenings in a small town called Four Winds.

Gabriel arrived at the crossroads, screeching to a stop. Then, standing by the side of the road, he fired three rounds into the soft bedding inside an arroyo where the bullets would impact safely. Before slipping into the driver's seat again, he reached into the back and handed Lanie a bulletproof vest. "Put this on and don't take it off until I tell you."

"But what about you?"

"I can shoot back—that makes me a harder target. You won't be armed."

She considered his logic, and it made sense. She wasn't sure if that was because of the fever, but she accepted his argument.

Gabriel drove to a ridge overlooking the abandoned ranch and looked at the dilapidated barn surrounded by pines that stood on the property. He studied everything that would be in their path as they slowly approached from the highway. "There's a third player in this—remember that. We could be walking into an ambush."

"Why don't they just make a run for it with the bowl?"

"They have to stack the deck a little more in their favor first. They want the roadblocks down first to make sure no one tracks them easily. With my Jeep, they can travel across terrain like these mountains without a problem. Using my police radio they can monitor communications, and with a few supplies on hand, the thief gives himself several options, including hiding out in the mountains until the heat is off. After things cool off for him, he'll undoubtedly ditch my vehicle, and take off in something that won't attract so much attention."

"Are the roadblocks down now?"

"No. They just moved farther back down the road. The state police will continue looking for someone of Ted's description, instead of stopping everyone. It isn't as effective, but it's better than nothing. Since the barn is up on a hill, Ted can see the main roads from there."

"Once they have the Jeep and we have the bowl, do you think they'll just leave us alone?"

"I won't lie to you, so don't ask a question like that unless you want a blunt answer."

"Tell me." Lanie tried to keep the fear from her voice, but her hands were shaking.

He took a deep breath, then let it out again. "We know that your death will increase the value of the bowl. It's to their advantage to get you out of the way before they leave the area." He paused and met her gaze. "But first they have to go through me."

THEY ARRIVED at the abandoned barn fifteen minutes later. Gabriel parked behind cover of some boulders. The area was dotted with piñon and juniper, and to their left, the forested area rose from the base of a hill. "Stay low to the ground until we know what we're up against," he said, grabbing the shotgun.

Gabriel slipped out and placed the shotgun on the ground by the base of the largest boulder, then crept forward. As he did, Ted came out from inside the barn.

"I've been waiting for you two long enough!" he yelled. "Come on, now, guys. I don't have all day." He held out the bowl, touching it gingerly by its sides. "I'm not packing a gun, so let's get going on this. Set down your side arm, Sheriff. Otherwise, I'm going to get nervous, and I doubt any of us here knows exactly what'll happen if I drop this bowl."

Gabriel stood where he could be seen, dangling the keys from his finger. "Here are the keys to my Jeep." He tossed them toward Ted, but made sure they landed just out of his reach. "Leave the bowl exactly where the keys landed."

"I want Lanie out in the open, too, then I want you both to step away from the vehicle," Ted ordered, setting the bowl down.

Gabriel motioned to Lanie, and they began edging sideways, weaving in and out among the boulders, making it impossible for anyone to get a clear shot at them. But a clearing stood directly in their path and was unavoidable. The moment they reached it, a bullet whizzed by and a rifle cracked.

Gabriel dove for cover, pushing Lanie to the ground beside him. "Stay down," he yelled, reaching for the backup revolver in his boot.

"You made it too easy, Sheriff." Ted laughed. "I'll have your vehicle, the bowl and both of you dead."

Gabriel saw Ted reach inside a dilapidated feeding trough and pull out a rifle. "You won't get away with this, Burns. The state police are still manning the roadblocks—they just moved back out of sight. They'll be on your tail the second I don't report in."

A barrage of gunfire pinned them down. Gabriel knew Ted was advancing, while his partner held them in position.

"Just in case you're thinking of shooting me, Sheriff," Ted yelled out, "keep in mind I've got the bowl in my jacket. If I fall, or if a stray bullet hits me, it's history."

Gabriel cursed under his breath as he helped Lanie crawl behind the base of a large stump. "Here," he said, handing her the small revolver. "Point and squeeze the trigger if there's no other option."

"Where will you be?"

"Hunting."

Gabriel slipped among the rocks and the trees, melding into the shadows. Stealth would be their only ally now. He considered going for the shotgun. It was less than ten yards away, but then opted against it. Instead, he reached for the knife at his belt. Ted would have to pass him here before reaching Lanie. If he could neutralize Ted, he'd even out the odds and take the bowl. He was sure Ted's partner would not risk damaging the artifact with more gunfire.

Ted advanced confidently while his partner continued to cover him. Gabriel waited, muscles tense.

As Ted passed by, Gabriel reached up and yanked him to the ground. After one well-placed punch, Ted's body grew limp. "See that, buddy boy? I didn't have to damage you or the bowl."

Gabriel took the bowl and his Jeep's keys from inside Ted's half-zipped jacket. The second he touched the bowl, a fiery blast of pain shot up his arm. Weakened, he rolled to his side, cursing himself for forgetting that the maker of the bowl had protected his creation from those of Gabriel's clan.

Lanie rushed up and scooped the bowl from the ground. "Come on, let's go!" she said, pulling Gabriel's arm.

Ted's eyes opened, and he staggered to his feet. Gabriel

reached out for him, but two quick rifle shots from the sniper forced him back. As they ducked behind the cover of a pine, a bullet grazed his cheek.

Gabriel heard Lanie gasp and felt the warm stream that ran down his face. "I'm okay. Stay down! Whoever's shooting can't keep missing at this range with a rifle. Stay here and keep the bowl safe. Ted was barely able to run. I think I can still catch him."

He'd sprinted only about fifty feet when an explosion hurled him to the ground. The roof of the barn rose twenty feet into the air, then fell back, shaking the structure. Flames appeared among the dust and debris.

Gabriel stayed down until all the flying lumber had settled to earth, then heard a vehicle speeding away. The explosion had been a diversion, but a good one. "Come on," he said, scrambling back up. "We've got to keep the fire from spreading to the wooded area."

Lanie ran up after him. "What fire?"

Gabriel saw that the explosion had smothered the fire, partially collapsing the barn. The ground was still damp enough from recent rains to prevent any spark that remained from catching. Gabriel hurried with Lanie back to his vehicle, retrieving his shotgun along the way. "Let's go. We still have the bowl to deal with."

Lanie brushed her palms against the sides of the bowl. "We finally got this beauty back, and for the first time in a long while, I feel completely well again."

"It has to be destroyed, my love. I don't want you to become dependent on that thing." He took one of her hands away from the bowl and pressed his lips to the center of her palm. "Depend on me. I *won't* let you down."

"I do depend on you." Her body shook with a fierce yearning. "I know what we have to do, but we still have a major problem. We don't know *where* the skinwalker was killed. I'd suggest researching that question in the library, but…"

"There's still the newspaper office."

Gabriel pressed down hard on the accelerator, and they arrived at Ralph's a short time later. The color had indeed come back into Lanie's face. She looked as beautiful as she had when she'd first come to Four Winds. He stole a furtive glance at the bowl in her hand. Suddenly, destroying it seemed foolish.

He shook free of the thought. Maybe the bowl was more dangerous than he'd given it credit for. He had thought himself above being influenced, but now he'd seen it wasn't so. "I'll sure be glad when that blasted thing is out of our lives," he said, mostly to himself.

As LANIE WALKED into the newspaper office, she felt decidedly awkward. She met Ralph's gaze and somehow sensed that he really had only been pretending to be asleep when she'd made her search.

Ralph listened to Gabriel's request. "I have a morgue, sure, but I'm not sure if it'll go back as far as you need." He led the way to a small adobe hut at the rear of the main building. "There are some wooden trunks in there that go back to the 1800s. I've never had time to search through everything, but if we have any newspapers that go back that far, that's where they'll be."

"Let's go check it out."

Gabriel followed Ralph inside the small building. Gabriel's gaze swept the room. More than a dozen wooden cartons filled the place. "This could take a while."

"They're stored by year, about a decade per carton. I can tell you it won't be in any of the boxes to the left of us. They only cover about the last fifty years. The oldest issues are on the right and in the back."

Gabriel spotted a large green wooden box in the far corner. It was layered with generations of cobwebs. "Let's start with that one, then."

As Lanie looked at the box, she felt as if a cold hand

were squeezing her heart. She touched the bowl and noticed it was icy cold.

"Why bother?" Ralph said. "Nothing could have survived inside there. It's got a big hole in its side."

"Let's check it anyway," Gabriel said. Crouching down, he pulled the unlocked lid open. As light streamed inside the box, a rattler reared its head, its coils shaking in a death song.

Face-to-face with the pit viper, Gabriel froze. If he ever needed the flint hawk to work, it was now. Curiously he felt the medicine bag at his belt almost vibrate, as if raw power had suddenly been called to life.

"You'd better not reach for your handgun," Ralph said quietly. "It's too close to the rattler. But my shotgun is inside the office. Don't move."

As Ralph left, Gabriel's eyes darted around the room. "There's a rake over there, to my left," Gabriel said to Lanie, his voice whisper soft. "Gently push the snake out of the box and away from me. Don't try to kill it—just get it out of striking range."

Lanie picked up the rake. As she drew close, the snake struck at the tongs. Taking advantage of the moment, Gabriel jumped clear.

Lanie breathed a sigh of relief as she stepped back, and the snake slithered sideways toward the door. "Let it go. It's over." Gabriel took the rake from Lanie's hands. "You okay?"

"Yes, I'm fine, but how about you?"

He smiled reassuringly, wishing for the day when he'd no longer see the taint of fear in her eyes. "I'm all right, though I have to tell you, Navajo and snakes don't mix. Some of the *dineh,* the people, even wipe out any tracks snakes leave behind."

"Why didn't you kill it, then?"

"Our tradition says that snakes are linked to the Lightning People. To kill them without reason would drive

away the rain. But it's more than that. We're taught not
to kill unless we're forced to, because everything is inter-
related.'' He waited until he could no longer see any sign
of the snake. ''I appreciate your help, though. It had me
dead to rights for disturbing its sleep.''

Ralph came rushing in. ''Where did it go?'' Ralph
asked quickly, lowering his shotgun.

''Outside,'' Gabriel answered.

''Let's take the box and go back inside the main building,'' Ralph suggested quickly. ''Watch your step,
though.''

Once in the newspaper office, they went through the
contents of the box. Newspapers, most of them in bad
condition, crumbled as soon as they were handled. But
near the middle of one stack, they found a headline that
captured their attention instantly.

''Lynching Averted,'' Gabriel read. ''Medicine Man
Calls For A Blessing On Four Winds.''

Lanie peered over his shoulder and read the story. ''The
skinwalker Flinthawk fought was found dead at a ranch
house outside town, by the well. But what ranch?''

''There is only one out in that area. We were just there.
That barn Ted blew up was constructed on the site of an
earlier one by neighboring farmers who needed to store
extra hay. The well must still be there near it. I hope it
wasn't buried in the barn rubble.''

''Let's go out there and see,'' Lanie said.

After thanking Ralph, Gabriel and Lanie drove back toward the abandoned ranch. ''Are you truly ready for what
you'll have to do?'' The hard lines of his mouth softened
as he gazed at Lanie for a moment before focusing back
on the road.

''Yes. Let's just finish it.''

''Take it one step at a time, and stay alert,'' he warned.
''That bowl, and the *chindi* it contains, has already done

much harm, to our town and to you and me. I have a feeling this final step isn't going to be easy."

Gabriel parked some distance from the old barn, then gave her hand a squeeze. "No matter what happens, remember I'll be by your side." He listened to the wind. But right now, it told him nothing.

"I can't see even a hint of movement out there," Lanie whispered. "It's so quiet. I think we're alone."

"Nature is rarely this silent," he mused, glancing around.

"Do you see any sign of a well?"

"No, but it should have been about halfway between the old ranch house and the barn."

"I bet that was the ranch house." Lanie pointed to a ruined stone foundation about a hundred yards away in a field.

Gabriel nodded and led the way, watching for signs of trouble.

Lanie reached in her bag and touched the bowl. It felt neither cold nor hot, almost as if it had given up and accepted its fate.

They reached a clearing between the ruined house and the barn and found a circle of stones nearly two feet above ground level, covered by some boards.

"This is it," Gabriel said. Pistol now in hand, he stood beside her.

Lanie reached into her tote bag and brought out the bowl. As she raised it, ready to smash it against the stones, Ted threw the boards aside and stood up, moving away from what remained of the well. His rifle was trained on Lanie. "I figured you'd come back here."

"How did you know?"

"My partner researched the history of that bowl. She was way ahead of you all along."

As Gabriel moved with lightning speed and kicked the rifle out of Ted's grip, Lanie drew back, ready to smash the bowl against the well. Suddenly the sharp crack of a rifle blast made her freeze in midmotion. The bullet impacted inches from her leg, spraying her with stinging sand.

"Don't even breathe, Lanie."

Lanie recognized the voice, and sorrow rippled through her as she turned to face Alma. "Why?" she asked in a strangled voice.

Alma stepped out of the shadows, a rifle in her hands. "That bowl is my ticket out of Four Winds for good. Don't you understand that it was meant for me all along? This town has always managed to make things work out for people, and now it's my turn. I spent years living out my sister's dreams. There was never a chance for me. After Emily died, I thought it was too late for me, that I was trapped. Then the bowl surfaced, and I knew I'd been given one last chance. I needed a stake in order to start anew elsewhere, and the bowl was my means to get it. I spent time getting the word out, making people think it would bring bad luck to anyone who didn't understand its magic. The incident with the paint barrels was designed to rattle you so you'd part with it and, at the same time, spread the word about its being a jinx.

"Then buyers began to contact me," she continued. "The chance to own a bowl that might have hidden powers was a powerful temptation to collectors. I knew Four Winds was finally going to make *my* dreams come true."

"You're wrong. Your research is incomplete," Gabriel said. "Things work out in Four Winds only for those whose motives are right and true. If the bowl had been meant for you, the peddler would have given it to you instead of Lanie."

"Alma, think about what you're doing," Lanie begged. "You'll spend the rest of your life looking over your shoulder. The bowl only corrupts. Look at yourself now. Nothing good ever comes of it."

"With what I'm going to make from its sale, I can go anywhere, and even reinvent myself," she said. "It's my last chance and I intend to take it. Give the bowl to Ted and step back."

Lanie saw Ted had retrieved his rifle and had it aimed at Gabriel's chest. "If I hand it over, then what?" Lanie pressed.

"If you don't, Ted will shoot Gabriel and I will shoot you," Alma replied. "Do as we say, and we'll all walk away from this."

Lanie reluctantly gave Ted the bowl. He handled it confidently, and even when his hand brushed against the roughened spot, the bowl did not injure him.

"You have what you wanted, now go," Gabriel said.

"Bring the bowl over here to me, Ted," Alma said sharply.

Ted stood rock still, holding the bowl in one hand and the rifle in the other. He moved his thumb in a caressing gesture over the smooth exterior of the bowl, as if entranced. Instead of coming toward Alma, he took a step back and swung his rifle barrel toward her. "I don't think so."

"Don't be a fool. You can't sell it on your own—you don't have the contacts."

"This shouldn't go to you," he said dully, his eyes on the bowl. "I took it from Lanie. You had me keeping an eye on the house, particularly in the morning, and it paid off. I saw Marlee pick up the paper after the sheriff left, and when I checked the door, it was unlocked. Nobody knew I was there. I was quiet, and careful. I was just outside the sheriff's door when I saw Lanie hide it in the closet. It was meant to be, don't you see? I'm the only one here who really understands, not just what it is, but what it can do."

"You're talking nonsense," Alma snarled. "Bring it to me, *now*."

Ted spun and ran as fast as he could toward the tree line. Alma fired off a shot, hitting Ted in the back.

Ted crumpled to his knees, still clutching the bowl. Then, crying out in anguish, he fell to the ground.

Alma stared at Ted's lifeless body, tears streaming down her face. "I didn't want to do that! He forced me!"

As Gabriel grabbed the rifle from Alma's stunned hands, Lanie ran to where Ted lay. She crouched by him, and touched the pulse point at his neck. Sadness filled her as she stared at the body. Ted had only been in his twenties, an adult with his whole life ahead of him. He'd chosen the wrong path long before now, but then the bowl had come into his life and given him the final push that had led to his downfall.

Lanie picked up the bowl, tears of anger and frustration stinging her eyes, and hurled it against the stones at the base of the well, smashing it into pieces.

Alma wrestled free from Gabriel's grasp and ran to where the shards lay scattered. Crying, she began to gather them up.

"No, don't touch those!" Gabriel ordered, his voice filled with alarm.

"What have you done?" Alma sobbed. "This was mine!"

As she held the clay fragments in her hand, a thin black cloud rose from the shards. Gabriel pulled Lanie to him, holding her close to his side. "The *chindi*," he said quietly, aware of the pulsing of the flint hawk inside his medicine pouch.

The smoke seemed to engulf Alma, then continued upward, swirling, into the air.

Gabriel's arm was wrapped securely around Lanie's waist. "It can't hurt us, not while I'm wearing the flint hawk and you're with me."

As they watched, the black smoke reversed directions,

drifting downward into the ground where Alma knelt, sobbing.

As the last wisp disappeared, Alma looked up at them, her face contorted with anger and fear. "You will not win!" Her voice was deep, filled with a rage that had crossed the barriers of time.

Alma jumped to her feet and sprinted across the field with an agility that took Gabriel and Lanie by surprise. They gave chase, trying to head her off. Forced straight ahead, Alma entered the wreckage of the barn. As they reached the entrance, Lanie heard beams overhead giving way. "Alma, get out!"

Lanie sprang toward the door, but Gabriel caught her in midair, pulling her clear of the barn. As they scrambled back, the structure collapsed completely.

Lanie tried to push Gabriel away and move toward the rubble, but he held on to her. "No, she's gone. You can't help her now," he said. "Look." He gestured toward the ruins. Black smoke lifted from a single source, then dissipated into the air.

"The *chindi* is gone," she whispered.

"Yes," Gabriel said. "Now one more duty remains."

Together they walked back to the well. Lanie's skin prickled as she gathered up what was left of the shards, but they no longer gave off the magic that had so drawn her. These pieces were now only a symbol of death and greed.

Gabriel dug a deep hole with his hands, then held open his medicine pouch as Lanie placed the shards inside with the flint hawk and sacred pollen. Tying the bag securely, Gabriel placed it deep into the hole.

The air was curiously silent as he finished the task. The breeze was still and the birds had stopped singing.

As he patted the last bit of dirt into place, the field came alive with the gentle chirping of birds and the breeze rustled through the nearby pines as if sharing their victory.

"It's finished for now," Gabriel said.

"For now?" Lanie repeated aghast.

"We have destroyed the bowl, but the peddler will be back. He's part of Four Winds."

Like she was. In thoughtful silence, Lanie walked with Gabriel back to his vehicle. Two lives had been lost to greed, but perhaps in death their troubled souls would finally find peace. Flinthawk's blessing on the town of Four Winds had stood true, and helped them defeat evil and restore harmony once more.

And now, as they headed back into town, she knew that it was time for her to either accept the gifts Four Winds offered her, or walk away forever. Lanie looked over at Gabriel, her heart telling her what she already knew. She loved this man more than she'd ever dreamed possible.

Gabriel drove to the top of the hill then, suddenly, he pulled to the side and stopped. "Come on. I want to show you something." Taking her hand, he led her out of the car and into the clearing that overlooked the town. As twilight settled onto the valley below, faint streamers of fading light fell over the houses and buildings, giving them a warm, welcoming glow. "Four Winds is calling out to you. You're needed here...I need you."

She smiled, and pressing his hand to her face, burrowed against it. "The past is behind me now. I want to find a place to call home. And I do have something to offer Four Winds. I'm going to apply for that teaching job that's open."

"There's a more important opening and it's one only you can fill." He tilted her chin upward, and captured her gaze. "I want you to be my wife."

A sense of destiny swept over her. She belonged here, with him. It was so right between them! She saw the love reflected in his gaze and knew it matched her own. "This is the way it was meant to be."

"Yes," he whispered, his breath teasing her lips. As a hawk cried shrilly overhead, he took her mouth with his own.

"You," he whispered this breath leaving his lips. As he leaned slowly overcame he took her mouth with his own.

Epilogue

Lanie stood before their new home. Gabriel was finishing a last-minute repair on the roof while Lucas put the last coat of paint on the porch trim. Joshua was loading left-over bundles of roofing shingles into his pickup, oblivious to the demands of such hard labor.

Marlee came up to stand beside Lanie, looking at Lucas wistfully. "You're a lucky woman, Lanie. You're now part of a very special family."

Finished painting the trim, Lucas sauntered by, picked up Lanie and twirled her around. "I want to be an uncle soon, okay?"

"Get married and start your own family," she shot back, laughing.

Lucas set her down, shaking his head. "Someday— maybe," he said, giving Marlee a wink, then walking off.

Marlee blushed and gave Lanie an embarrassed smile. "My guess is that Joshua will marry next. Lucas will be the last of the Blackhorse brothers to settle down. You mark my words."

"Joshua? You think so?" She looked at the muscular giant holding the ladder as Gabriel climbed down from the roof. "But he doesn't even have a girlfriend."

"Four Winds will fix that. You wait," she said, walking over to help Lucas clean up the paintbrushes.

Gabriel came up and, taking Lanie's hand, led her to the shadow of a tall pine. Standing behind her, he pulled her close against his chest. "Well, pretty wife, what do you think? Is everything the way you wanted?" he asked as his gaze settled on their new home. "If there's anything missing, just say the word," he whispered.

"Only one thing is needed to truly make it *feel* like home." She leaned back, resting against his chest. "And I have a feeling you'll know exactly what to do about that, once we're alone."

"Oh, yeah," he said, raining a trail of moist kisses down the column of her neck.

As she felt the warmth of his breath against her skin, a shiver ran up her spine. "I couldn't ask for more," Lanie said, then sighed as he nuzzled her ear, setting her blood on fire. "But I probably will."

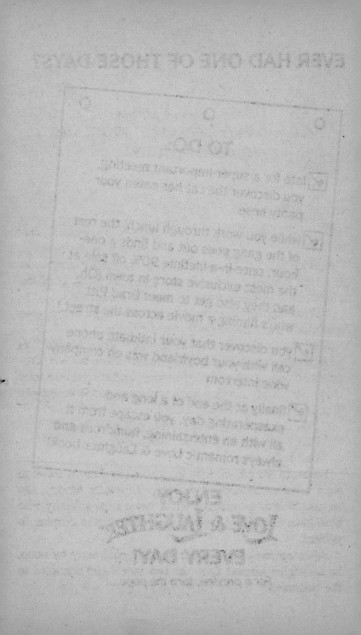

Here's a sneak peek at
Colleen Collins's RIGHT CHEST, WRONG NAME
Available August 1997...

"DARLING, YOU SOUND like a broken cappuccino machine," murmured Charlotte, her voice oozing disapproval.

Russell juggled the receiver while attempting to sit up in bed, but couldn't. If he *sounded* like a wreck over the phone, he could only imagine what he looked like.

"What mischief did you and your friends get into at your bachelor's party last night?" she continued.

She always had a way of saying "your friends" as though they were a pack of degenerate water buffalo. Professors deserved to be several notches higher up on the food chain, he thought. Which he would have said if his tongue wasn't swollen to twice its size.

"You didn't do anything...bad...did you, Russell?"

"Bad." His laugh came out like a bark.

"Bad as in *naughty*."

He heard her piqued tone but knew she'd never admit to such a base emotion as jealousy. Charlotte Maday, the woman he was to wed in a week, came from a family who bled blue. Exhibiting raw emotion was akin to burping in public.

After agreeing to be at her parents' pool party by noon, he untangled himself from the bed sheets and stumbled to the bathroom.

"Pool party," he reminded himself. He'd put on his best front and accommodate Char's request. Make the family rounds, exchange a few pleasantries, play the role she liked best: the erudite, cultured English literature professor. After fulfilling his duties, he'd slink into some lawn chair, preferably one in the shade, and nurse his hangover.

He tossed back a few aspirin and splashed cold water on his face. Grappling for a towel, he squinted into the mirror.

Then he jerked upright and stared at his reflection, blinking back drops of water. "Good Lord. They stuck me in a wind tunnel."

His hair, usually neatly parted and combed, sprang from his head as though he'd been struck by lightning. "Can too many Wild Turkeys do that?" he asked himself as he stared with horror at his reflection.

Something caught his eye in the mirror. Russell's gaze dropped.

"What in the—"

Over his pectoral muscle was a small patch of white. A bandage. Gingerly, he pulled it off.

Underneath, on his skin, was not a wound but a small, neat drawing.

"A red heart?" His voice cracked on the word *heart.* Something—a word?—was scrawled across it.

"Good Lord," he croaked. "I got a tattoo. A heart tattoo with the name Liz on it."

Not Charlotte. Liz!

HARLEQUIN WOMEN KNOW ROMANCE WHEN THEY SEE IT.

And they'll see it on **ROMANCE CLASSICS**, the new 24-hour TV channel devoted to romantic movies and original programs like the special **Harlequin®️ Showcase of Authors & Stories.**

The **Harlequin®️ Showcase of Authors & Stories** introduces you to many of your favorite romance authors in a program developed exclusively for Harlequin®️ readers.

Watch for the **Harlequin®️ Showcase of Authors & Stories** series beginning in the summer of 1997.

If you're not receiving ROMANCE CLASSICS, call your local cable operator or satellite provider and ask for it today!

Escape to the network of your dreams.

A woman alone—
What can she do…?
Whom can she trust…?
Where can she run…?
Straight into the arms of

HER PROTECTOR

HE SAID

SHE SAID

Explore the mystery of male/female communication in this extraordinary new book from two of your favorite Harlequin authors.

Jasmine Cresswell and Margaret St. George bring you the exciting story of two romantic adversaries—each from their own point of view!

DEV'S STORY. CATHY'S STORY.
As he sees it. As she sees it.
Both sides of the story!

The heat is definitely on, and these two can't stay out of the kitchen!

Don't miss **HE SAID, SHE SAID.**
Available in July wherever Harlequin books are sold.

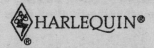

Let's Celebrate!

LOVE & LAUGHTER™

invites you to
the party of the season!

Grab your popcorn and be prepared to laugh as we celebrate with **LOVE & LAUGHTER**.

Harlequin's newest series is going Hollywood!

Let us make you laugh with three months of terrific books, authors and romance, plus a chance to win a FREE 15-copy video collection of the best romantic comedies ever made.

For more details look in the back pages of any Love & Laughter title, from July to September, at your favorite retail outlet.

Don't forget the popcorn!

Available wherever
Harlequin books are sold.

 HARLEQUIN®

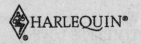